Suddenly That Summer

Suddenly That Summer

Lizzie Byron

CORONET

First published in Great Britain in 2022 by Coronet
An Imprint of Hodder & Stoughton
An Hachette UK company

This paperback edition published in 2022

1

A CIP catalogue record for this title is available from the British Library

Paperback ISBN 9781529360349
eBook ISBN 9781529360356

Typeset in Plantin Light by Manipal Technologies Limited

Printed and bound in Great Britain by Clays Ltd, Elocraf S.p.A.

Hodder & Stoughton policy is to use papers that are natural,
renewable and recyclable products and made from wood grown in
sustainable forests. The logging and manufacturing processes
are expected to conform to the environmental regulations
of the country of origin.

Hodder & Stoughton Ltd
Carmelite House
50 Victoria Embankment
London EC4Y 0DZ

www.hodder.co.uk

For all the misfits
and those lucky enough to be loved by them

Chapter 1

There's something about London in May, Nora always says.

Every year, there's a day before the softness of spring surrenders to the urgency of summer. A day when she finally feels the turn that London has been struggling towards since March, when the clocks go forward and the city begins to shuffle off the cold coil of winter.

Until then, it seems to take *forever*. After the glow of Christmas and the promise of the new year comes the reality of winter with its months of dim, dragging days and dark, dark nights. Months of runny noses and stiff fingers. Months of porridge for breakfast and soup for dinner and, for a while, it feels like it will be that way for ever. That the days will always be too short and the nights too long and Nora will never remember what it's like to feel the sun on the back of her neck or to spend a Sunday afternoon sitting in the park with her friends.

But then – finally – spring arrives and everything begins to feel brand new. Colour returns. Even in London. The real London, anyway. The London Nora knows, with its 24-hour off-licences and tower blocks and narrow, grubby canals that the tourists don't deem worthy of Instagram.

Drifts of daffodils appear in the parks and the trees fill out, their bare branches disappearing under the weight of new leaves and clouds of blossom.

Then Nora and her friends start to linger outside the pub, promising they'll only stay for one more. There are tables outside the cafés again and they dare speak of holidays and barbecues and picnics: outside no longer something to avoid, rather to embrace.

That's why May is her favourite month. Not just because it's her birthday tomorrow, but because of those first few perfect days when the sun is bright, but not burning, and you can feel your bones thawing. Soon it will be June, and the park benches will be too hot to sit on, the beer gardens too hot to stand in, and just right will become too much.

Not today, though.

Today is the first perfect day of the year.

What makes it even more perfect is that her boss, Roland, is out for most of it. She has no idea what he's doing, but she's sure he'll come back to the gallery later, drunk on gin, to regale her with stories about people she doesn't know doing things she doesn't care about.

Until then, she has a few hours of peace. One of the best things about the gallery is that it's appointment only and there isn't another until three o'clock, so Nora slips out for lunch. The sudden sunshine is such a surprise that she didn't think to grab her sunglasses when she left the house this morning, so she buys a cheap pair from the corner shop, gets a falafel wrap and her first iced coffee of the year, then heads to Mark Street Gardens.

She walks the long way to Mark Street Gardens in an effort to avoid the building site on the corner of Curtain Road after that builder shouted, 'Hey, chocolate queen!' when she passed yesterday. He seemed so genuinely bemused that she didn't stop and ask him to climb down from the scaffolding and take her right there in the street that she couldn't help but ask herself if that approach has worked for him in the past.

Maybe it has.

Gardens is a grand word for what is essentially a narrow patch of grass, and a few benches, but it's exactly ten minutes' walk from the gallery, ten minutes from the hair salon her friend Luce works in, and ten minutes from her brother Ben's flat. So, as underwhelming as it is, Mark Street Gardens has become their spot to have lunch, when the weather allows. Or, when it's not sunny, somewhere to meet and bicker over where they're going that evening, even if they almost always end up in the pub across the road.

It's the nearest patch of grass, so Nora isn't surprised when she gets there to find it full. All the benches are taken so Nora claims a spot under one of the trees, kicks off her heels, shrugs off her leather jacket, then sits on the grass with her legs stretched out in the hope that it will discourage anyone from sitting near her.

She's tempted to tuck into her falafel wrap, but sips her iced coffee and checks her email. When she sees that she has one from Carol Talley at the Tate, her heart hurls itself against her ribs and she says a little prayer to whoever the god of jobs is before she opens it.

Nora reads it, then lets out a squeal. When she looks up, Luce is sauntering towards her and it's all she can do not to jump up and run over to her. Of all the people she wants to see at this moment, it's Luce Nicolaou.

They met in the queue outside Chick 'N' Sours on Kingsland Road three years ago and, after a passionate discussion over what they were going to order, have been inseparable ever since. Her brother, Ben, always says he doesn't know how they're friends, given how different they are. And he's right. They seem to exist in exact opposition to one another. Where Luce is tiny and fierce, Nora is tall and quiet. Considerate, Luce calls her, which, Nora knows, is a kind way of saying that she has a horrible habit of overthinking everything.

The funny thing is, Nora's family thinks she's this flighty, fickle free spirit and, compared to them, she is, she supposes. After all, her mother teaches economics at LSE, her father works for PricewaterhouseCoopers and her brother is training to be a doctor, so they have no idea where she came from. Compared to Luce, though, she isn't a free spirit at all. Brave, relentlessly restless Luce, who is a hairdresser today (and makes sure that she emphasises *today* when she tells people) but two years ago she was a graphic designer, and when she and Nora met, she was in a band. Now she wants to be a tattoo artist, and she will be because Luce's philosophy is that you have to try everything. You don't need to master it or even be good at it, you just have to try, and if you don't enjoy it, try something else.

Nora wishes she could be more like that, but such is her need to be good at everything that she won't even try unless she knows she's going to succeed. Like the job at the Tate. She would never have bowed to the pressure from Luce and Ben to apply if she hadn't known she was abundantly, almost excessively, qualified for it.

It's better to have not tried and not failed, that's what Nora says.

But every now and then, she feels a wild, uncontainable urge to tell Roland to shove his job. To move out and see what happens, sleep on Luce's sofa if she has to. To risk it all to find out if she can have something more.

That's why she loves Luce: she reminds her that it doesn't matter that she's twenty-seven tomorrow and she doesn't have it figured out yet. The joy is in *trying*. So how could Nora not love her? Even if, by her own admission, Luce is pure Shoreditch trash. Like now. She's wearing a pair of yellow tartan cropped trousers, Vans and an Aaliyah T-shirt.

And her hair.

That's the only thing they truly have in common: their hair. Shoulder length, curly and unruly. Except Luce's is a different colour from when Nora last saw her. Yesterday it was *macaron* pink and today it's dirty lavender. That, paired with the tartan trousers-Vans-Aaliyah-T-shirt combo, makes Nora look positively demure in her leopard-print shirt dress.

'Loving the purple,' she tells Luce, as she approaches.

'Thanks.' She dips her head and shakes her curls. 'I just did it.'

'What colour are we calling this?'

'I was thinking space grey.'

'How about Vulcan Violet?'

5

'Vulcan Violet.' She plonks herself on the grass in front of Nora. 'Love it.' She nods, putting the paper bag she's carrying between them. 'I'm stealing that.'

'What can I say? I'm a wordsmith.'

Luce nods at Nora's phone, which is still in her hand. 'Why so happy, wordsmith?'

'What?' She tries to stop smiling, but can't.

'Come on. Spill, Armstrong.'

'Well,' Nora says, with a wistful sigh, her nose in the air, 'I was just sitting here thinking about how I won't have to put up with Roland much longer.'

Luce looks confused as she reaches into the paper bag and pulls out a bottle of orange juice. She opens it and, as she's taking a sip, her face lights up.

She points the bottle at Nora. 'You got the job at the Tate!'

'I got the job at the Tate!'

Luce sends an arc of orange juice flying across the grass as she throws her arms around Nora. It narrowly misses a couple who are clearly in the middle of an argument. Luckily, they're too distracted to notice.

'Hey. Why we hugging?'

Luce lets go of Nora and they look up to find Ben standing over them.

She raises the now half-empty bottle to him. 'Nora got the job at the Tate!'

'No way!' He looks genuinely thrilled. 'Well done, sis. I knew you'd get it!'

She clambers to her feet to give him a huge, swaying hug. When they step back, Luce tugs at the hem of Nora's dress with a grin. 'You can finally tell Roland to suck it!'

'Yeah, maybe don't use those words,' Ben says, arching an eyebrow at Nora as she sits down. 'But can I be there when you do it? He'll have a stroke.'

'You have to go full Jerry Maguire!' Luce tells her, with a wicked grin.

'Yes!' Ben rubs his hands together. 'Make him cry. I hope he cries.'

'The best bit is,' Luce realises, 'this means you can *finally* move in with me!' She throws out her arms, her grin noticeably more cheesy.

Ben nods. 'I think Mum and Dad will be more thrilled about that than anything.'

Nora glares at him, but Luce squeezes her arm until she looks at her. 'Listen. I've fallen in love with this flat in a converted factory on Nile Street. We can barely afford it. Like, *barely*. But we don't need to eat, right? Or go out. Or use hot water and electricity.'

'Yeah, who needs hot water and electricity?' Ben mutters.

'It'll be like *Friends*!' Luce squeezes Nora's arm again. 'Except, you know, just the two of us. And we'll have to keep the door locked because it's Hackney.'

'Two stabbings last night.' Ben points at Luce, then holds up two fingers at Nora while he shoulders off his bag and sits on the grass with them. 'Two.'

'Wait,' Luce says, gesturing at his bag. 'Are you going to the gym?'

'Just been.'

'Didn't you get off night shift?'

He scratches his temple. 'Yeah, but I'm too wired. I had to burn off some energy or I'll never sleep. I don't even

7

know if it's worth it now, though. I'll only get a few hours' before Nora's birthday dinner later so I might finish the paper I'm reading on zebrafish. Did you know . . .' he stops to take the sports bottle out of the pocket of his gym bag '. . . that translucent zebrafish can regrow their own tissue and repair wounds? Like, they can repair their own hearts.' He gestures at his chest. 'So if we can work out *how* they do that, the medical ramifications are staggering. We could achieve scar-free healing within a generation.' He takes a chug of water, and when he looks up, they're both staring at him. 'What?'

Nora sighs theatrically. 'I love you, little bro, but you're such a nerd.'

'Hi, I'm Ben,' Luce says, putting on his deep voice. 'I just finished a ninety-two-hour shift in A and E, saving lives, and after I've been to the gym to work on my abs, I'm going home to discover how to achieve scar-free healing in the few hours before my sister's birthday dinner. After that, I'll probably rescue a cat from a tree and cure world hunger.'

'I do have a cure for world hunger, actually,' he tells them, as he unzips his bag and pulls out a small cardboard box. 'It involves rich people paying their taxes and employers providing a wage their workers can actually live on.'

Luce rolls her eyes at Nora. 'And now he's eating salad.'

'What?' Ben looks down at the cardboard box with a frown. 'I like salad.'

'You don't win friends with salad,' Nora sings, with a shoulder-shimmy.

8

'You don't win friends with salad,' Luce joins in, unwrapping her panini.

Ben just stabs at a cherry tomato with a wooden fork.

'You win, okay?' Nora tells him, as she opens her falafel wrap. 'You're perfect.'

'I am certainly not perfect.'

'You are! You know you are! I love you, but being your big sister sucks sometimes.'

'What?' He looks horrified. 'Why?'

'You're the Golden Boy! You went to Oxford. You're training to be a doctor. You're marrying your fellow Oxford-educated girlfriend next year. You're the Guyanese Dream.'

'I am not.'

'You are! I'm a year *older* than you and I'm still single.' She counts off each thing on her fingers. 'Still living at home. Still a gallery assistant getting Roland's matcha lattes for twenty-two thousand pounds a year. So, the least you can do is admit that you'd rather have *that*.' She stops to point at Luce's panini then at his salad. 'Than *that*.'

'What? It has sourdough croûtons.'

Before Nora can scream, Luce says, 'First of all, who cares if you're single? Just because Dr Kale here is engaged doesn't mean you have to be. Second of all, may I remind you that you have a first from Central Saint Martins, one of the best art schools in the world. And you're not going to be a gallery assistant for much longer, are you? By the end of today, you'll be telling Roland where to stick his matcha lattes and, pretty soon, you'll be moving in with me and you won't be living at home any more. So there,' she says, with a satisfied nod.

'She's right, you know.' Ben points his fork at Nora. 'You're killing it. Redchurch is one the coolest galleries in London because of you. You spend your evenings and weekends going to exhibitions and trawling Instagram, finding new artists and putting them under Roland's nose so he can swan about, taking the credit and accepting all the adulation for launching their careers. You love art and you make other people love it too. The Tate are lucky to have you. You're going to show those kids that they can make and *be* art as well.'

Nora's cheeks flush. She's so overwhelmed that all she can do is kick him.

He kicks her back and returns to his salad. 'So, come on,' he says, biting into a piece of grilled chicken. 'Read us the email from the Tate.'

Nora grins as she opens it again, shivering as she reads, '"It was a pleasure meeting you yesterday and hearing your ideas. You were far and away the strongest candidate."'

'The strongest candidate, you know!' Ben interrupts.

'With the best hair!' Luce is quick to point out.

But, then, she's biased: she gave Nora a deep condition before her interview.

'"Your experience working at Redchurch Gallery,"' Nora continues, '"combined with your passion for inclusivity and making sure all children, whatever their background, have an opportunity to explore and express their creativity as well as to see themselves in the art that surrounds them is exactly in line with what we're trying to do with our schools programme.'"

That's greeted by a chorus of cheers and 'I told you you'd smash it!' from Luce.

Nora reads out the rest of the email: '"I think you will be a valuable and much-needed addition to the team so I am putting your name forward as my recommendation for this role at our senior management team meeting later today."'

That's enough to make Ben and Luce abandon their lunch to clap furiously as Luce leans over and hugs her so tightly that a falafel pops out of Nora's wrap.

'What else did she say?' Luce asks, when she sits back again.

'Just that the meeting is at two and she'll be in touch after that.'

'Do you know when they want you to start?' Luce asks, pulling a string of cheese from her panini. 'Do you have to give Roland notice or can you just walk out? I say just walk out.'

'She's not walking out. She's not doing anything until she's signed a contract,' Ben says. When he raises his eyebrows at Nora, he's never looked more like their mother. 'I know you're dying to tell Roland to suck it, but don't say a word until you have something in writing.'

She draws a cross on her chest with her finger. 'I won't, I promise.'

Chapter 2

'Mummy, please, I'm not going to be late for my own birthday dinner,' Nora reassures her, as she stops on the pavement outside the gallery. 'I'll get the fast train.'

She's trying to temper her tone, but her mother's timing, as always, is impeccable. It's a minute to three so their next appointment is about to arrive. Mercifully, she can see through the glass door of the gallery that Roland isn't back yet, but if their client arrives now – while she's on the phone to her mother – he'll be furious if he finds out.

'Please do, Nora,' her mother says, clearly unconvinced. 'Mark and James are here and—'

'They're there already?'

'Yes,' her mother says, in a way that lets Nora know she's noticed her switch from surly to delighted at the mere mention of her uncles.

'Are they *back* back? That's it, right? They're not going back to Cornwall?'

'As far as I'm aware. Mark's in the kitchen now.'

'What's he making?'

'I have no idea, but it smells divine.'

Nora does an excited shimmy. 'Definitely not going to be late now.'

'Oh, so you'll be on time for your uncles, huh?' Jennifer says, then blows three quick kisses to her daughter down the phone and warns her not to miss the fast train.

When she sweeps into the gallery, she catches herself grinning at the thought of announcing over dinner that she's got the job at the Tate.

As soon as the door closes behind her and the sound of Redchurch Street softens to a hum, she lets go of a breath. *Bliss*, she thinks, her shoulders lowering. No more bored-looking influencers posing for photos in front of the graffiti-smeared shutters of the fondue place on the corner. No more bicycles or buggies or Deliveroo scooters buzzing back and forth.

Just silence.

As much as she hates Roland, she doesn't hate this place.

Now she thinks about it, it's the only reason she's put up with him for the last four years. One day she'll have a place like this but, for now, she's content to love this one as though it were her own. She adjusts the canvases when she comes in each morning and arranges for the walls to be repainted between exhibitions and for the parquet floors to be buffed until the dots of red wine disappear. Roland may be the face of Redchurch, but Nora is the heart. She's the one who remembers the clients' names and makes sure there's space for as many artists as possible, not just Roland's friends. So, despite his enviable reputation, her brother's right: she's a big part of the reason he has that reputation.

She takes off her sunglasses and glances around. She knows her parents don't get why she loves this place so much but, sometimes, she wishes they did. It's not that they don't see the beauty – and joy – of the gallery, it's that they still don't quite understand what she does. They know she wants a gallery of her own one day, but they don't get why she spent three years at Central Saint Martin's to sell other people's art.

Her brother's career choice they understand. Ben's going to be a doctor. That makes sense to them. And they know, as Roland keeps telling her, she needs to learn the ropes, but it's been four years and she's still getting him coffee and picking up his dry cleaning.

Not for much longer, though, she thinks, with a shiver of excitement.

'Hey, Nor,' Charlie says, without looking up from his phone.

He's exactly where she left him, still stretched out on the battered black leather chesterfield by the window, his head on one arm of it, his ankles crossed neatly on the other.

Nora has what she politely describes as an *uneasy* relationship with Charlie. He's a nice guy. He's even quieter than Nora – almost monosyllabic – until he starts talking about something he loves. The pair of them often get into long, spirited discussions about the snobbery around street art or how unfair it is that Georgia O'Keeffe's sister, Ida, a brilliant artist herself, could never quite step out from under her older sister's shadow.

So, when Nora is feeling generous, she'll confess to quite liking Charlie. Most of the time, she's not feeling generous. Which isn't Charlie's fault, she concedes. But after telling Nora since she started at Redchurch that she needed to learn the ropes before he could promote her to a dealer, Roland hired Charlie six months ago.

That stung but, she assumed, Charlie had more experience – and clients – than her. So, when this twenty-one-year-old strolled into the gallery a week later and Roland told her he'd just graduated from the Slade, Nora was confounded.

Until she discovered that he was Roland's best friend's son.

She should have left then. Again, that isn't Charlie's fault, but she still can't help resenting him. Even if he's utterly oblivious to it. But Charlie is utterly oblivious to most things. If Roland is a triple espresso, then Charlie is constantly on the verge of falling asleep.

'Hey, Charlie,' she says coolly, as she heads over to her desk.

She glances down at her phone to find a voicemail from Carol at the Tate. *How did I miss that?* She curses, under her breath, then curses again when she realises that Carol must have called while she was talking to her mother.

This is it, she thinks, suddenly so excited she feels light-headed. *This is it.*

But before Nora can call Carol back, Roland barrels in with his arm slung across the shoulders of a painfully cool Shoreditch type, who looks as if he could be one of Charlie's friends. They're dressed almost the same. Black skinny jeans, grey at the knees. Black suede Chelsea boots. Except where Charlie is wearing a white shirt buttoned to the neck, this guy is wearing a white T-shirt under a baggy, open-weave black jumper, the sleeves tugged up to the elbows to reveal tattoos on each forearm and a silver ring on each finger.

Shoreditch Deluxe. That's what Luce calls Charlie. She'd probably call this guy that as well because it's all a bit too carefully curated. His jeans are Acne and his boots are Saint Laurent and his long hair is pulled up into a top-knot that is just the right side of untidy.

Roland punches the guy's shoulder. 'Look who I just found at the bar at the Ace!'

He always does this and it's excruciating. There's an air of possessive pride about the way Roland is holding onto the guy, his eyes bright and his lips turned up into a smile so wide he may as well be jumping up and down shouting, *Look who I'm friends with!*

'Charlie Boy!' the guy bellows, when he sees him lying on the sofa.

Of course he knows Charlie.

'JoBo!' Charlie bellows back, in a rare moment of enthusiasm.

Jonathan Bodham.

Their three o'clock, Nora realises, as Charlie swings his legs off the sofa and stands up, the dent in his shoulder-length blond hair betraying how long he's been lying down.

Jonathan and Charlie hug enthusiastically, clapping each another on the back.

'How you doing, JoBo?' Charlie asks. 'Haven't seen you since Christmas.'

When they step apart, Jonathan takes off his sunglasses and flashes Charlie a sly smile. 'I went to Thailand for New Year's. Met a girl. Fell in love. You know. The usual.'

'When did you get back?'

'Last week.'

'And the girl?'

'Lost her somewhere between Dubai and here.'

'JoBo, you devil!' Roland clasps his hand around the back of Jonathan's neck and shakes him so hard a strand of hair falls out of his topknot. 'Oh, to be twenty-one again!'

Twenty-one? Nora tries not to gasp. When she was twenty-one, she was working in the cloakroom at the Royal Academy because it was the only job she could find that was remotely related to the arts and buying lunch with her Boots Advantage points. She certainly couldn't afford to spend New Year's in Thailand or buy artwork from somewhere like Redchurch.

Roland laughs loudly enough to let Nora know he's had a couple of drinks with lunch as he slaps Jonathan on the back and asks, 'What brings you in today, JoBo?'

'Looking for some stuff for my new place.'

'Where you living now?'

'I just bought somewhere on Fournier Street.'

Bought, Nora notes. Not rented.

'Nice.' Roland nods. 'I love that street.'

Nora does too.

'It's nice.' Jonathan tilts his head from side to side. 'But I need to make it more me.'

'Well, we can help with that.' Roland beams. 'I'll leave you with Charlie, but shout if you have any questions.' He slaps him on the back again and points at him as he walks backwards towards Nora's desk. 'Give your father my love, yeah? He still owes me for Ibiza!'

Jonathan clearly has no idea what he's talking about, rolling his eyes at Charlie as soon as Roland turns his back and marches over to Nora.

He stops in front of her. 'Messages?'

She plucks a neon green Post-it note from her desk. 'Just Anna from the *Guardian*. She wants to know if you're going to the Magritte preview at the Hayward tonight.'

He waves away the Post-it. 'She got me on my mobile. Anything else?'

Her smile tightens. 'We need to discuss the wine for the Chris Cash launch next week.'

'Nora, it's wine. I don't care. Just pick one. It's not difficult. *God*,' he hisses, as he turns and paces to the other side of the gallery. 'Do I have to do everything?'

She closes her eyes and takes a deep breath.

When she lets it out and opens her eyes again, he's behind his desk and she watches as he throws himself into the large black leather swivel chair. He pulls his phone out of the inside pocket of his suit jacket and when he says, 'Lawrence, you old bastard! How are you?' Nora glances at her own phone, every bit of her aching to listen to Carol's voicemail so she can march over to his desk and tell him where to stick his wine.

But she reaches for the gallery phone instead and calls the wine merchant. There's no answer, so she leaves a message. As she's writing an email, ordering four cases of the red they get for *every* exhibition, her gaze drifts to Charlie and Jonathan as they wander around.

'I like this. Who's it by?' Jonathan asks, gesturing at a charcoal of a woman's face.

'An artist called Natasha Nowak.' Charlie sweeps his hair back with his hand and nods towards the door. 'She's local. She lives in Spitalfields. Not far from your new place, actually.'

'Is it a self-portrait?'

'No, this is her girlfriend, Adjua.'

'She kind of looks like Erykah Badu.'

Charlie nods. 'She does, actually.'

'It'll look good in the hall. What about this one?'

Charlie follows as Jonathan walks over to a watercolour of a raw red mouth, the paint dripping down off the edge of the canvas. 'This is Eliot Turnball. He's one of Roland's friends.'

Jonathan turns his head to Roland, who's still guffawing into his phone, then looks back at the painting. 'Yeah. I like it. It's perfect for the master bathroom. Who's this?'

He turns to the other wall and Charlie raises his hand to a series of portraits of Black men, their faces obscured by swirls of different-coloured paint. But before he can say anything, Roland stops his conversation to bark, 'Daniel Adebayor. I found him on Instagram.'

You *found him on Instagram?* Nora almost barks back.

'He's going to be the next big thing!' Roland tells Jonathan. 'Trust me!'

'I'll take all three, then.'

Roland winks at him. 'Good man!'

Jonathan saunters over to Nora's desk. He takes his wallet out of the back pocket of his jeans, but when he opens it and holds out his Coutts card, Roland waves his hand in the air and bellows, 'Don't worry, JoBo. We'll invoice you. We know you're good for it!'

He closes his wallet, then thumbs at Charlie. 'Hey, mind if I steal this one for a drink?'

Roland doesn't hesitate. 'Of course. It's Friday. You guys go.'

Sure, Nora thinks. *It's my birthday dinner tonight, but let Charlie go home early.*

Mind you, the commission he just earned is probably more than she takes home in a month. *Not bad for nine minutes' work, eh?* she thinks, as Charlie goes to grab his stuff.

As soon as he does, Jonathan turns to her with a loose smile. 'Hey, Nora. I've got a spare ticket for Damian Marley at Brixton Academy later, if you fancy it. Should be fun.'

'I'd love to,' Nora lies, with a much stiffer smile, 'but I have a dinner thing tonight.'

Jonathan arches an eyebrow at that. 'A *date* dinner thing?'

'A *birthday* dinner thing,' she says, loud enough for Roland to hear.

'Is it your birthday?' Jonathan licks his lips. 'Happy birthday, Nora.'

'It's tomorrow actually.'

'Happy birthday for tomorrow, then. Where are you going for dinner tonight?'

'It's a family thing. My uncle's cooking.'

'Yeah? Jollof rice and Egusi soup?'

Nora stares at him, momentarily stunned. She's guessing that Jonathan has one Black friend and they're Nigerian.

'I'm Guyanese, actually.'

He looks confused. 'They have jollof rice in Ghana, right?'

'No, *Guy*-ana.' She points to the left. 'In the West Indies.'

'Okay.' He tips his chin at her. 'Cool. Cool. Cool.'

Charlie returns from out back holding his denim jacket and saves him. Then they're gone and it's just her and Roland and her phone, which is still face down on the desk. She turns it over to find another missed call from Carol and her heart stutters.

Just the thought of it – of Carol saying, *You got the job, Nora* – makes her hands shake. But as she's about to make an excuse so she can slip out and call her, Roland looks up.

'Nora,' he says, far too loudly given they're the only ones there. 'I've emailed you a link to Caesar and Charlotte's wedding registry,' he says, like she should know who Caesar and Charlotte are. 'Pick something out. I don't care what, just make sure that it's between two and three hundred pounds. And look into flights to Barcelona in mid-July,' he adds, tugging at his earlobe as he reaches for his phone with his other hand. 'I think I might go to Benicàssim this year. Oh, and call the tailor to see if my Tom Ford suit's ready.'

Guess I won't be ringing Carol, then, Nora thinks as she turns back to her screen.

~*~

By the time she's done, it's almost five o'clock and Roland's given her another four things to do. She looks down at her phone and scrambles for an excuse to leave and call Carol, but Roland barks, 'Have you done Jonathan's invoice yet?'

Of course she hasn't. Why would she have done Jonathan's invoice? He and Charlie do their own and she pays the artists. That's how it goes. It's the one bit of work they actually do. They're weirdly territorial about them. Probably because they don't want her to know how much commission they earn.

Not that she couldn't find out if she wanted to, but why torture herself?

As such, Nora hasn't done an invoice since she started at the gallery, but given she designed the template herself, it should be pretty straightforward, so she pulls it up on her computer. It autofills so all she has to do is type in Jonathan's name and his address pops up. Or it *should* pop up, but the address that does must be Jonathan's old one because it's not a Fournier Street address. So she texts Charlie to check. Then she types 'Natasha Nowak' on the first line of the invoice and selects the piece from the drop down, then does the same for Eliot Turnball and the three Daniel Adebayor paintings Jonathan also bought.

That makes Nora smile. Daniel will be thrilled. She can't resist calling to tell him.

He answers with a gruff. 'Hello?'

'Hey, Daniel. It's Nora Armstrong from Redchurch.'

'Hey, Nora.' He softens immediately. 'How's it going?'

'Good. Great, actually. We sold your paintings.'

'What? You're kidding! But it's only been, what? Three days?'

'Uh-huh.'

'Which ones did you sell?'

'All of them,' she tells him, her cheeks warm with pride.

'*All* of them?' He whistles. 'Nora! That's amazing! Thank you so much.'

'I should be thanking you for giving Redchurch a chance to exhibit them.'

'Not Redchurch, *you*, Nora,' he corrects. Then mutters something she won't repeat about Roland. 'I hate he's making money off me, but I'm desperate. My car just broke down.'

Nora promises to process his payment as soon as possible. Technically, she's not allowed to pay the artist until they receive the payment from the client, but as Roland said, Jonathan is good for it. Besides, she needs a distraction from looking at her phone every three seconds. It's agonising. One phone call. *One* and she won't have to do any of this any more – ordering wine she doesn't like and buying Fornasetti candles for people she doesn't know and looking up flights to places she can't afford to go.

She does the sales receipt for Eliot first, because she's done a few for him already, but when she's creating new ones for Daniel and Natasha, she notices something strange. There are no price tags on anything at the gallery because, as Roland says, *If they have to ask, they can't afford it*. So, because she doesn't do Charlie and Roland's invoices, she doesn't know what anything sells for, only what they pay the artist.

Still, even with Redchurch's healthy forty per cent commission, something's not right.

'Roland.'

He doesn't look up from his phone. 'What?'

'I'm doing the sales receipts for the pieces Jonathan just bought.'

'Yeah?'

'And the cost price for Daniel and Natasha's paintings is a lot less than Eliot's.'

'Yeah?'

'We're only paying them two hundred and fifty for each piece, whereas we're paying Eliot two and a half grand.'

'The artist sets the price for their work, not us,' he reminds her.

That's true, but if she had known Daniel and Natasha were only charging two hundred and fifty pounds, she would have told them to up it.

'I know, Roland, but we're selling their work for the same price as Eliot's.'

'So?'

'*So* we're selling their pieces for three and a half grand each and only paying them two hundred and fifty pounds.'

'Yeah?'

'*So*, that's *a lot* more than forty per cent commission.'

He doesn't respond to that, just continues to scroll through his phone.

He obviously wants her to let it go, but she can't. 'If an artist is underselling themselves, don't we have an obligation to tell them?' She waits for him to look at her, but when he doesn't, she persists: 'A lot of these guys have never sold their stuff in a gallery before. They don't know what it's worth. We shouldn't take advantage of that.'

'Uh-huh.'

It's all Nora can do not to charge over to his desk and snatch the phone out of his hand. The least he can do is look at her, given these artists are the ones she found. The ones *he* brags about giving their start when their careers take off.

So *this* is how he gives them their start, huh?

Nora takes a deep breath and presses her lips together, telling herself to calm down. But she can't. She's furious. How dare he? How dare he profit off these artists who are just as good and just as talented – if not more so – than his friends?

'If Daniel and Natasha are worth the same as Eliot, they should earn the same as Eliot.'

Roland ignores her, his lips pursed as he reads something on his phone.

'Why should Eliot earn ten times more than them?'

'Eliot went to Goldsmiths.'

He's your mate's nephew, more like, she almost says, but stops herself. 'Natasha went to Goldsmiths as well,' she reminds him.

'Well, Daniel barely passed his GCSEs.'

Nora stares at him, horrified. 'So?'

'*So.*' Roland looks up, at last. 'When I found Daniel—'

'When *you* found Daniel?'

His face hardens. 'If it wasn't for me, that kid would be spray-painting the side of a chicken shop in Leytonstone. Whatever I pay him, he's lucky to be getting it.'

There's a moment of silence while Nora stares at him. She waits, and when he doesn't blush or apologise or look even the least bit contrite, she finally snaps. 'You know what?' she says, pushing back her chair and standing up. 'You are vile.'

He finally falters. 'Excuse me?'

'Vile!' She snatches her phone and sunglasses off the desk. 'You're happy to take credit for launching the careers of artists like Daniel. Artists who, I may add,' she stops to open the bottom drawer and take out her bag, 'you would never have heard of if it wasn't for me. But you don't have the decency to pay them what they're worth. You're disgusting, Roland.'

He looks around the empty gallery as though waiting for someone to defend him.

'Disgusting.' Nora makes sure she looks him in the eye when she says it this time as she tugs the strap of her bag onto her shoulder. '*Four years*, Roland!' She holds up four fingers suddenly ashamed of herself that it's taken her so long to say it. 'Four years of spending every night and weekend trying to find artists like Daniel and Natasha and Kofi.' She nods at him when his face changes at the mention of his name. 'Yeah, your precious Kofi Campbell, who was nominated for the Hepworth Prize last year and got you and this place that profile in the *Sunday Times*. Well, *I* saw his degree show at Chelsea *three years* ago.'

She holds up three fingers this time. When his cheeks redden, she points her phone at her chest before he can tell her otherwise. '*I* told you about him, Roland. *Me*. And for what? So *you* can profit off *his* work while I get your dry cleaning and your matcha lattes on the promise that, one day, you might promote me beyond your glorified PA. Well, *enough*!'

She says it so loudly Roland actually recoils.

'The sad thing is,' she goes on, walking around her desk and stopping in the middle of the gallery, 'I think you actually believe you're this *genius*,' she waves her hands at him, 'when the truth is you don't have a creative bone in your body. You wouldn't know the Next Big Thing if they walked up to you wearing a T-shirt saying, *I'M THE NEXT BIG THING*.'

He's so stunned that he puts his phone down.

When he does, Nora waits. Waits for him to hear her, for him to have just a tiny moment of self-reflection and realise what she's saying. But he just snatches his phone off the desk again, then nods towards the door. 'Fine. You don't like it? Get out.'

So she does.

Nora doesn't look back, just puts on her sunglasses and strides out of the gallery. She doesn't stop until she gets to the fondue place on the corner, her whole body singing with the thrill of finally telling Roland what she thinks of him. She can't even remember what she said, but she wishes Ben and Luce had been there to see it.

She feels so good – so light, so free – that she's ashamed of herself for not doing it sooner. In fairness, she hadn't known that Roland was profiting so shame-lessly off the artists she'd brought him, although she knew he was profiting off them in other ways. But she let him because she thought they were getting a much-needed platform. Looking back on it now, though, they're so talented that they were probably going to make it anyway.

They don't need Roland, she thinks, as she feels her phone buzz in her hand.

She looks down to see that it's Carol Talley and almost drops it in her haste to answer.

'Carol! Hey! Hi! It's Nora,' she says, breathless, because this is it.

This is it.

'Nora, hi,' Carol says, sounding out of breath herself. 'I'm sorry to keep calling.'

'No. No, it's fine. So. How was the meeting? Do you have good news for me?'

There's an endless stretch of silence. Then Carol sighs and says, 'Nora, about that.'

Chapter 3

When Nora gets to Clapham Junction she has exactly three minutes to make it up the stairs at platform two and down them again at platform six if she's going to make the fast train.

I should have waited for the next one, she thinks, when her dress almost gets caught in the doors as they close behind her. At least then she would have had time to walk to the end of the platform and get into the first carriage, where she might have found a seat. There's no chance of that here, as she finds herself pressed against the doors between two men.

At least it's the fast train so she has to stand for only nine minutes.

As soon as it pulls away from the station, she calls Luce. She'd rather not have this conversation in a packed train carriage, but if she's going to have a meltdown, she wants to get it out of the way now so she can go home and pretend that everything is okay.

'You didn't get the job?' Luce literally *shrieks*. So loudly that Nora has to hold the phone away from her ear. 'But that email said she was recommending you for the role!'

'I know.'

'What happened?' Luce asks, in her best *Don't freak out, Nora* voice. But given that she has to raise her voice over the racket at the salon, it isn't quite as soothing as it usually is. The salon is always rowdy, but it's Friday night so it's *raucous* with everyone – clients and staff – getting ready to go out. It sounds like bedlam. Hairdryers and laughing and the radio roaring.

Nora exhales through her nose. 'She was overruled by her boss, apparently.'

'Why?'

'He found someone *more suitable* on Instagram.'

'Who?'

'Someone …' Nora stops, unable to bring herself to say it '… younger.'

'*Younger?*' Luce shrieks again.

Nora shivers with horror as her gaze flicks around the huddle of exhausted commuters, with their grey suits and grey hair and grey skin. As much as she abhors this part of her commute she does enjoy the withering stares she gets each time she skips onto the train. Especially in the summer when she's wearing a yellow playsuit or, like today, a leopard-print shirt dress. It makes her feel like a parakeet in a flock of pigeons. Like they're staring because they know she doesn't belong there and, one day, she'll fly away.

That was the plan. Commuting – living with her parents and being a gallery assistant – wasn't for ever. *It'll only be for a year or so*, Roland told her, when he offered her the job at Redchurch. *A year or so while you learn the ropes.* Then she'd be promoted to dealer and move in with Luce. But *a year or so* became four and she doesn't know how that happened, just that now she's too old for the job at the Tate.

I'm not too old. I'm only twenty-seven tomorrow. Twenty-seven isn't old.

Is it?

The thought makes her shudder as she asks, 'Luce, are we old?'

She doesn't hesitate. 'Yes!'

'What? No, we're not!' She says it so loudly that the man next to her peers over his copy of the *FT*. It's enough to make her want to take a step back, but there's nowhere to go.

She turns her cheek away as Luce says, 'You try working in a salon with a bunch of eighteen-year-olds talking about bands you've never heard of. I've made my peace with it.'

'When did this happen?' Nora leans back against the doors with a tender sigh. 'I feel like I graduated from uni last year.'

'That was six years ago, Nor.'

That can't be right.

Can it?

'And you're just okay with this?' Nora sighs again. 'With being ...'

She doesn't say it, but she can feel the word hanging over her head like a neon light.

Old.

'What can we do, Nor? It's the circle of life. Or youth, in this case.'

Nora knows Luce is teasing her, but it still stings.

'So,' Luce pushes, when she doesn't say anything, 'who'd they give your job to?'

'Some guy called Tatum Green.'

'Tatum Green?'

'Do you know him?'

'Course! Everyone in the salon is *obsessed* with him.'

'Who is he?'

'A photographer. Mostly street stuff, but he did the cover for JME's new album.'

'Why haven't I heard of him, then?' Nora asks, even more furious.

'Because you're—'

'Don't say it!' Nora warns, before Luce does, the neon light flashing over her head again.

Luce cackles unrepentantly. 'Probably because he's known more in the music industry than the art world. He started out taking photos of his mates. He grew up with Rex.'

'The grime artist?'

'Yeah. When Rex blew up, so did he. Now he has, like, three million followers on Insta.'

'Three million?'

That puts Nora's 2,011 to shame.

'He seems pretty cool. I've been following him for a while,' Luce admits, raising her voice again as someone in the salon starts singing along to a Megan Thee Stallion song. 'Every couple of months or so, he puts a call out on Live, telling people to meet him somewhere and bring their camera, and he teaches them how to do street photography.'

He sounds perfect for the Tate schools programme, she thinks. But instead she says, 'That sounds dangerous.'

'I suppose,' Luce admits. 'But I don't think anyone's tried to murder him yet.'

Nora can feel tears gathering in the corners of her eyes. She needs to pull herself together because she doesn't want to cry. Not because she's embarrassed to do it in front of a carriage full of strangers, but because if she starts, she doesn't know if she'll be able to stop.

'Nor?' Luce says, when she goes quiet.

She turns to face the train doors and whispers, 'I did something bad.'

'How bad? Nora bad or me bad?'

Nora makes herself take a deep breath. 'I walked out of Redchurch.'

'Oh, no, Nora. Oh, no. Oh, no. Oh, no.'

'I know.'

'But Ben said …'

'I know what Ben said.' Nora closes her eyes and presses her hand to her forehead. 'But Roland was being *Roland* and I snapped, okay? I thought I had the job at the Tate and I … Oh, God, Luce.' She winces as the horror of it sets in. 'What am I going to do?'

'It's okay,' she tells her, deploying her *Don't freak out, Nora* voice again. 'I quit jobs all the time.'

'Yeah, but you don't have my parents, do you?'

'Listen. Don't stress. Just enjoy your birthday.'

Nora takes her hand away from her forehead, eyes wide. 'How am I supposed to enjoy my birthday? I just quit my job and I don't have another one to go to!'

'I know, but it's done. There's nothing you can do about it now, is there? Short of going back to Redchurch and begging for your job back. Which,' Luce says sternly, obviously knowing that Nora's asking herself if that isn't such a terrible idea, 'you are not going to do.'

'I can't.'

She can't.

Can she?

'You can't, Nor. You have more dignity than that.'

Do I? she thinks, as she considers how she's going to tell her parents.

'Yes, you do, Nora Patricia Armstrong. Besides, if things were bad at the gallery before, imagine how bad they'll be if you have to grovel to Roland for your job back.'

That's true.

'Like I said, just enjoy your birthday and we'll come up with a plan on Monday. You know what your parents are like. They worry. If you have a plan, they'll be fine.'

Nora nods. 'I just need a plan.'

'Exactly. In the meantime, you'll be okay. It's not like you have kids or a mortgage, or anything. You live at home. So, whatever happens, you'll have a roof over your head and you're not going to starve, are you? Yeah, your parents are going to be pissed that you walked out of Redchurch, but they'll get over it. You'll find another job and all this will be a funny story you tell *The Times* in five years when they do a profile on you and your gallery.'

Nora manages a chuckle.

'In the meantime, you have an overdraft, right? So you're not *broke* broke.'

'True.'

'I know you don't like going overdrawn, but you'll have to use that to live on.'

'It's only, like, a couple of grand, though. That's not going to last long.'

'It'll last a month. Maybe two, if you're careful.' Nora isn't convinced until she adds, 'You're not going to work so you're not paying for travel. Or lunch. Or coffee. It'll last.'

'And if it doesn't?'

'What about that art blog you write for sometimes?'

'It doesn't pay much. Only, like, fifty quid an article.'

'It'll pay your phone bill, at least,' Luce reminds her. 'Besides, it's not about the money. It's about getting your name out there. Remember that piece you wrote about those sisters?'

'Georgia and Ida O'Keeffe?'

'Yes! Didn't you end up going out for a coffee with someone who read it?'

That's right. She did.

'Rowan from the Arts Council. She loved it.'

'You said everyone in the industry reads that blog, so who knows who you'll meet?'

That makes her feel slightly better. Slightly steadier.

'So, don't worry about money,' Luce tells her. 'I don't have much, but if you need to borrow something to keep you going, you know I've got you.'

'Luce, I love you.'

'It's going to be okay. Plus, your uncles are back from Cornwall, right?'

'Yes!' Nora lets go of a breath. 'Thank God.'

'Talk to them,' Luce suggests. 'They'll know what to do. They always know what to do.'

Chapter 4

Nora buys a KitKat at the station and eats it so quickly she almost swallows a piece of foil. She feels like a naughty schoolkid stuffing sweets before dinner – which is exactly what she's doing – but it gives her the energy she needs to make the walk from the station.

When she finally gets to the top of her street, she tells herself it will be okay. Her uncles are there. They'll know what to do. Besides, she'll find something else. She just needs to sort out her Instagram, make it less about other people's dogs and what she had for lunch and more about what she does. After all, her phone is full of photos of street art she's stumbled across, exhibitions and graduate shows she's been to.

Then tomorrow she'll email the editor of the art blog, pitch her piece about the commercialisation of Frida Kahlo. And she can reach out to some smaller galleries, see if they need help. Plus, it's summer. There's loads of festivals and art fairs coming up, and the Royal Academy Summer Exhibition starts next month. Even if she volunteers to be a greeter, that's something. Luce is right: her parents just need to know that she'll be okay.

They just need a plan.

With that, Nora feels better. Even if she has to spend her birthday emailing everyone she knows who works in the arts, she'll have a plan for her parents by Monday.

I just need to get through the weekend, she thinks, as she stops outside her house and looks up at it. Her chin shivers as she thinks about the flat in that converted factory on Nile Street. There will be other flats, but it still hurts. Why, she isn't sure. After all, she's never lived anywhere other than at home – even when she was at uni, she got the train into London every day – so she shouldn't be mourning the loss of a flat she's never lived in.

Perhaps it was the promise of it. The promise of moving forward, for once, rather than remaining in this holding pattern she's been in since she graduated. The promise of feeling like a grown-up, at last. Paying bills and calling an emergency plumber when the boiler breaks down, and bickering with Luce about whose turn it is to buy loo roll.

Silly, mundane things she'll no doubt be sick of in a few months, but will be easier when it's just her and Luce and no one to ask what time she's getting home. No more getting her ASOS orders delivered to the gallery so her parents don't see. No more *Have you eaten today?* Or *Is that a new handbag?* Or *Are you going out* again *tonight?*

As Nora looks at her big red-brick house, she feels awful. She doesn't mean to sound ungrateful. After all, her parents have been uncharacteristically patient with her. They've certainly been more patient than her grandparents would have been. All of this – art school, the internships, working at Redchurch – wouldn't have been possible without their help.

Nora stops to give Ron, her burgundy Peugeot 307, a loving pat on the roof in the driveway, then looks at the front door and smiles. It was her idea to repaint it this nude calamine pink and, while it looks lovely with the chequerboard path, it caused quite a stir on their street. So much of a stir, in fact, that it almost got her parents kicked out of the Cadogan Gardens WhatsApp group. A year later, though, and nearly everyone else has repainted their door. Everything from subtle shades of cook's blue and sage green to a not-so-subtle brassy red at number thirty-seven. Nora had no idea that Mrs Sutton had it in her.

She's biased, but it's the nicest house on the street. The only one with a turret, which, Nora was delighted to learn as a child, is also called a witch's hat. And the only one with an original wrought-iron balcony at the front, over the front door and living-room windows.

Nora grew up thinking all houses were like that. It wasn't until she went to uni and saw *how much* she'd have to pay for a room barely big enough for a single bed with a shared bathroom that she came to realise how lucky she was. Even now, compared to the flats she and Luce have considered, it's a veritable palace. A detached, five-bedroom Victorian with sash windows and a long garden that rolls down to the banks of the Thames. There's even a boat. They inherited it from the previous owners so, given it's older than Nora, it's unfit to leave the dock but is the perfect spot to sit and watch the other boats float past.

More than that, though, it's her home. The only one Nora has ever known. She learned to ride her bike on this street and broke her arm trying to climb the tree in the garden, and she knows which part of the staircase to avoid stepping on when she's trying to sneak in.

So, as much as she wants to move out, it's not that she isn't happy here. There are moments – like now – when she asks herself, *What's the rush?* But then she'll have to fork out sixty quid for a cab because she's missed the last train to Richmond. Or she'll be at Ben's, watching him and his fiancée moving smoothly around the kitchen, laughing and chopping vegetables while Nora chooses a record to play and she'll think, *I want this.*

Somewhere of her own.

Somewhere to hang the canvases and prints she's collected over the years. Somewhere with shelves for her books and an armchair to read them on. The yellow velvet one she saw in that antiques shop on Columbia Road that's probably sold now. Somewhere with a black wrought-iron balcony that she can sit on in the summer with a glass of white wine and watch the commuters rush by, where she can grow – and no doubt kill – tomatoes and chillies and basil in mismatched terracotta pots.

One day, she thinks.

But not today.

Not yet.

~★~

'Nora?' her mother calls from the kitchen, as she closes the front door.

'Hey, Mummy,' she calls back, kicking off her heels. She exhales as she presses the tender soles of her feet to the cool tiled floor, her toes curling with relief.

Jennifer emerges from the kitchen doorway at the end of the hall. 'Nora,' she says again, looking startled. 'You're on time.'

Nora turns to hang her bag and leather jacket on the coatstand. 'I said I would be.'

'Yeah, for your uncles.' She arches an eyebrow at her, then smiles.

On cue, she can hear them calling her from the kitchen. She recognises Mark's voice immediately. 'Nora! Get your arse in here!'

Followed by James singing, 'Nooooorrrraaaaaa!'

And, just like that, things aren't so bad. She's home. Her mother is happy and her uncles are here so it smells like home, like onions, garlic and ginger frying in a Dutch pot, like every birthday she's ever had. Every birthday and Friday-night dinner, the six of them huddled around the dining table, elbows and knees knocking together as they talk over one another.

'Me first!' Jennifer demands, beckoning Nora over. She immediately throws her arms around her daughter. Nora reciprocates, grinning as her mother presses a kiss to her cheek and says, 'Welcome home, baby girl.' She smells of home as well, of shea butter and Chanel No 5. She kisses Nora's cheek again. 'I can't believe you're *twenty-seven* tomorrow!'

'Don't remind me,' she mutters, when her mother finally lets go. After the Tatum Green thing, it stings more than it should.

'Come.' Jennifer slips her arm around Nora's waist and leads her into the kitchen.

There they are. Her uncles. Mark at the stove, stirring something, and James at the island, pouring her a glass of wine while Duke Ellington plays softly in the background.

And just like that something realigns. Her uncles have been married for twelve years and together for three before that. Since Nora was a teenager, they've only ever been two streets away. Always there for Friday-night dinner and to meet for breakfast on a Saturday morning in that café on the high street, the one with the maddening smell of warm, buttery croissants that makes her want to undo whatever she's just achieved in spin class.

Their house, while much smaller and less tidy than hers, with its stacks and stacks of books and vinyl and an instrument in each room – a drum kit in the bedroom, guitars in the living room, a cello in the dining room – has become her sanctuary. They're never surprised to see her. They feed her homemade cinnamon rolls while she complains about Roland or being broke or whatever other horror is going on in her life, and she loves that. Loves how there's always coffee. Always an article in the *New Yorker* she should read or a podcast she should listen to. Always music. Something classical to soothe her nerves or something more buoyant when she just needs to dance until she can't catch her breath.

But they've been in Cornwall for the last *five months*, caring for a sick friend, and while Nora would never complain about that, she's felt utterly unmoored without them.

But they're back.

Everything is okay.

Everything will be okay.

'You're home!' Nora grins, clapping and jumping up and down. She hasn't seen them for *so long*, but they look the same. Mark, bald, tall and solid with her mother's dark skin and brown eyes. James, taller, but lean with short, neat blond hair. He's even paler than he was before he left. To the point that Nora wants to ask if there's sun in Cornwall.

'There she is!' Mark grins, turning away from the stove to hug her first.

Nora still has her phone in her hand and almost drops it in her haste to hug him back. When she presses her cheek to his big, warm chest, it's enough to bring tears to her eyes as she considers staying like that for the rest of the evening. But he lets go and steps back so James can hug her. He kisses the top of her head and when she presses her cheek to his chest as well, she remembers how he smells like Mark, of the same washing powder.

He steps back and takes the glass of wine off the island. 'Happy almost birthday, Nora!'

She puts her phone down and accepts it with a loose smile. 'Thanks, Uncle James!'

'Your father's on his way,' her mother says from the doorway, and when Nora turns to her, she nods down the hall. 'I'm going to freshen up. How long until dinner, Mark?'

He rubs the back of his head. 'Half an hour?'

'Perfect.' Jennifer nods, then is gone.

'What are you making?' Nora asks, walking around the island to peer into the pots.

'Mark's rediscovered his Persiana recipe book,' James says, rolling his eyes.

Mark lifts one of the lids to reveal something that smells so good Nora gasps. 'Lamb and sour cherry meatballs.' Then he points at the bowls and platters. 'Chargrilled aubergines with saffron yoghurt, tomato salad with pomegranate molasses and homemade flatbreads.'

It all looks amazing, so Nora feels bad when she tentatively asks, 'Is there rice?'

Mark laughs. 'Of course.' He points to one of the saucepans. 'We're Guyanese.'

'You didn't have to go to all this trouble,' she says, even if she is very grateful that he did. 'We're going to the Wolseley tomorrow night for my actual birthday, remember?'

'Oh, he loves it. He'd make all of this even if it was just me and him,' James tells her, then pats the stool next to his at the island. 'Now come, Nora. Distract Mark so he doesn't realise I've done nothing to contribute to this supper I'll be claiming half the credit for later.'

'I'm so sorry about Meredith,' she says softly, as she hops onto it.

He and Mark exchange a glance and they look so sad it makes her chest hurt.

'Thanks,' James says, looking away as he tops up his glass.

'We knew we were going to lose her.' Mark reaches for his own. 'I'm just glad we got to spend some time with her before ...' When he trails off, James reaches for his hand.

'Anyway.' Mark forces a smile. 'Come. Tell us, darling. What have you been up to while we've been gone?

Remind an old married couple what it's like to be young and cool.'

That hits a nerve and Nora swallows a huge gulp of wine.

'What?' James asks, when she puts the glass down.

She glances over her shoulder at the door to check her mother isn't there, then tells them about the job at the Tate, about walking out of Redchurch because she thought she'd got it, then finding out about Tatum Green. They're furious, but don't seem surprised.

'I can't do it again,' she tells them, knocking back another mouthful of wine. 'Remember what it was like when I graduated from uni?'

They groan, letting her know that they do.

'All those exhibitions and fairs I helped with and the coffees I went for and *nothing*.' She shakes her head. 'All those interviews. The research I did and the presentations I prepared, and for what? The only job I could find was in the cloakroom at the Royal Academy.'

'We remember,' Mark tells her, with a heavy sigh, as he lets go of his husband's hand so he can check on one of the pots.

'And then I finally got the job at Redchurch and I thought, *This is it! This is exactly what I want to do*. And Roland *promised*.' James nods when she points her wine glass at him. 'He *promised* to teach me everything he knew. So, I did *everything* he said. I managed his diary and got his turmeric and ginger shots every morning, which he'd wash down with a *pain au raisin*, and what did he do?' she asks, even though they already know. 'He hired Charlie!'

45

'He hired Charlie,' her uncles say in unison.

'I should have left then,' she tells them, finishing her wine.

It's them, so they have the grace not to remind her that they did tell her to leave.

Instead, James refills her glass while Mark nods sympathetically.

'So, I applied for the job at the Tate and guess what?' She snatches her glass from the island. 'Here I am again. Back to square one.' She's suddenly so angry that she has to tell herself to lower her voice in case her mother hears. 'I've *wasted* the last four years.'

'No, you haven't,' James says. 'Roland is an unrepentant arsehole, but you did learn something from him. And you made *a lot* of contacts while you were there.'

That's true.

'So, you're not back at square one,' Mark reminds her. 'You have four years' experience working at one of the coolest galleries in London with some of the coolest artists.'

'Okay. Yes.' She sits a little straighter. 'This is working. Keeping saying stuff like that.'

'And all of this hasn't been for nothing, has it?' James assures her. 'You ran Redchurch. So, when the time comes for you to open your own gallery, you know exactly what to do.'

Nora slumps again. 'If Mum and Dad don't kill me first.'

'Don't worry about them.' Mark waves his hand. 'They just want you to be happy.'

James nudges her with his elbow. 'You've got to remember that all they know is you coming home every night complaining about how much you hate Roland. They just don't understand why you put up with him when you're miserable at Redchurch.'

'I'm not miserable,' Nora says, then softens. She's never thought about what it looked like to her parents. 'I only put up with Roland because I thought it was leading somewhere.'

'I know. And he took advantage of that,' James says, picking a pomegranate seed from the salad in front of him and popping it into his mouth. 'But now you know that people like him do that and you won't let it happen again, will you?'

'Listen, darling,' Mark chips in, as he cuts a lemon in half, 'I know you don't think so because you're constantly comparing yourself to Ben, but your parents are proud of you. We've seen them. Haven't we, James?' He points the knife at him. 'Every time we go to one of your exhibitions at Redchurch, they tell everyone, *Our daughter did this!*'

That's true. They do that.

'So, I'm not worried,' Mark tells her, putting the knife down and grabbing one half of the lemon. 'And you shouldn't be, either. You'll find something else. I know you will.'

James steals another pomegranate seed before his husband squeezes the lemon over the salad. 'You just need to come up with a plan before you tell Jennifer and Alex.'

Mark nods. 'As long as you have a plan, they'll be fine.'

Before she can thank her uncles, her phone buzzes on the island.

She looks down to see that it's Ben.

'Hey. You almost home?'

'Yeah.' There's a long pause before he adds, 'Sounds like you are already, though.'

'I just got in.'

'Are you alone?'

'No, I'm in the kitchen with Uncle Mark and Uncle James. Why?'

There's another long pause. Then he says, 'Don't worry. I'll see you soon, yeah?'

~*~

Dinner is exactly what she wanted. The six of them haven't been together since Christmas so it's lovely to be around the dining table again, passing plates and bowls back and forth.

Or, at least, it's lovely until her father asks her if there's any news from the Tate.

Ben winks at her across the table and she remembers he doesn't know. So, she just smiles sweetly and says, 'Not yet.'

Her uncles intervene before there are any more questions, regaling them with tales of Pidwell, the tiny village in west Cornwall where they were staying. How beautiful it is. How magical. How they need to visit, go back to Mousehole and see how much it's changed since

Mark and Jennifer were kids. They used to go to Mousehole every summer – but since Nora's grandfather passed and her grandmother moved into a retirement home nearby, to be closer to Mark and Jennifer, there's no need to go back.

Mark clearly doesn't agree and while he needs to calm down about how wonderful Pidwell is, Nora is grateful, glad that her parents can't get a word in to ask her anything else.

Ben is being uncharacteristically quiet, though. Nora watches him across the table as his face tightens and tightens until he's sitting there, arms crossed and jaw clenched.

Mark must notice as well because he finally stops gushing and says, 'You saw.'

Ben nods. 'I saw.'

Nora looks at her brother, then at her uncles. 'Saw what?'

They exchange a glance, then James clears his throat and says, 'We weren't going to say anything tonight, what with it being Nora's birthday. We were going to wait—'

'Did Ben see you at the hospital?' Jennifer interrupts. 'Is one of you sick?'

'No! No!' James holds his hands up. 'Nothing like that.'

Her uncles look at each other again and Mark says brightly, 'It's good news, actually.'

Jennifer doesn't look convinced. 'What did Ben see?'

Mark runs a hand over his head and sighs, his shoulders sinking. 'The for-sale sign.'

Chapter 5

Nora's phone buzzes as she's leaving the house the next morning and she doesn't even check, assuming it's Luce. So, when she answers, it takes her a second to realise it's Charlie.

'Oh. Hey,' she says, unsure why he's calling her. She didn't know he had her number.

'Hey,' he says, in that slow, sleepy way he does, like he's about to yawn. 'Roland told me what happened yesterday. I'm sure you have a different version of events, though.'

Apparently, Roland's 'version of events' is that she couldn't hack it, had a tantrum and walked out. Nora is seething, but given Charlie's connection to Roland, she's never been sure if she can trust him. But she's left Redchurch now and, she figures, isn't likely to see either of them again, so gives in to the urge to tell him what actually happened. About Roland and the obscene commission he added to Natasha and Daniel's work and his vile chicken-shop comment.

To his credit, Charlie sounds genuinely appalled. 'God, he's such a dick.'

'He really is.' Nora chuckles, softening at the unexpected solidarity.

He curses under his breath, then mutters, 'Listen. He's back so I'd better go. Don't worry, yeah? I'll put the feelers out, see if there's anything going. I went to uni with someone who does loads of digital stuff for the V and A. I'll text her now.'

'Thanks, Charlie,' she says, taken aback by his generosity.

'It'll be okay, yeah? You're brilliant. You deserve much better than this place.'

Then he's gone and Nora has to cough the lump from her throat as she heads to the café, the one that always smells of croissants. This morning it smells of burned sugar as well and, given that all she's eaten so far today is a banana, it's more than a little overwhelming.

It's Saturday, so it's packed, but she finds her uncles sitting at a table in the corner.

'Have you forgiven us, darling?' Mark asks, with a pout.

Nora ignores him, sitting next to James when he slides along the wooden bench to make room for her. And she ignores the plate with the almond croissant the size of her head that Mark pushes her way. So, he tries a different tack, reaching down and producing a baby pink gift bag with large red spots and holding it over the table at her.

'Happy birthday, darling!'

It's pure bribery, she knows, but takes it anyway.

It's them, so the gift is perfect. A book about Modigliani and a Space NK voucher that, combined with the one her parents gave her, means she can have a much-needed splurge. Even the card is perfect. An illustration of Moira Rose that says, *HAPPY BIRTHDAY, BÉBÉ.*

'Thank you,' she says, then thanks the waiter when he arrives with a latte.

'So,' Mark tries again, as she reaches for a sugar, 'are you going to let us explain?'

'Explain what?' she asks, with a pointed sigh, shaking the packet, then tearing it open and pouring it into her coffee. 'How you're abandoning me to live in Cornwall?'

He rolls his eyes at her theatrics. 'We're not abandoning you, Nora.'

She stirs her coffee, nose in the air in mock-indignation. 'Hmm.'

'We're … we're … I don't know…' He looks across the table at James for back-up.

James finishes Mark's thought. 'Starting a new chapter of our life.'

She looks down and opens the Modigliani book. 'How nice.'

'The thing is …' Mark starts, then stops, clearly waiting for Nora to look up again, but when she starts flipping through the book, pretending to be absorbed, he tries again. 'The thing is, Nora, watching someone you love die puts things into perspective.'

That makes her stop and look at him.

When he catches her peering at him from under her eyelashes, he tries to smile. 'You never met Meredith, but she was a *force*. She had this energy. You could feel it before she even walked into the room. I honestly thought she'd live for ever, but she didn't, and …'

He looks at James, then carries on: 'I know you don't get why I … why *we*,' he looks at James again, 'love Pidwell so much. It's not just because of Meredith and her wife, Annabelle, although they were a huge, huge part of it. It's because ...'

When he trails off again, Nora looks him in the eye for the first time.

Earning her attention obviously gives him the courage to continue because he flashes her a grateful smile and says, 'I know you haven't been back to Mousehole since Pops died ten years ago and Mum moved here. But you remember it, right?'

She nods.

'Well, as pretty as Mousehole is, growing up there as a Black kid who was into the Cure and wore eyeliner wasn't easy. I already felt like a misfit, so when I realised I more than just *admired* Rob Lowe because he was a great actor, I felt completely lost.'

Mark chuckles warmly and says, 'Just try to picture it, Nora. There was me, a Black gay eyeliner-wearing Goth, living in Mousehole, the most un-Black, un-gay, un-Goth corner of the earth. Needless to say, I was miserable. So, one afternoon in the summer holidays, when I had nothing to do and no friends to do it with, I decided to go for a walk.

'So, I'm walking along the top of a cliff, Pidwell Cove beneath, listening to Kate Bush and considering throwing myself into the sea ...' Mark pretends to swoon and presses the back of his hand to his forehead '. . . like only a misunderstood fifteen-year-old Goth can, when someone calls out to me. For a moment, I wondered if it was God, telling me not to jump.'

James laughs, almost choking on his coffee. Nora dreads to think how many times he's heard this story, but he's still enthralled.

'But it's not God, it's Meredith, in a white, flowing kaftan, her dark hair *everywhere*. So then I think it's Kate Bush. That I've conjured her and she's there to save me!'

James laughs again, which makes Nora laugh as well this time.

'It had to be an apparition, right?' Mark insists. 'Pidwell is literally at the edge of the earth. I didn't think anyone lived there. It used to be a busy village back when the quarry was in operation. But when it shut, everyone left to find other jobs and Pidwell just kind of died.'

'There's nothing there, Nora,' James tells her, 'just the valley and the cove, but you wouldn't pass it unless you were walking along the South West Coast Path, like Mark was.'

'Even if you're driving, you turn off the main road,' Mark says, gesturing to the left, 'when you see the sign for Pidwell and drive until you see the sea. That's it. There's just one road that cuts through the valley. So, there's no reason to go there and nothing there when you do. Only a handful of fisherman's cottages and a shop. And the Trefelyn Inn, which was the quarry manager's house when it was built. It was converted in the twenties, but it hasn't been a hotel since Meredith bought it in the sixties. It was just she and Annabelle living in it until about ten years ago, when it became too much for them and they bought a cottage.'

'The odd tourist stops by,' James tells her with a shrug, as he finishes his coffee, 'usually in the summer, when they're walking the Path. But the sea in Pidwell is too calm to surf and the cove's tiny, so there's not enough to keep them entertained. They just stop, get an ice cream from the shop, take some photos and carry on to Mousehole or Penzance.'

'Which is why I didn't think anyone lived in Pidwell. So, you can't blame me for thinking I was hallucinating and Kate Bush had come to take me away from it all,' Mark insists. 'So, when she beckoned me over, of course I went.'

'Why wouldn't you? It was Kate Bush,' Nora agrees, sipping her coffee.

Mark ignores her tone – and James's snort – and carries on with the story: 'So, I go over, she looks me up and down and says, "Hey, kid. Know how to peel a potato?"' He raises his cappuccino cup. 'And that's how I started working in the kitchen of the Trefelyn.'

James points at the Modigliani book. 'It used to be an artist colony, you know.'

'The Trefelyn?' Nora asks, with a frown.

'Pidwell. It's not as famous as the others in Cornwall, but some of the artists from the Newlyn School came to join it. It was started by an artist called Malcolm Montgomery in the thirties. He loved it so much, he changed his name to Malcolm Pidwell.'

'That's how Meredith ended up there,' Mark adds. 'She heard about the colony and went to see why Pidwell was so special. She always says ...' the corners of his mouth droop as he corrects himself '... *said* that the light was different there because there's nothing in the way, so the sun is uninterrupted and at its purest.'

'When was this?' Nora asks, picking a flaked almond off the croissant.

''Sixty-five, I think. She was sick of the scene in London and—'

'Wait,' she interrupts, pointing at Mark across the table. Something's been nudging her and she realises then what it is.

'*Wait*,' she points at him again. 'Is Meredith *Meredith Murphy*?'

'Yes,' her uncles say in unison.

'Who's married to the sculptor Annabelle French?'

They nod.

'Annabelle French who won the Turner Prize?'

'Yes.' James lifts his right shoulder and lets it drop. 'In 1992, I think.'

Nora wants to shake them. 'Why didn't you tell me?'

'We did!' they insist.

'*When?* There's *no way* you could have told me you're friends with Meredith Murphy and Annabelle French and I wouldn't remember!'

James points at his husband, then at her. 'We told you last night!'

'You weren't listening,' Mark hisses, and he's never looked so much like her mother.

'Last night?' She waves her hand at them. 'Of course I wasn't listening. I was distracted by the Tate thing. You should have told me before. I can't believe you kept that from me.'

'We didn't keep anything from you.' James puts his hands in his hair and fists them. 'We talk about Meredith and Annabelle *all the time*, Nora.'

'Meredith and Annabelle,' she clarifies. 'Not Meredith Murphy and Annabelle French.'

James looks at Mark, who looks equally confused. 'What's the difference?'

'Um. Hi. Hello?' Nora points at herself, then plucks another flaked almond from the top of the croissant. 'Have you forgotten what I do?'

'We told you they're artists,' Mark reminds her.

That's true, she thinks, as she drops the almond onto her tongue. They did tell her that Meredith and Annabelle were artists. She just figured they were like every other elderly couple in Cornwall, wiling away their days painting pretty pictures of the sea.

'Artists? Have you been on Instagram? *Everyone*'s an artist,' she huffs, giving in and reaching for the croissant. 'You didn't tell me that one of them won the Turner Prize!' She tips her chin at her uncles, before she takes bite. 'So, your good friend world-renowned pop artist Meredith Murphy was sick of the scene in London and ...'

'*And*,' Mark echoes her tone as he crosses his arms and sits back in his chair, 'as soon as she got to Pidwell, she fell in love with it. So, she bought the Trefelyn Inn and started the Pidwell Arts Club. She charmed a few other artists into joining her, including Annabelle.'

'Then what happened?' she asks, putting the croissant down and finishing her coffee.

'Well, from the stories she and Annabelle tell, by the late sixties the Trefelyn had become Cornwall's equivalent of the Silver Factory. Hunter S. Thompson visited briefly in the early seventies, apparently, because he was going to write a piece about the Pidwell Arts Club, but Meredith and Annabelle weren't interested.'

'What? Why?' Nora asks, as she tries to get the waiter's attention to order more coffee, but it's so busy that he passes their table without so much as a glance.

'Because it was never meant to be this *thing*, you know. Meredith left London because she hated the scene, so she had no intention of starting another. It just happened.' Mark stops to think about it, then says, 'The Pidwell Arts Club wasn't supposed to be The Pidwell Arts Club. It was supposed to be a port in a storm. Somewhere misfits, like me, were safe to be whoever we were and whoever we wanted to be. Meredith always says,' he doesn't correct himself this time, Nora notes with a sad smile, 'that home is where you're understood. So, if you weren't understood where you lived, you always had a home in Pidwell.'

'Is it still that to people?'

'To some, yeah. But you know what the art world's like, Nora. It's constantly evolving. So, when the artists moved on, James and I were the only ones who still visited regularly.'

'Meredith and Annabelle always say we're the sons they never had.' James shrugs. 'So, we shouldn't have been surprised that Meredith left us the Trefelyn when she died.'

Nora stares at him. 'But what about Annabelle?'

'She's thrilled.' Mark shifts in his chair. 'She had no idea what to do with it.'

'Yeah, but *still*,' Nora says, her eyes wide. 'Wasn't that their home?'

Mark clears his throat. 'It was. But like I said, they bought a cottage in the valley so the Trefelyn has just been sitting there, empty, for the last ten years.'

James's gaze flicks to Mark, clearly uneasy about their unexpected windfall. 'Besides, the pair of them have spent the last fifty years living like hippies, so have accrued quite a fortune without realising it. Annabelle never has to work again, if she doesn't want to.'

'Meredith left us the Trefelyn because she wants us to bring it back to its former glory,' Mark explains. 'Which we intend to do. She also left us the money to do it, but according to the quotes we've had, it will barely cover the cost of repairing it. It's in a right state, Nora.'

'The Inn's bones are good, though,' James smiles at her, then at Mark, 'so it doesn't look like there will be any major repairs. It's mainly cosmetic, but still. It's a lot of work.'

'So, what's the plan?' Nora asks, as she finally gets the waiter's attention.

'The plan was to spend the summer doing it up, then put it on the market,' James says.

Nora notes the *was* and holds her breath as James looks across at Mark.

'But after spending so much time in Pidwell with Meredith and Annabelle since the new year, we've realised how unhappy we are.'

'Unhappy?'

They're not unhappy.

Nora has never known two people with so much energy. They're always moving. Always laughing. Always teasing one another. Being around them is such a joy.

They're not unhappy.

'Of course we're happy,' James reassures her, when her shoulders sink, slowly rubbing her back with his hand. 'I love our life and I love being a music teacher, but our budget has been cut so much that from September I'll be working across three different schools.'

'And while I,' Mark says, with a wistful sigh, 'dreamed of working in procurement for the London Borough of Richmond upon Thames when I was a kid, it's not that fulfilling.'

They chuckle, but Nora feels a pinch of panic as she waits for them to say it.

'So, now we're thinking …' Mark says gently.

Here we go, Nora thinks, when he pauses, the pinch a little sharper this time.

'. . . we're going to keep it. Run it ourselves. It's what Meredith would have wanted.'

'Yeah. But.' Nora tries not to sound sour, but she can feel her whole face tightening into a scowl. 'You don't know the first thing about running an inn. It's hard work.'

'That's true,' Mark concedes. 'But we'll learn.'

'It'll be an adventure!' James says, in the too-bright, too-loud tone her mother used when Nora was a kid and she was trying to persuade Nora that okra wasn't evil. When it doesn't work, he takes it down a notch. 'I'm going to manage the Trefelyn and Mark's going to run the kitchen. We're going to bring some life back to the village.'

'It's already started!' Mark grins. 'Artists have been coming back to Pidwell for the last few years, since Annabelle did the Fourth Plinth. It's got this *energy* again. It's palpable.'

'It must be like how the village felt when Meredith started the Pidwell Arts Club.' James beams, his cheeks flushed. 'One of the artists, a sculptor who showed up three years ago, looking for Annabelle, is starting the New Pidwell Arts Club in Meredith's honour. So, it feels like the perfect time to be there. To be part of the new wave, you know?'

Okay. This is happy, Nora realises, as she listens to them, breathless and giddy.

Mark looks at James, then at her. 'It won't be long until people hear and want to visit again. So the new plan is to reopen the Trefelyn for the August bank-holiday weekend.'

Nora isn't convinced. 'That's in *three months*! Isn't that a bit ambitious?'

'Yeah,' James says. 'But if everyone helps out …'

'Everyone?' She senses where this is going.

Mark holds up his hands. 'Don't worry, Nora. We're not going to ask you to knock down any walls or sand the floorboards, or anything.'

'Oh, God, no!' James snorts at the thought, then smiles up at the waiter as he returns with their coffee. 'We have another proposition for you, actually.'

'Yeah?' she asks warily, as she reaches for a packet of sugar.

'We've been thinking about your plan.'

'Does it involve a plane ticket to Mexico?' she asks, shaking the sugar.

'You need something to tide you over until you find something else, right?'

She continues to eye James warily, the packet stilling between her fingers. 'Yeah?'

'Well,' her uncle Mark tags in, 'in the sixties, Meredith and Annabelle hosted the Pidwell Arts Festival. You know the sort of thing. Local artists, showing their work.'

'It used to be every August bank-holiday weekend,' James joins in, when Nora continues to stare at them suspiciously. 'Before we left Pidwell, we were talking to Annabelle, and she said it would be a fitting tribute to Meredith if we were to revive the festival.'

'Okay,' Nora says.

'We thought we could coincide it with the reopening of the Trefelyn,' James tells her, the bench shivering as he turns his knees towards her.

'That's a good idea, actually,' Nora admits.

'We're glad you think so.' Mark gives her full jazz hands, which isn't like him at all, so he must be excited. 'Because we want you to run it!'

'What?' She sniggers. 'The Trefelyn? I thought you were managing it, James?'

He snorts. 'No! Not the inn. The festival!'

'I mean, it's not the Venice Biennale,' Mark says, tilting his head from side to side as he reaches for his cup, 'but thanks to a generous donation from a local artist—'

'Which,' James interrupts, raising a finger to him, 'is a blessing and a curse, because it means that Nora will have to find space for Kate's *awful* paintings.'

'God. Yes. True,' Mark says. Nora dreads to think how awful these paintings are because he looks horrified, but he softens the blow: 'But it does mean that we can pay you.'

James nudges her and waggles his eyebrows.

They're proving to be quite the double act.

'*And*,' Mark adds, answering the question before she even thinks to ask it, 'we know someone who is spending the summer in the South of France and needs a house-sitter.'

'A house-sitter?' Nora asks, struggling to keep up. A moment ago, she thought they were going to ask her to run the inn. Now she's house-sitting and organising an arts festival.

'Yes!' James claps. 'All you need to do is keep her cat alive. You can do that, right?'

'Of course she can!' Mark tells him. 'Cats are easy. Much easier than dogs. At least you don't have to walk them. All you have to do is feed them and not interfere with their plans for world domination.'

They grin at one another, then turn to her and say at once, 'It's the perfect plan!'

'Is it?' she asks.

But Nora can already feel the shock giving way to something else. Excitement, she realises, as she feels the fizz of it in her chest. Yeah, it's only a local arts festival, but Meredith Murphy and Annabelle French are hardly local. And, if she's running it, that means she can do all the things she loves. Meet the artists. Choose and hang the art. Devise the programme.

And she'd be paid for it?

Nora immediately starts doing a pro-con list in her head.

Pro. She'll be doing something proactive, rather than waiting around for another job.

Con. What if she misses out on a job because she's in Cornwall for three months?

Pro. She's never managed a festival before so it will look great on her CV.

Con. It's only a local festival so she'll probably be doing everything herself.

Pro. She'll be doing everything herself so she'll learn more than she did at Redchurch.

Con. It's a whole summer without Ben and Luce.

Pro. It's a whole summer with her uncles.

'Well?' James asks, with an eager smile. 'What do you reckon, Nora?'

'The timing is perfect, darling. This is just what you need.' Mark tilts his head at her. 'Remember what your mum always says whenever you get knocked off course?'

Rest.

Reset.

Regroup.

Nora rips into the sugar packet and pours the contents into her latte. 'Okay.'

Her uncles gasp, clearly expecting to have to do more to persuade her.

'Okay?' James almost leaps off the bench. 'You'll do it?'

'I'll do it.'

Mark reaches across the table for her hand and squeezes it. 'Thank you, Nora.'

James slings his arm around her shoulders and says the same as he kisses her cheek.

'No, thank *you*. You're right, it's the perfect plan,' she tells them, then pulls a face. 'I'll have to google *How to keep a cat alive*, though. Remember that succulent you got me?'

James shakes his head solemnly. 'Please don't do that to Mrs Stroud's cat.'

Chapter 6

The following evening, Nora and Ron – the elderly burgundy Peugeot 307 she inherited from her mother six years ago – are on the B3315 looking for the sign to Pidwell.

It had all happened in such a rush. One minute she was in the café, offering to help with the festival and promising not to kill Mrs Stroud's cat, and the next her uncles were telling her that there was so little time – and so much to do – before the August bank-holiday weekend that she found herself agreeing to leave for Pidwell the next day.

With hindsight, that was good, because it meant she had no time to procrastinate. The plan was to tell her parents that evening over dinner when she'd have Ben and her uncles there to back her up. But, really, it was more to do with the fact that if she did it somewhere public – especially somewhere as nice as the Wolseley – she hoped there would be less yelling about her walking out of Redchurch before she was sure about the job at the Tate. But when she told Ben her plan, he said it wasn't fair to announce it in a busy restaurant with waiters hovering and someone proposing to their girlfriend at the next table.

He was right, so Nora told her parents as soon as she got home from the café. They were unnervingly quiet.

Then her father demanded to see the email Nora had received from Carol. When she handed him her phone, to her astonishment, he peered over his glasses and said, 'If I'd received this, I would have thought I had the job as well.'

'Very unprofessional,' her mother agreed, with a sharp huff.

When they asked her what she was going to do and Nora told them about Pidwell and the arts festival, they were, like everyone said they would be, comforted that she had a plan.

'This is just what you need, darling,' her father told her, kissing her cheek.

'Yes. Rest. Reset. Regroup,' her mother said, kissing the other one.

So, her birthday dinner at the Wolseley became a farewell one, with her family toasting her summer sojourn in Pidwell, while Mark told the Kate Bush story again.

But if her parents were quietly concerned, Luce was utterly hysterical at the prospect of a summer without Nora. Luckily, she calmed down after a couple of cocktails and, by the time the bar closed, she was already planning to take the August bank-holiday weekend off work to come to the festival and was looking up trains to Penzance.

After that, everything was a blur of packing and goodbyes and now here she is, on the B3315, looking for the sign to Pidwell.

Turn when you see the sign and drive until you see the sea. That was all Mark had said, so when she finally spots the turn-off to Pidwell, she does as she's told, but after driving through a dense valley of trees for several minutes, Nora begins to panic.

It doesn't help that it's so dark. Not London dark, which is never actually dark, not with its lamppost-lined streets and the neon glow from the kebab shops. Here it's dark in the purest, most menacing sense. There's no light at all. Just an endless tunnel of trees that part for the road, a layer of leaves between her and the sky so she can't see the moon any more. Only Ron's headlights, like twin lighthouses pointed out across a black ocean.

Perhaps if it wasn't dark she wouldn't be so concerned. It's her own fault. She should have followed her uncles when they left this morning. But she'd wanted one last brunch with Ben and Luce and now she's lost. In fairness, she should have been here three hours ago when there was still the prospect of daylight. But, thanks to an overturned lorry and having to stop to use the toilet and grab what was quite possibly the saddest cheese sandwich ever made, it's now almost eleven o'clock and everything looks the same. The steady, trundling treadmill of the road beneath the wheels of her car just black, black, black.

Nora is about to call her uncles when there's a break in the trees. A cottage. The lights are on and the small sign of life is so reassuring that she lets go of a breath. A few minutes later there's another. Then another. Then another. Then nothing for almost half a mile.

But just as Nora begins to panic again, the trees stop, the road ends and there it is.

The sea.

For a moment the relief makes her eyes swim out of focus as she stops at the top of the slip down to the beach and looks out ahead of her. At last, there's the moon, high and bright in the sky, picking out the tips of the waves beneath it so they're gilded with silver.

She's here.

Ron lets out a curmudgeonly creak as she opens the door and clambers out. Her legs are stiff from driving for almost nine hours and her head foggy from too many cups of dire petrol-station coffee, but she still has to fight the urge to run down the slip towards the sea.

Instead, she stands there, listening to the crickety-click of Ron's engine as it cools while she takes it all in. Not that there's much to see in the dark. Just the curl of the cove and the sweep of the cliffs. And the sea, of course, the moon over it, white and uninterrupted.

So this is Pidwell, is it?

When she turns away from the shore to look at it for the first time, it's just as her uncles described, the cove a perfect crescent. In the middle, directly in front of her, is a solid granite building that looks like it used to be a house and is now Pidwell's only shop. Then, farther to the right, there's a row of three fishermen's cottages, one of which she's staying in. And, on the other side, to the left of the shop, carved high into the cliff, there it is.

The Trefelyn.

The lights are on and she pictures her uncles side by side in bed, each with a book, trying not to fall asleep as they wait for her to call. She will but, for now, she just wants to get to the cottage and inspect where she'll be calling home for the next three months.

It's so close that she could walk, but she probably shouldn't abandon Ron at the top of the slip, so she drives the few feet to the cottages. She's almost there when Ron's headlights pick out a cat as it crosses her path. She screams and hits the brakes.

Oliver.

The cat she's tasked with keeping alive for the summer.

Not a great start, she thinks, as she grips the steering wheel and tries to catch her breath. He stops outside the front door of one of the cottages, letting her know which is hers.

He looks exactly like the photo her uncles sent her. A pale grey pudding of a cat with faint black stripes, folded-down ears and a permanently startled expression. He's a Scottish Fold, apparently. Nora knows nothing about them but, thanks to Luce's cat, Miffy, she knows enough to approach with caution. So, when she grabs her suitcase from the boot of the car, she walks over to where he's sitting on the doorstep and greets him with a careful nod.

'Oliver. Pleasure to meet you. I'm Nora. Please don't walk in front of any more cars.'

He responds with a yowl.

She realises then that she doesn't have a key, but when she tries the door, it's open. Apparently, there are still places in England where you don't have to lock your front door.

She can't wait to tell Ben.

The lights are on. Her uncles' doing, she assumes, as Oliver trots past and leaps onto the arm of the sofa, still eyeing her with that slightly startled, slightly curious expression.

The cottage isn't what she expected. She thought everything would be white with big, wide windows framing views of the sea and bare floorboards. Why, she doesn't know. According to her uncles, Mrs Stroud is in her eighties, so Nora should have prepared herself for chintz. Dried flowers and doilies and delicate, dusty chotskies she's terrified to touch.

But this isn't that, either. It's small. No big, wide windows. No white walls. No linen sofa that she can recline on while drinking tea and looking out to sea. It's essentially one room with the kitchen at one end, the living room at the other, and a small, round dining table separating the two. The living area is dominated by a red sofa with a mustard yellow blanket slung over the back. It and the other furniture – a battered brown leather chair, a wooden coffee table, a velvet footstool the same colour as the blanket with a pile of *Aesthetica* magazines on top of it – focused on a well-used wood-burning stove.

It's lit with lamps, which gives the cottage a warm, gentle glow that isn't uninviting, even if it isn't the cheery seaside hideaway she'd been hoping for. The walls are white like she'd pictured, though – what she can see of them, anyway – each one crowded with bright, abstract canvases and framed prints. And the floorboards are bare, but they're hidden under several worn, overlapping rugs that are a mess of different colours. Terracotta red and blush pink and duck egg blue, that all seem to go, somehow.

That's the thing, she realises. As mismatched as it is, everything works together. Like that cluttered bookshop around the corner from Redchurch that looks like chaos, but the guy who owns it can put his hands on whatever you ask for within a few minutes.

Her mother would hate it. She'd start tidying as soon as she walked in, like she does at Mark and James' house. Mrs Stroud's cottage is just as untidy, but untidy in that well-worn, well-loved kind of way her uncles' house is. Stuff everywhere. Not just stuff, but things.

Memories.

If Mrs Stroud was here, Nora's sure she'd introduce her to each thing as though it was an old friend. The strange statute on the sideboard. The antique binoculars on the window sill. The Clarice Cliff teapot on the kitchen counter. 'I found this in Mexico,' she'd say. 'I found these at a flea market in Penzance.' 'I found this when I was clearing out my mother's house after she died. She had no idea what it was worth and made tea in it every day.'

It's kind of comforting, Nora thinks, as she checks her phone to see what time it is. There's signal, Nora is thrilled to discover – she was terrified there would be none – and smiles when she finds a string of messages from Luce, checking if she and Ron made it, and one from her brother with a link to an article in the *Guardian* announcing an Elizabeth Taylor exhibition at the V&A, which she'd already read while she was stuck on the A30.

She fires off a text to let Luce know she's okay, then calls her parents to do the same. They're obviously in bed, waiting up to hear from her, so she promises to be in touch again in the morning, then realises she'd better call her uncles before they send out a search party.

Mark answers on the second ring. 'Are you here?'

'I'm here.'

'Beautiful, isn't it?'

Nora chuckles as she peers out of the living-room window. 'I can't actually see it.'

'Just wait until morning. It'll take your breath away, I promise.'

'Right now, I'd settle for some sleep.'

'The drive that bad, huh?'

'It wasn't *bad*,' Nora concedes with a yawn. 'Just long.'

'We must have just missed that accident on the A30. I told you to follow us.'

'I know, but I wanted one last brunch with Ben and Luce.'

'Hope the chicken and waffles were worth it.'

'Absolutely. No regrets.'

Mark chuckles. 'Go. Sleep. We've left some milk in the fridge, in case you want a coffee in the morning. And there are some fairings in the cookie jar.'

'What are fairings?'

'You'll see. Did you notice the shop?'

'Yeah.'

'We'll meet you there tomorrow morning at ten. Alice does a mean omelette.'

'Okay.' She stops, overwhelmed by another huge yawn. 'The shop. Tomorrow at ten.'

'Then we're going to Annabelle's for lunch so you can meet your team.'

'My team?'

'For the arts festival. I wouldn't get too excited, though,' he warns her. 'They're all volunteers and quite a motley crew. But I hope they'll be more of a help than a hindrance.'

'That doesn't sound ominous at all.'

'See you in the morning, darling. Now sleep.'

'Sleep.'

'Oh and, Nora,' he says, before he hangs up, 'we're so glad you're here.'

She smiles and wanders into the kitchen to see what fairings are. She can't find the cookie jar, though. Or anything from Mrs Stroud. No key. No instructions for what to do with Oliver. There's a charger, though, so she plugs in her phone and heads to the fridge.

She opens it to find that her uncles have left more than milk. There's also butter, beer and cheese. The essentials. Plus loads of vegetables. Onions. Spinach. An aubergine. A craggy thumb of ginger. A bulb of garlic with several cloves missing. A paper bag that she opens to find full of thin vicious-looking red chillies. *What am I supposed to do with these?* she asks herself, then realises there probably isn't much chance of Deliveroo in Pidwell.

She wanders through the living room towards a door that leads to what she assumes is the bedroom. She turns the light on to discover that it is, in fact, the bedroom, and it's as untidy as the rest of the cottage. Again, there are books and magazines everywhere, the walls covered with more canvases and framed prints.

The big, antique-looking dark wooden sleigh bed isn't made, and when Nora turns up her nose, she tells herself not to be a princess. This isn't a hotel, she reminds herself, as she heads over to the door on the other side of the room to find a small, bright bathroom.

Again, she's not being a princess, but she had hoped Mrs Stroud would have stripped the bed before she left. Or put out some clean towels. The only one she can find is hanging on the back of the bathroom door and is still damp.

Mercifully, Nora finds the airing cupboard and changes the sheets, then gets into the shower. At least the water's hot and there's a decent amount of pressure so she can wash the day off her. She emerges fifteen minutes later, but as she's tugging off her shower cap to free her curls, she hears the front door open, then close, and her heart skids to a halt.

She peers through the crack in the half-open bedroom door as someone passes it, and her heart starts again, twice as fast. *It's Uncle Mark*, she tells herself, as she looks around the room for her phone. *He's come to check on me*. But they've just agreed to meet in the morning. Besides, he would knock, or at least announce himself so as not to give her the panic attack she's on the verge of now. She tells herself to keep calm as she looks for her phone, then curses herself as she remembers it's charging in the kitchen. Panic licks her palms as she looks around the bedroom for a landline. Mrs Stroud is old. She must have one.

Somewhere over the sound of her heart hammering in her ears, she can hear movement in the kitchen. Cupboards opening and closing. The fridge door. A drawer.

They're looking for a knife, she thinks. But then she hears the hiss of a beer bottle being opened and that makes her miss a step as she paces over to the window, trying to open it and can't. It's painted shut. The one in the bathroom isn't, she remembers. She just opened it to let out the steam from her shower. She hurries in there to discover that it's tiny. Even if she could somehow navigate herself over the washbasin in just a towel, she's never going to get her arse through it. She considers staying where she is so there's at least a door between whoever it is and whatever they're going to do to her, but there's no lock, of course.

Nora is looking for something to prop the door closed when she hears music playing. Loud enough for her to realise it's Nina Simone. It makes her whole body shudder because it's like that 'arty' bit in a film when something horrifically violent is soundtracked by a misplaced classic song that'll be for ever associated with *that* scene in *that* film.

Her demise, it seems, will be soundtracked by Nina Simone's 'Sinnerman'.

And all she'll be wearing is some old lady's towel.

Chapter 7

*N*o, Nora thinks. *I am not going out like this. I am not
dying in someone else's towel.*

All she has to do is make it to the front door. If she can
make it to the front door, she can make it outside, and if
she can make it outside, she can make it to the Trefelyn,
to her uncles. The cottage is tiny, so it can't be more than
fifteen steps. She can run fifteen steps.

If I can survive the last train from Clapham Junction, she
thinks, *I can survive this.*

She just needs a weapon.

Nora considers the toilet brush, but can't bring herself
to touch it, so opts for a can of deodorant. She uncaps it
and, one hand clutching the top of the towel, the other
curled around the can, she creeps out of the bathroom
and across the bedroom. She stops at the door and waits,
peering through the crack to see the path to the front door.
She just needs to navigate the gap between the coffee-table and sofa, then she's there. So she opens the door with
her foot and charges out, holding up the can of deodorant,
finger poised, ready to spray.

Nora sees him then, the man.

He's standing behind the kitchen counter, flipping through a stack of post. He doesn't flinch when he looks up to see her brandishing the can of deodorant. Just picks up a remote from the counter and points it at the sideboard until 'Sinnerman' softens to a murmur.

'Hello,' he says, looking at the can of deodorant, then at Nora.

'Hello,' she says back, but has no idea why.

Nora shouldn't be saying hello, she should be running so she has no idea why she's stopped to look at him. *For the police*, she tells herself. She'll need a description for the police.

He's tall, she notes. Six foot one. Maybe two. Dark hair. Dark eyes. Tattoos down to his wrists and no doubt more under the sleeves of his black T-shirt. That's distinctive. She can tell the police that. And he looks South Asian, Indian maybe, his skin a shade or two lighter than her own.

He doesn't look like a serial killer, though. He's too thin to be a serial killer. Toothpick thin with far too much hair that clearly hasn't seen a comb for a while. She could take him. Even in a towel. And he's barefoot. Oh, God. Is that what they call him? The Barefoot Killer?

She's listened to enough true crime podcasts to know how this ends.

'I'm going now,' she tells him, her voice far steadier than she feels. 'And you're going to let me. My uncles own the Trefelyn Inn. I just called them. They're on their way,' she lies, pointing the can of deodorant at him. 'They'll be here any minute.'

Again, he doesn't flinch, just holds his hands up and says, 'Don't spray.'

Nora doesn't know if that's supposed to throw her off or reassure her that he's harmless, but it's enough to make her hesitate. His voice is deep but gentler than she expected. He talks like Charlie. That slow, syrupy drawl, like he's about to fall asleep.

But he has an accent.

Irish, she realises.

He's Irish.

'What do you want?' she asks, as she notes that to tell the police as well.

Why is she asking him that? She should already be out of the front door and fleeing to the Trefelyn. Or in Ron, heading back to London, where it's safe.

He reaches for the bottle of beer in front of him on the counter. 'Nora, I assume?'

That makes her falter. 'How do you know my name?'

'James and Mark told me you were arriving today.'

'And who are you?' Her gaze narrows. 'The welcome wagon?'

He stops to take a long sip of beer. 'I'm your neighbour.'

'My what?'

'Your neighbour.'

'Well, *neighbour*. I appreciate you coming over to ...'

Nora trails off, unsure what exactly he's come over to do. But there's something about how easily he moves around the kitchen that makes her heart settle because maybe this is what they do here. Maybe Mrs Stroud is the Monica Geller of Pidwell with people coming in and out of her cottage all day, drinking her beer and nosing through her post.

'Well, it's very nice of you to stop by,' Nora says, lowering the can of deodorant as she remembers that Mrs Stroud is in her eighties, so he's probably used to checking on her and may have promised her uncles that he'd the same for her. 'but, it's late and, as you can see, I've just got out of the shower.'

The corners of his mouth twitch. 'Yes, I can see that.'

God, he's pretty, Nora thinks, which is a ridiculous thing to notice given that a few minutes ago, she was sure that he was going to murder her. But it's impossible to ignore. He's not handsome, just *pretty*. Nothing but dark hair and big eyes and a frankly *obscene* mouth that he draws attention to by dragging the pad of his thumb along his bottom lip.

'Well.' Nora ignores the slight smirk tugging at the corners of his mouth, her hand tightening around the towel. 'I appreciate the welcome, but I'm tired and I'd like to go to bed.'

He takes another long sip of beer, then says, 'Nora, you know I live here, right?'

'Here *where*? Pidwell?'

'No, here *here*. In this cottage.'

She almost drops the can of deodorant. 'Excuse me?'

'This is my cottage. Mrs Stroud lives next door.'

She stares at him. 'I'm sorry, *what*?'

He points the bottle of beer at the wall behind her. 'That's your cottage.'

'What? No.' She looks behind her, then back at him. 'But the front door was open.'

'No one locks their doors here.' The corners of his mouth twitch again. 'It's very safe.'

'But the cat.' She points at Oliver who is still perched on the arm of the sofa, observing them like he's watching a particularly tense game of tennis. 'He was on the door-step.'

'That's my cat, Dodger.' This time he points the bottle at the cat curled up asleep on the sideboard by the strange statue, oblivious to what's unfolding. 'That's Oliver.'

Nora looks at the cat on the sideboard, then at the one on the sofa, then back at him.

'They look *exactly* the same.'

'They're brothers.'

'How do you tell them apart?'

'You'll get used to them.'

The horror of it dawns on her then, and it's as chilling as getting out of the shower to hear him walking through the front door. Nora turns in a circle, frowning at each thing, her lips pursed into a small O. The orange peel on the coffee-table. The open Murakami novel face down on the sofa. The photo of him and a woman with an easy smile on the mantelpiece.

Oh, God.

Oh, no.

'Oh, no.' She stops as a wave of shame passes over her. 'Oh, no.'

He doesn't seem bothered, though. ''S all right.'

'I'm gonna . . .' is all she can manage as she thumbs over her shoulder at the bedroom.

But he just goes back to drinking his beer.

Chapter 8

Nora wakes with such a start that it takes her a moment or two to realise where she is. But when she sits up to find Oliver – or, at least, she hopes it's Oliver – perched on the end of the bed, watching her, she lies down again with a groan as what happened the night before comes flooding back to her with such force she pulls the duvet over her head.

Oh, God.

She didn't.

She did *not* go into someone else's house and take a shower?

And change their sheets, she remembers, with another groan, as she sinks further down the bed, vowing never to come out.

She doesn't remember what she said to him before she fled, just that she charged into the bedroom to pull on what she'd been wearing before she got into the shower, then charged out again with her suitcase, waving the towel at him and promising to wash it.

Her trainers were on the doormat, where she'd left them, so she grabbed them, and her phone, which he'd left on the arm of the sofa, and ran out. She headed to her cottage – the first one, she knew it was the first, her uncles had *told her* it was the first – to find, once again, that it was unlocked. She closed the door behind her and stood with her back to it.

When her breathing had returned to a pace less likely to kill her, she took a deep breath. But it took a couple more before her eyes would refocus. When they did, there it was.

Mrs Stroud's cottage.

The one she was supposed to be in.

The layout was identical to the one she'd just run out of. Except where her neighbour's cottage was a heavenly mess of stuff he'd collected over the years, Mrs Stroud's was more carefully curated. Everything had its place and looked like it had been there for years. The floors looked original, but the white marble fireplace almost certainly wasn't, the heavy gold mirror over it reflecting the neat wooden kitchen that, much like the one next door, looked as if it had been hand-built, this one painted a warm stone white.

It was cosy. Comfortable, but elegant. More like a country pile than a beach house, the walls painted a pale Parma grey-blue, the oil paintings hanging on them in neat, evenly spaced rows. There was a large wicker basket of wood next to the woodburning stove and each area – living, dining, kitchen – was separated by a different antique rug.

Like next door, the cottage was lit with table lamps, each one a different shape, but here they all had blue and white porcelain bases and cream shades so they matched, but not quite. They were on, thanks to her uncles. And she was sure that they had also had something to do with the vases of pale pink roses and peonies dotted everywhere.

Nora went into the kitchen to find it was immaculate. No dirty plates and mugs in the sink, like next door, everything put away, the fridge clean and empty, apart from the bottle of milk her uncles had left. She also found the cookie jar and the fairings, which, she learned, after stress-eating five, were ginger biscuits and very nice.

While she devoured another, Nora found a letter from Mrs Stroud on the kitchen counter with detailed instructions on how to feed Oliver. She had also written down the numbers for his vet in Penzance, a local electrician and plumber, but no Wi-Fi code, even though Nora could see the router on the desk, which was just cruel.

Best of all, though, Nora had her big cream linen sofa that faced the sea.

She was tempted to throw herself onto it, but was drawn to the living-room window, and the moon hanging high in the sky. She stood there for a while, looking out at it until her breathing realigned and her nerves finally settled into place. As soon as they did, she yawned and remembered how tired she was. So, she grabbed her suitcase and headed into the bedroom to find the bed neatly made and two clean towels folded on the end.

Now, here she is, hiding under the duvet as her alarm goes off.

She peeks out from under it to retrieve her phone from the bedside table. When she sees that it's only six thirty, she asks herself why on earth she set it to go off so early.

But then she remembers it's Monday, so this is usually when she wakes up for work.

She has a text from Luce and is tempted to call her and tell her what happened last night, but she'll never let Nora live it down. It'll be like that time she had her photo taken with Jack Grealish in a pub. Except it wasn't Jack Grealish. It was some random bloke with good hair, which Luce knew full well, but went along with because she thought it was hilarious. Until he tried to get Nora's number, that is, which was when Luce dragged her away.

Actually, this is worse. At least she never saw him again. Her neighbour is *right next door* and, she's guessing, in a village as small as Pidwell, is going to be impossible to avoid.

'This is your fault,' she tells Oliver, pulling back the duvet just enough to glare at him.

He's still sitting on the end of the bed and doesn't look contrite in the slightest.

It's impossible to be cross with him, though, as he sits there, licking his paw and purring contently. He looks so soft that she might have been brave enough to stroke him if she hadn't decided to stay under the duvet until the memory of last night quietens.

But then he stops licking his paw and trots up the bed to sit where Nora is curled up, peeking out from the cocoon of the duvet. He stares at her for a moment, his big yellow eyes on hers, then throws back his head and lets out a pained miaow.

Nora isn't sure what the cat for *Feed me* is, but she's pretty sure that's it. 'Don't make me come out from here,' she pleads. 'This is where I live now.'

He miaows again, letting her know that he doesn't care.

'Fine,' Nora mutters, untangling herself from the duvet and crawling out of bed.

She glances at the bedroom window to find the sky the flattest, most perfect blue she has ever seen and stops to stare at it. *It must be even better over the sea*, she thinks, turning and walking towards the open door. She steps into the living room to find the morning light spilling in, the window a rectangle of pure blue, separated in two – the lighter sky resting on the slightly darker sea – like a Rothko. And her uncle was right: it takes her breath away.

Sadly, she doesn't get to enjoy her first glimpse of Pidwell, because Oliver is at her feet, reminding her about his breakfast. She gives in, following Mrs Stroud's instructions to the letter while he miaows hysterically, as though he's telling her to hurry up.

When Nora puts his bowl down, he eats with such enthusiasm that she waits to make sure he doesn't choke, before she heads back into the bedroom and gets in the shower. She curses herself again as she replays the whole ordeal in her head, but, by the time she emerges, she's determined to move on. After all, she can't avoid her neighbour for the next three months, can she? It was just a silly mistake, she tells herself as she heads out of the bedroom. She's not going to let it ruin her time here before it's even started.

So Nora doesn't tell her mother when she calls, just stands by the living window, smiling at the sea, trying to describe how beautiful it is as her mother sighs dreamily and says that she can't wait to see it for herself when she and Nora's father come for the festival.

When they blow each other three kisses and say their goodbyes, Nora turns away from the window to find Oliver dozing in a puddle of sunshine on the rug. He lifts his little head as she passes, blinking slowly, then lets it fall again as she begins opening the cabinets in the kitchen, looking for coffee. Any coffee. She doesn't care what Mrs Stroud has – instant will do – so she gasps when she finds a cafetière, then gasps again when she pulls it off the shelf to find a canister sitting behind it. She flips open the lid and the relief is immediate, the smell as comforting as it's familiar when she sticks her nose into it and inhales.

My only friend, she thinks, as she scoops more than is healthy into the cafetière.

By the time the kettle's boiled, she's found a travel mug in another cabinet. A few minutes later, she's out the door with her phone and coffee, itching to explore the village.

She has no idea why she locks the front door. After all, it's Pidwell. What's the worst that can happen? Someone will break in while she's gone and change the sheets?

At least you can laugh about it, Nora, she tells herself, as she heads towards the shop.

It's seven thirty, so the shop isn't open yet, but there's a few tables outside, a potted succulent on each. Nora peers inside to find that it's all white with white-painted shelves and a long wooden table in the middle topped with baskets. Glossy red apples in one. Garlic in another. A great green cloud of what she thinks is watercress frothing from a third.

With the sun hitting the window, she can't see the rest of the shop in any detail, but she can see enough to discover it's surprisingly well stocked. She'd figured it would be like any other shop in a village this small. Somewhere you can grab a pint of milk and a newspaper. But this shop wouldn't look out of place on the high street in Richmond. The shelves are lined with neat rows of cans and bags of pasta, and there's a fridge that looks full. She can't see with what, but she's relieved to realise she's not going to starve as she turns to face the sea.

This is what I came for, she thinks with a dreamy sigh.

The light really is different here. She knew it the moment she stepped into the living room earlier, but now the sun is in full force it's no less astonishing, just in a different way. Meredith was right. The light is purer here. It isn't dulled from having to push between tower blocks and office buildings, like in London. The sky is an unbroken stretch of blue that goes from dark to light to lighter then back to dark, brilliant blue when it meets the sea.

It's as still as bathwater, the cove curling around it and the cliffs sweeping up on either side, lush and green, the tops blushing with pink. And it's so quiet. There's no traffic. No bicycles or buggies or Deliveroo scooters buzzing back and forth. No drilling or lorries beeping as they back up. Just the whisper of the sea and the gulls wheeling overhead.

Nora continues around the cove and stops at the top of the slip down to the beach, where she parked when she arrived last night. The water looks calm. Calm enough for Nora to consider taking a swim if it warms up enough over the next few weeks. Maybe she can persuade her uncles to join her, she thinks, as she turns to face the Trefelyn Inn. She smiles when she finally sees it in the light, high on the hill, looking out across the cove. Like the shop and the cottages, it has the same pitched slate roof and white wooden windows, facing the sea. But unlike the shop and the cottages it is a crisp, wedding-cake white.

She has no idea what else they need to do but, from here, it looks in pretty good shape. No smashed windows or bowing roof. She's dying to see inside. *Maybe they'll give me the grand tour after breakfast*, she thinks, as she continues around the crescent of the cove.

At the furthest tip, she finds a sign for the South West Coast Path with *Land's End* on it and an arrow pointing up a slope. She smiles when she reaches the top and asks herself if this was where her uncle first saw Meredith in that flowing white kaftan and thought she was Kate Bush. Now she's up here, she can see why. Between the sweep of the cliffs and the call of the sea beneath, it kind of feels like the edge of the earth, like she's the only one left, so Nora doesn't blame him for thinking Meredith was an apparition.

When she looks to her right, she can see the Path, its edges softened with yellow flowers that look alight in the sunshine. It's narrower than she imagined and uncomfortably close to the edge of the cliff, but she can see why her uncles love this place so much.

She's honestly never seen anything like it.

Now Nora thinks about it, they might be on to something with the Trefelyn. From what they told her, the South West Coast Path stops here, passes around the cove and picks up again on the other side, past the cottages. The only way to rejoin it is by passing through Pidwell. The tourists *have* to pass through, so if they can be persuaded to stop for lunch – or even to stay the night – the Trefelyn could be an absolute goldmine, especially in the summer.

That makes Nora feel better about them moving here. She was slightly concerned that they'd be stuck by themselves running the Cornish equivalent of the Overlook Hotel. *But who wouldn't want to wake up to this every morning?* She takes one last look at the sea before she turns, steps away from the edge of the cliff, and heads back down the slope.

Nora's about halfway down when she hears a rustle in the bushes beside her and stops, turning her head, the travel cup poised. To do what, she doesn't know, but luckily it's only a grey and white speckled bird that emerges from the wall of leaves. She had no idea such a tiny bird could make so much noise, pressing her hand to her chest as it flies off.

As it does, she notices a path veering off the slope that she didn't see on her way up. It feels much steeper, especially in flip-flops, but she makes it to the top to find a copse of trees, their branches twisting towards the sea. She takes a tentative step forward, peering between their trunks, and her courage is immediately rewarded when they part to reveal a patch of thick grass studded with small pink flowers.

Nora's expertise extends as far as buying the odd bouquet from the florist on Richmond High Street, so she has no idea what the flowers are, just that they're so pretty: dense clumps of long stems topped with balls of bright pink blooms.

Nora walks in further, careful not to trample on the flowers, and finds a long wooden bench. Actually, it's not even a bench, rather a tree that's either fallen in a storm or because it couldn't support its weight any longer, and the trunk has been made into a seat.

As she approaches it, she sees that someone has carved 'MM + AF' with a heart around it in the middle of the seat. Nora traces it with the tips of her fingers, hoping that Meredith and Annabelle won't mind if she borrows their bench for a while. She sits, and it's perfect. Absolutely perfect. Ahead of her is an unbroken view of the sea, beneath her feet a lush carpet of green and pink. And, over her head, a thick canopy of leaves that whisper gently in the breeze, the sunlight sieving through them, warming her face.

She opens the travel cup and that's perfect as well, the coffee immediately mingling with the sea salt and damp grass so it's like nothing she has ever smelt before.

Like the beach and the forest, all at once.

Between the nine-hour drive and the *incident* with her neighbour, her introduction to Pidwell has hardly been relaxing. Nora leans back, stretches out her legs, inhales a deep breath and exhales as she looks out at the sea. As soon as she does, she feels something in her settle in way she doesn't think it ever has before. Not since she was fourteen and she went on that school trip to the Musée d'Orsay and stood staring at Monet's *Blue Water Lilies* for so long that her art teacher, Mrs Bignall, had to come and find her.

That was the day she'd known she wanted to be around paintings like that all the time. This morning, she feels the same thing as she reminds herself that working in – and owning – a gallery was never supposed to be a career. It was never supposed to be about endearing herself to people like Roland or about how many contacts she has or how much she earns. It was supposed to be about *this*, she realises, as she looks at the sea and remembers that afternoon spent staring at Monet's *Blue Water Lilies*. About seeing the most beautiful thing she had ever seen and wishing that everyone could see it as well.

~*~

Nora heads back to the cottage to freshen up before she meets her uncles for breakfast. She finds Oliver in exactly the same spot in the living room. Again, he lifts his little head when she walks in but, this time, she's brave enough to bend down and let him sniff her fingers. When he nudges them with his cheek, she gives him a quick scratch on the top of the head.

'Sweet boy,' she says, as he purrs loudly and stretches.

When she walks into the bedroom, she finds Dodger in a similar position, except he's sleeping inside her open suitcase, but doesn't bother to acknowledge her as she passes.

'Comfortable?' she asks, as she heads into the bathroom. And he just mews, as if to say, *Very*.

~*~

Nora should have got ready before she went out earlier because now she has only fifteen minutes before she meets her uncles. Still, it's enough time to put on some makeup and change into something other than yoga pants and a baggy grey T-shirt.

It's not warm enough yet for her yellow playsuit, so she opts for something simple. Jeans and an old Misfits T-shirt, that she knows her uncle Mark will appreciate. She pairs it with gold hoops that are immediately lost in her cloud of cola-coloured curls, and the gold Saint Christopher medal her parents gave her for her thirteenth birthday.

By the time she finds her sunglasses, she really is running late. She grabs her phone, keys and leather jacket, in case it gets cooler later, and barrels out of the front door. She's in such a hurry that she doesn't look where she's going and walks straight into her neighbour.

'Oh, my God!' she gasps, dropping her keys as they collide.

He's cradling a loaf of bread that he manages to hold on to, clutching it to his chest, but when he moves it away, there's a dusting of flour on his black T-shirt.

'I'm sorry!' she gasps again. 'I'm so sorry!'

''S okay,' he mutters, brushing himself with his other hand.

'And I'm sorry about last night,' she blurts out, then doesn't know what to say next. She was hoping to have time to come up with something more substantial than *sorry*, but she wasn't expecting to open her front door and see him, so it's all she's got.

''S okay,' he says again, this time with a shrug.

'Listen …' she says, then stops because why did she say that?

What exactly does she want him to listen to?

Just keep it simple, she thinks. *Just say sorry. Just say it was a misunderstanding. Just say something*, she tells herself, conscious that she's standing there, staring at him as he roots through the pockets of his jeans. He pulls out a set of keys and when he looks up, peering at her through his tangle of dark hair, Nora gulps – actually, full-on cartoon gulps – because, *good Lord*, he looks even better in daylight. The sun hitting his skin so it gleams like a brand new penny, the light picking out his Cupid's bow, drawing her attention to his mouth.

Then she's staring at it – his mouth – watching his lips pull into a pout as he brings his hand up to scratch his left temple with a finger, keys jangling as he does. When she tells herself to stop staring, she looks up to find him frowning, as he waits for her to finish the thought, the word – *Listen* – still hanging in the air between them.

'Towel,' she blurts out.

His frown deepens. 'Towel?'

'Your towel. I'll give it back to you later.' She thumbs back at her cottage.

'Okay.'

Then he's gone, his keys still jangling as he ambles towards his cottage.

Good talk, Nora thinks, giving herself a thumbs-up as she hurries away.

She looks up to find her uncles sitting at one of the tables outside the shop. She can hear them cackling from there and she doesn't think she's ever seen them look so happy.

'Nora!' They cheer and wave when they see her coming.

They jump up and hug her as she approaches. Mark notices her T-shirt immediately, saying it's perfect for Pidwell, and James tells her that Annabelle will love it as he gestures at her to sit. They ask how her morning has been, but before she can tell them, a woman strolls out of the shop and Nora stops, sure that she recognises her, but she has no idea from where.

Then she smiles and Nora's heart hiccups.

The woman from the black-and-white photograph on her neighbour's mantelpiece.

Except here she is, in glorious technicolour.

She's small and blonde, that California blonde from Instagram ads for yoga mats. More sun-kissed than bleached and still drying, like she should have a surf board under her arm.

Her neighbour's girlfriend, Nora assumes, the back of her neck burning as she realises the woman must know what she did the night before.

Great first impression, Nora, she thinks, tempted to give herself another thumbs-up.

'Hey, guys!' she says, stopping at their table and squeezing James's shoulder.

She has the same accent as her neighbour, Nora notes.

'Alice!' they say, in unison.

Then the three are talking at once, asking how each other is doing and saying how lovely the weather is before Mark and James tell her about their return to London.

Then Alice turns to her. 'You must be Nora!'

Yes, I'm the one who broke into your boyfriend's place and took a shower, Nora thinks, her smile not as easy. At least she can hide behind her sunglasses.

'Welcome to Pidwell!' Alice says, her green eyes disappearing she's smiling so hard.

'Thank you,' Nora says sheepishly.

'We really need your help with the arts festival. None of us know what we're doing!'

Her uncles laugh, nudging and pointing at one another. When James rolls his eyes and shakes his head at Mark, Nora senses a story, which she's sure she'll hear later.

'You hungry?' Alice asks.

She is actually. *Starving.*

'What's the omelette today?' Mark asks, pushing his sunglasses back up his nose.

'Feta and basil.'

Mark turns to Nora and nods. 'That sounds good.'

She nods back. 'Yeah, perfect.'

Mark thumbs at James. 'And we'll have the full Cornish with extra bacon.'

Alice doesn't write it down, but then, Nora supposes, they're her only customers.

'I know you guys will have a latte and a cappuccino, right?' Alice points between her uncles, who nod enthusiastically, then she points at Nora. 'What would you like?'

'I'll have a latte as well, please.'

'What kind of milk?'

'Normal is fine,' she says, somewhat startled.

She wasn't expecting to be asked that in Pidwell.

Mark gestures at Alice. 'She makes her own oat milk.'

'And pesto,' James adds. 'And almond butter. And bread.'

'We're very self-sufficient around here, thanks to Meredith and Annabelle,' Mark explains, adjusting his sunglasses. 'They've been members of Greenpeace since the sixties so Pidwell's always been ahead of its time when it comes to environmental stuff. You can't see them, because they're around the back, but the Trefelyn was one of the first places in Cornwall to get solar panels. Now almost everyone here has them.'

He points at her neighbour's roof and Nora sees the panels soaking up the sunshine.

When she turns back, Alice indicates the slatted wooden box outside the shop. 'We compost our kitchen waste. You're welcome to use it if you have any cooking scraps.'

'Cooking scraps?'

'You know. Eggshells. Vegetable peelings. Apple cores. That sort of thing.'

Mark knows Nora well enough to say, 'Coffee grounds.'

'Oh. Okay.'

'Here's Megan!' James cheers, at someone walking out of the shop.

97

She's white as well, but almost the opposite of Alice. Tall with broad shoulders and full hips. She's dressed in jeans and a dark green polo shirt, with *Albert Orchard* embroidered on it in small white cursive letters, and looks fresh from the shower, her short dark hair wet and her cheeks pink. Her smile isn't as easy as Alice's, though. Not in an unfriendly way, more in an *I wish all these people weren't looking at me* sort of way.

James nods at her when she stops at the table. 'Nora, this is Megan, Alice's wife.'

Wife? So Alice isn't her neighbour's girlfriend?

Maybe she doesn't know about last night, then.

Nora waves at her, slightly relieved. 'Lovely to meet you, Megan.'

'Megan's from New Zealand,' Mark says, then chuckles. '*Kia ora*, Nora!' He's clearly thrilled with himself, but Megan looks like she wants to run away.

'What's up?' James asks, when she and Alice head back into the shop.

Nora frowns. 'What?'

'You're being weird.'

'Am I?'

'She's being weird?' Her uncle Mark looks confused. 'Why are you being weird, Nora?'

'I'm not!'

They don't believe her, though, so she confesses to what happened the night before.

They sit there, their mouths getting wider and wider, until she stops.

'That's why I was weird,' she admits. 'Because I thought he'd told Alice about it.'

Her uncles turn to one another, then mock-scream.

'You didn't!' Mark gasps, covering his mouth with his hands.

James looks at him, then at Nora. 'You did not change the sheets!'

Mark barks out a laugh. 'We told you it was the first cottage, Nora!'

'I know,' she hisses. 'But you didn't tell me there were two cats!'

Her uncles are hysterical then, shrieking with laughter as she tries to shush them.

Mark holds his hands up. 'This is the best thing that's ever happened!'

'I can't wait to tell Annabelle!' James agrees, mirroring him.

'You can't!' Nora tells them, through her teeth. 'You can't tell anyone! I am *mortified*.'

'Sorry.' James takes off his sunglasses and wipes his eyes with the back of his hand.

Mark does the same, still wheezing as he says, 'Yeah, sorry, Nora.'

'I'm sorry, but ...' James starts, then splutters, covering his mouth with his hand.

'You tell her,' Mark tells him, as his shoulders start shaking again.

James lowers his voice. 'I thought you of all people would have recognised him.'

'Who?' she asks, her eyes wide with panic.

James leans forward and says, 'Your neighbour. He's Sendhil Achari.'

'No!' The shock of it makes Nora knock over a salt shaker with her hand. 'He is *not* Sendhil Achari.' It can't be. They have to be winding her up. 'You're lying!'

They shake their heads as she picks up the salt shaker and stands it back up.

'No!' She points at James, then at Mark. 'Sendhil Achari, the sculptor?'

They nod.

'No!'

Sendhil Achari is intensely private so she's never seen a photo of him (although, in fairness, she's never sought one out) but she thought he was, like, fifty, or something.

'Wait. Didn't he win the Turner Prize, like, three years ago?' When her uncles nod again, Nora throws up her hands. 'Has everyone in Pidwell won the Turner Prize?'

'You don't have to have won it to live here, but it helps.' James shrugs.

Mark looks over his shoulder to check if Alice is coming and says, 'Sendhil's the one we were telling you about. The one who's starting the New Pidwell Arts Club.'

'You told me *that*, but you neglected to tell me *who* he was.'

It's the Meredith and Annabelle thing all over again.

'At least we don't have to introduce you now,' Mark offers.

But then James roars with laughter again, slapping his arm. 'Of *all the people* in Pidwell Nora could have done that to, it had to be Sendhil, didn't it?'

Mark slaps him back and barks out another laugh.

When they finally settle down, Nora asks, 'Why is it so funny that it was him?'

'He's a bit . . .' Mark stops to look at his husband, then back at her '. . . shy.'

'I heard he was elusive,' Nora says, lowering her voice. 'He never does interviews.'

'Elusive?' James snorts. 'I'm not saying he's the Unabomber, but ...'

Mark pinches him until he cackles. 'He's just not very good with people, Nora.'

'Or talking,' James adds.

Mark corrects him. 'He talks to Annabelle and Alice.'

'*Everyone* talks to Annabelle and he grew up next door to Alice. Whereas I've only spoken to him twice, since he moved here three years ago and that was just "Morning."'

'He's just private. Reticent,' Mark tells her, rubbing the back of his head. 'You know what artists are like, Nora. He's sensitive. He likes to be left alone.'

'Great. So, I'm sure he loved me breaking into his place to take a shower.'

They fall apart laughing again, and Nora immediately regrets telling them.

So much for chalking it up as a silly mistake and moving on.

When they finally stop, James looks at her with a wicked smile. 'Peng, isn't he?'

Nora glares at him. 'Don't ever say that word again, Uncle James.'

'What?' He looks wounded. 'That's what the kids at school say.'

Chapter 9

When they've finally finished breakfast, it's time to head to Annabelle's for lunch.

I could get used to this, Nora thinks, as they amble up the road towards the valley.

As they're approaching the Trefelyn, her phone buzzes in her hand and Nora grins when she looks down to see that it's Luce calling.

'Sorry!' she answers. 'I was going to ring you later, I promise.'

'Oh, no worries. I was just checking you're okay.'

'Yeah,' she mutters, hissing at her uncles when they laugh and point down the road at Sendhil, who is ambling towards the shop, the cats trotting behind him, their tails in the air.

'You sure?' Luce asks, obviously noticing Nora's shift in tone.

'I'm fine, I promise,' she assures her, then glares at her uncles and swats at them to stop in case Sendhil sees them. 'I'll tell you later, okay? I'm on my way to lunch.'

When Nora hangs up, her eyes widen as she realises they must be in the valley. It's *huge*. Much bigger than she'd thought when she'd driven through it last night, and dense with trees that seem to go on and on and on. And, with that, the light shifts, the midday sun spilling through the gaps in the shifting leaves over their heads, scattering delicate, lacy shadows in every direction as they walk under them, bathing everything in a soft green light.

'I wasn't expecting this. I knew about the sea, but ...' She trails off, a little breathless, as she tries to pick out each shade of green they pass. Not just verdigris and jade, but apple and monstera and avocado skin, and so many others, she'd never be able to count them all.

'This is quite rare in Cornwall,' James says, waving at the trees circling them. 'To have a valley like this so close to the sea. It's kind of magical. Every time we walk through here, it's slightly different. In the spring, the grass is dotted with snowdrops, then early primroses and white anemones, and by mid-April, it's awash with bluebells.'

'I didn't think it would be so colourful here,' Nora admits, wishing she'd seen the bluebells last month. 'Like those pink flowers on the tops of the cliffs.'

'Thrift.' Mark raises his voice over the rush of the stream. 'Or sea pinks. Pretty, right?'

'So pretty. What are the yellow ones lining the path? Mimosa?' she asks, remembering the bunch she'd bought in March that had made her room smell like spring.

'Gorse, actually.'

'How do you know all this? You've only just moved here,' Nora asks, with a frown.

'We've been boning up,' Mark tells her, slinging his arm around her shoulders.

'We're growing our own herbs for the kitchen at the Trefelyn,' James says, as he ducks under a branch. 'We want everything to be local. Nothing from more than thirty miles away.'

'Here we are,' Mark says, and when Nora looks up, she sees it.

A house.

It seems to appear from nowhere, like in a fairy tale. It looks like all the others in Pidwell. Square, solid, with a slate roof, the front door in the middle with four white, wood-framed windows, two up and two down. Except this one is circled by a waist-high wall with what looks like a fuchsia hedge on the other side of it.

A head pops up as they approach. 'You're here!'

'Annabelle!' Nora's uncles say, cheering at the sight of her.

Nora tries to be cool, but it's Annabelle French. One of the country's most famous sculptors, who turned down an OBE in 1993 because, according to an article she read before she left London, *It was a club she would not have been welcome to join if she were unable to manipulate clay*, which made Nora fall hopelessly in love with her.

She had pictured a tall, serene soul who carried herself with the sort of confidence that only comes with having nothing left to prove. But Annabelle is tiny. All soft cheeks and wrinkly eyes with this itchy sort of energy that makes Nora wonder if she ever sits still.

When Annabelle steps back from the hedge, Nora sees that she's wearing denim dungarees that are muddy at the knees, with a pale blue linen shirt that's the same colour as her eyes, her thick grey curls trying desperately to escape from the bun at the back of her head. She wipes her brow with the back of one of her gardening gloves. 'Just having a tidy!'

There's a chorus of *Hey! Hello! How's it going?* as Annabelle and her uncles greet one another. Then Annabelle strides over to her. 'Nora!' She kisses her on both cheeks and pulls her into a big, blanketing hug. Given that they've never met and Annabelle is holding a pair of secateurs, Nora would usually balk, so she's surprised that she finds herself melting into it.

When Annabelle steps back, she puts her hands on Nora's shoulders and looks at her. 'Listen to me, Nora Armstrong,' she says. 'Fuck Roland and fuck the Tate.'

'Okay,' Nora says, too startled to say anything else.

'Their loss is our gain, dear,' Annabelle tells her. 'Now come.'

She compliments her Misfits T-shirt, then slips her arm around Nora's waist, leading her up the path to the open front door.

When Annabelle stops in the hall to step out of her wellies, Nora sneaks a look around. The living room, to the left, and the dining room, to the right, are painted black, as are the hall and staircase. That should make downstairs look dark, but the sunlight spilling through the windows and open front door seems to bounce off it, making it brighter.

There's a long wooden table in the dining room with a crystal chandelier over it and a large round mirror that, once again, makes the midday sun bounce in every direction. In the living room, there are two white sofas, not unlike the ones in Mrs Stroud's cottage, facing one another on a black-and-white Moroccan print rug, a black lacquered coffee-table between them that's topped with glossy hardbacks, a few succulents in small grey pots and a large candle, which is lit. There's another chandelier and another large round mirror, this time over the mantelpiece, which is painted the same black as the walls.

Everything is there for a reason. To be seen. Amplified. Appreciated. The books on the shelves a perfect line, hardbacks together, paperbacks together, some on their sides, some upright. Each vase and candlestick carefully placed. The cushions on the sofas mirroring one another. Every splash of colour – yellow here, turquoise there, orange up there – pops.

'Meredith's obsessed with Abigail Ahern,' Annabelle explains, waving her hand.

Nora isn't aware of an artist called Abigail Ahern, making a mental note to google her later. But then James mouths, 'Interior designer,' as they follow Annabelle down the hall.

'Oh,' Nora mouths back, immediately distracted as she tries – and fails – not to stare at the artwork. Like Sendhil's cottage, the walls are covered with canvases, prints and photographs. *Memories of a life well lived*, Nora thinks, when Annabelle tugs off her gardening gloves and leaves them, with the secateurs, on the table opposite the staircase.

When Nora glances back down the hall and wonders whether they should shut the front door, she sees the canvas hanging over it. It's coarse with thick, green paint. Layers and layers of it in every possible shade that, combined, almost manages to mirror the colour of the valley. In the middle the words, *COME AS YOU ARE*, are scraped deep into the paint.

The greens of the canvas are reflected in every corner of the house, Nora notices. There are plants *everywhere*. Puffs of ferns. A tall, sharp palm. A monstera by the window in the living room with wide, glossy leaves. As though some of the outside has made its way in.

Is that a Peter Blake? Nora asks herself, as she follows the others into the kitchen to discover that it isn't black, rather a bright, brilliant white. So white, in fact, that the green from the garden seems to reflect off the glossy cabinets. The green from the garden and even more plants. Pots of basil, mint and thyme on the windowsill and yet more succulents.

'It's a lovely day.' Annabelle marches over to the fridge and opens it. 'Let's sit outside.' She pulls out a bottle of Veuve Clicquot and, by the time she shuts the fridge door, James has grabbed the tray with four champagne saucers that is sitting on the counter.

As soon as they follow Annabelle outside, Nora spots the huge, round mirror in the corner of the garden that's tilted up to reflect the canopy of the valley, and turns her back on Annabelle to reach for the sleeve of her uncle Mark's shirt.

'That is *not* an Anish Kapoor,' she whispers, her fingers clutching the denim.

He shrugs and she despairs of him as she turns back to Annabelle, who has stopped to tuck one of the thick grey curls that has escaped from her bun behind her ear.

'This is lovely,' Nora tells her, with a dreamy smile.

The lawn is the lushest she has ever seen and the garden is obviously lovingly tended. There's an elderly apple tree in the corner, papery white roses, a big, bolshie hydrangea bush, and, like in her parents' garden, a row of purple allium along the back wall.

Annabelle leads them to a large, worn teak table, and that's when Nora sees the pair of wooden horses to her left, in the corner. She was so distracted by the Anish Kapoor that she failed to notice them, although she doesn't know how given they're *huge*. The size of real horses and just as magnificent, made of thick pieces of greying, twisted driftwood and carved to look as if they're in motion, like they're galloping towards the wall.

Annabelle must notice her staring at them, because she says, 'I just finished them.' She doesn't look at them, only Nora. 'They're supposed to be me and Meredith. A bit cliché, I suppose, but she loved that song, "Wild Horses". Do you know it?'

'The one by the Rolling Stones?'

Annabelle nods. 'They're for the festival. I thought we could put them on the beach, so it looks like they're running into the sea.'

'That would be beautiful.'

'It would,' James says, taking the champagne from Annabelle. 'But how will you get them to stay put? They're heavy, but you know what the wind is like here.'

She simply shrugs. 'They'll stay there until they're ready to go.'

Nora and James share a sad smile as he opens the champagne.

'Speaking of the festival,' Annabelle says, the light back in her eyes as she gestures at Nora to sit. 'We should get this out of the way before the others arrive.' Annabelle sits next to her and presses her hands to her chest. 'I can't even begin to tell you how touched I am that you've agreed to spend your summer here, in Pidwell, helping us to revive Meredith's festival. Thank you.' She reaches for her champagne saucer, raising it in the air. 'To Nora!'

'To Nora!' her uncles cheer, clinking their glasses with her.

She's so touched she doesn't know what to say, but adds, 'And to Meredith.'

That makes Annabelle's chin shiver as they clink again. 'To Meredith!'

'Lovely,' Mark leans in and whispers, kissing Nora's cheek.

Annabelle taps the table with her hand. 'So, do you want to hear about your team?'

Nora's fingers flutter with a mix of excitement and a touch of dread.

Annabelle swallows a mouthful of champagne, then exhales sharply. 'First of all, I think it's only fair to warn you about Kate.'

'Oh, God, yes,' James mutters, which doesn't bode well.

'Lady Kate Albert.' Annabelle waves her hand theatrically.

'She really is a lady,' Mark confirms. 'She's a distant relative of Camilla Parker Bowles.'

'What can I say about Kate?' Annabelle stops to take another sip of champagne as she thinks about it. 'Lady Kate doesn't live in Pidwell. She owns a farm, an estate, actually, between here and Mousehole with a farm shop that's popular with locals wanting homegrown stuff and tourists looking for a seven-pound bottle of hand-pressed apple juice.'

'It's stunning,' Mark says. 'You must ask her to show you around. There's a dairy and an orchard. They grow everything from cauliflowers to daffodils and ship all over the country.'

'That's how we can do the thirty-mile thing at the Trefelyn,' James explains.

'She's an artist, right?' Nora asks.

'And a staunch supporter of the arts,' Annabelle puts in. 'She's slightly eccentric, but, then, aren't we all? She's a sweetheart, so don't worry. We're lucky to have her. She's a dream benefactor. All she wants in return is for you to find somewhere to exhibit her work.'

'I'm sure I can do that,' Nora says.

'But it's worth noting,' Annabelle adds, 'that what makes Kate such a dream benefactor is that she has more money than she knows what to do with. She's a widow with one feckless son, who's a politician, I believe. A Tory, of course,' she's careful to clarify, then stops to take another sip of champagne. 'Between Kate's donation and the Arts Council funding, we should be fine. But if at some point you find the budget dwindling, just compliment one of her paintings and she'll sign a blank cheque.'

Good to know, Nora thinks.

'Then, there's Tommy,' Annabelle continues. 'He came here in the late eighties and never left. He was in a heavy-metal band that had one hit song he's been living off ever since.'

Mark nudges her. 'Get him to tell you the story about Ozzy Osbourne and the Twix.'

Nora stares at him and Mark just cackles.

'Tommy isn't an artist,' Annabelle says, 'but if you give him a bottle of Jack Daniels and a hammer, he can build anything. Let him do the heavy lifting. That's what he's there for.'

Nora wishes she'd thought to write this down. 'Okay.'

'Then there's Alice Duffy and Megan Healy, whom you met this morning, right?'

'Yes.'

'Megan is from New Zealand and came to London to work for Deloitte and was doing rather well for herself. She was earning an obscene amount of money, but then hit thirty and had a bit of a breakdown. Last year, when she came out the other side of it, she gave it all up and now manages the orchard for Kate. Then she met Alice and, well ...'

'She only met Alice last year and they're already married?' Nora asks, with a frown.

Annabelle rolls her eyes. 'Lesbians. We go on three good dates and move in together.'

Mark and James nudge one another and chuckle merrily.

'*Anyway.*' She stops to mock-glare at them. 'Megan's busy with the orchard and Alice has her hands full with the shop, but they really do want to help, so don't be afraid to ask.'

'Plus she'd never tell you this,' James adds, 'but Alice is a brilliant painter.'

'Yes!' Annabelle points her glass at Nora. 'But she suffers terribly with self-confidence, which is hardly surprising given that her best friend won the Turner Prize.'

'Didn't you win the Turner Prize as well?' Nora reminds her, with a cheeky smile.

'Years ago, darling,' Annabelle says, as if it doesn't count. 'Sendhil won it three years ago when he was twenty-seven. A month after winning the Hepworth Prize for Sculpture.'

Blimey, Nora thinks. *He won the Turner and the Hepworth within a month?*

'He's a *genius*.' Another curl falls out of Annabelle's bun. 'And I don't say that lightly, believe me. But more about him later,' she warns, arching an eyebrow at Nora. 'Back to Alice. James is right. Do persuade her to show something at the festival.'

Mark doesn't look concerned. 'Nora will charm her, I'm sure.'

'Which leaves Mr Achari.' Annabelle stops to close her eyes and take a deep breath. When she opens them again, she says, 'I want to preface this by saying that I adore Sendhil.'

Oh, God, Nora thinks. This isn't going to be good, is it?

'He's brilliant. But, like Megan, when he arrived here, he wasn't in a good way.' Annabelle stops to rub the bridge of her nose, then lets out a small sigh. 'I won't go into why, because it isn't my place to say, but I don't think Sendhil would mind if I told you that winning the Turner and the Hepworth was the best and the worst thing that ever happened to him. He came here not long after, looking for me. And he was right to. After all, I know more than anyone what winning a prize like that does to you. The pressure to keep producing at that level is, quite frankly, impossible to sustain.'

Annabelle lowers her voice then, even though they're the only ones in the garden. 'I'm fiercely protective of him, so I'd appreciate your discretion, Nora.'

She sits a little straighter. 'Of course.'

'I'm only telling you this,' Annabelle reaches for her hand and holds it tightly, 'because I don't want you to worry. He's agreed to produce something for the festival but you have to leave him alone.' She shakes her head firmly. 'You mustn't put any pressure on him.'

'I never would,' Nora promises.

'Although,' Annabelle says, squeezing Nora's hand with a cheeky smile, 'If you want to threaten him with a can of deodorant again, please do. I think he quite liked it.'

Chapter 10

Getting lunch ready before the others arrive is chaotic, like it would be with her family on any other sunny bank-holiday Monday, everyone asking for and reaching for things.

Nora wishes her parents were here because they'd love this. The big green garden and big full table. The bowls of salad and couscous studded with pomegranate seeds, and plates with slabs of grilled halloumi drenched in olive oil, and amber wedges of roasted butternut squash, dusted with feta cheese. And they'd love how much her uncles are laughing and stopping for quick kisses while they check on the lamb chops on the barbecue.

Kate is the first to arrive, bang on one o'clock. After their discussion earlier, Nora thought she'd look like Camilla Parker Bowles. Fluffy white hair. A practised smile. A delicate handshake. She'd expected Kate to show up in a pair of filthy green Hunter wellies and a worn tweed jacket, but she's tall with a sharp grey Anna Wintour bob. She's equally immaculate in an ankle-length, black-and-white graphic-print dress that's far too nice for lunch in Annabelle's garden, and a pair of sunglasses that add to her Wintouresque command.

She saunters into the garden, a bottle of champagne in each hand, and makes a beeline for Nora, as her uncles had said she would. 'You're the one who decides where her paintings go,' they had warned, a few minutes before. 'She'll want to keep you sweet.'

Sure enough, Kate is nothing but kisses and compliments.

Tommy is next, this time with six bottles of Doom Bar ale that he proceeds to drink by himself. He looks exactly as Nora had pictured, as if he hasn't had a bath or a hot meal in some time. With his pale skin, long grey hair and black clothes, he isn't unlike Jonathan Bodham, the kid who came into Redchurch the day she quit and bought all that artwork.

Or, at least, Jonathan Bodham in forty years.

Tommy doesn't say much, which is no bad thing given all the other chatter, but he says enough to let Nora know he's a south Londoner and a vegan.

Finally, Alice and Megan bustle in with a box of stuff, including one of Alice's infamous stargazy pies. Infamous only because her uncles had dared Nora to Google it when Annabelle said she was bringing one and she was horrified to be confronted by a pie with fish heads and tails poking out of it. Mercifully, Alice's is vegetarian, so is made with baby carrot tops instead.

They're quite the motley crew, Nora thinks, this disparate group of souls whose paths should never have crossed. She gets why her uncles think Pidwell is so special, because here they all are. Whether they found their way by accident, like Mark, or came looking for it, like

Tommy, they're here now and no one seems in any hurry to leave.

And why would they? What was it Meredith said? Home is where you're understood? They're understood here. Annabelle, in her muddy dungarees, with dirt under her fingernails, standing next to Lady Kate in her silk dress and diamond earrings. Tommy and Megan, who haven't said a word and are just standing, side by side, sipping their drinks, watching while Alice and Nora's uncles bicker over how long to leave the lamb chops on the barbecue.

None of them go together, yet they do. Annabelle's easy generosity balances Kate's focused intensity. Tommy and Megan's watchful silence balances Alice and Nora's uncles' disregard for the linen tablecloth as they squeeze lemon juice over everything. There's this tender, unspoken harmony as they orbit one another. There's no distrust, no uncertainty, no hesitation, no need to make space for one another. Annabelle doesn't feel the need to change out of her dungarees. Tommy and Megan don't feel the need to comment on the lamb chops. Alice and Nora's uncles don't feel the need to be more careful with the vintage wine glasses as they gesticulate wildly at each other.

They just are and that's okay.

Come as you are, Nora thinks, remembering the canvas hanging over the front door.

If this place had a motto, that would be it.

Pidwell. Come as you are.

~★~

When they sit down to eat, Annabelle is very careful about the seating plan. She sits at the head of the table and puts Nora at the other end. In Meredith's seat, Nora wonders, her cheeks warm as she sits where she's told. Annabelle puts Kate to her right and Tommy to her left, with Nora's uncles opposite one another in the middle, Alice and Megan next to them.

It means that Nora can't be cornered by Kate, which is a relief. As is the fact that Alice doesn't let Kate dominate the conversation when she tries to, taking quietly to Nora instead. She quickly learns that Alice, much like Luce, has no filter whatsoever, so they hit it off immediately. Annabelle must have known they would, which is why, Nora suspects, she was so keen for them to sit next to one another.

'Sendhil told me about last night,' Alice admits, popping a raspberry into her mouth.

She waits until dessert to say it and they know each other a bit better, but still.

'Oh, God.' Nora groans, reaching for her coffee and hiding her face behind the cup.

'Ah, come on! It could be worse.' She thumbs at herself. 'At least you didn't get your period at the Clonakilty Street Carnival when you were fourteen. In white jeans, no less.'

Nora almost spills her coffee trying not to laugh.

'He thought it was hilarious,' she assures her. 'I haven't heard him laugh that hard in ages. You threatened him with a can of deodorant, Nora. Death by Dove. What a way to go!'

Tommy stands up then, the shock of it enough to silence the table.

He nods towards the French windows and says, 'I'd better get back to Archie.'

Then he's gone.

'Who's Archie?' Nora asks Alice, when he disappears into the kitchen. 'His husband?'

She pops another raspberry into her mouth. 'His dog.'

'*I'd better get back to Archie* is code for *I've had enough of you lot*.' Annabelle winks.

Everyone around the table chuckles warmly.

'Still,' Mark says, finishing his champagne, 'he did well to make it to half five.'

'Four and a half hours,' Annabelle concedes. 'That's pretty good going.'

There's another ripple of laughter, then Mark and James are on their feet, collecting the empty plates. They stop Annabelle when she tries to help, while everyone else does. Everyone but Kate, who generously offers to keep Annabelle company while they head into the kitchen to wash up and Megan sorts out the barbecue.

Between the four of them – Nora, her uncles and Alice – they make light work of it and put everything back in its rightful place without any breakages.

When they're done, Nora checks the clock on the oven to see that it's almost half past six and she's late feeding Oliver. She nips to the loo, assuming it's time to go, but when she gets back outside, they're tucking into a cheeseboard while James opens a bottle of red wine.

Alice tells her she has to try the Cornish Yarg. Before Nora knows it, the garden is dark and gasps when she checks her phone. 'It's eight seventeen! I haven't fed Oliver!'

It's only her first day in Pidwell and she's already forgotten to feed the cat.

'Ah, don't worry about it,' Alice tells her around a mouthful of Yarg. 'Sendhil knows you're here. He'll have done it. There's no way those monsters will let him forget their dinner.'

~*~

By ten o'clock, Kate is regaling them with a story about being kidnapped while visiting a farm in Kentucky. She was there sourcing Wagyu beef for the farm, and was on her way to meet a farmer about purchasing a couple of cows when some locals, realising she was loaded, bundled her into the back of a van as she was leaving her hotel. They demanded a million-dollar ransom from her husband, but he just told them to ask her if she had his passport.

'They let me go a few hours later,' she says, when everyone stops laughing. 'Poor things had no idea I had ten thousand dollars' cash in my bag as a deposit for the cows.'

There's another peal of laughter, which Kate laps up. But before she can launch into another story, Nora's uncles clear away the cheeseboard as Alice grabs the last piece of Brie.

Then they're back in the kitchen, doing the next round of dishes, before finally saying their goodbyes. They agree to be at the town hall the next morning at ten for the first meeting about the arts festival. Nora had no idea Pidwell had a town hall, but she's sure she'll find it.

Alice and Megan live on the farm, so Megan leaves with Kate, who has a driver, which is probably for the best given how much champagne she's had. And Alice goes with Nora and her uncles because she needs to relieve Sendhil, who has been keeping an eye on the shop.

It's too dark to walk through the valley now so they have to take the road. Annabelle gives them a torch from the stash she keeps in the cupboard under the stairs, which, they learn, after several minutes of trying them, are mostly out of batteries.

Nora is anxious about the road, sure they'll be ploughed down by a tractor. But they don't see a soul. Only a fox that crosses their path so suddenly that Nora shrieks, sending the birds in the trees over their heads fleeing. Her uncles and Alice think it's hilarious and are still teasing her about it, mock-shrieking and waving their arms when they finally reach the Cove.

Nora can't really see the sea now, only the heavy moon hanging over it and the tips of the waves as they push slowly back and forth. But she can hear it, this gentle hush, like white noise, that's punctuated by the gulls calling as they bob over their heads.

'We'll give you the grand tour tomorrow, okay?' Mark thumbs at the Trefelyn. 'Swing by after the meeting. We can go to the shop after for lunch. What's the special tomorrow?'

Alice gives them the double-finger guns and grins. 'Taco Tuesday!'

Her uncles cheer, then head up the path to the Trefelyn.

'The shop's still open!' Alice throws up her hands when they reach the bottom of the road. 'It's gone eleven! He should have locked up by now!'

'Maybe Sendhil lost track of time,' Nora offers.

'He'd better not have gone home and left it like that,' Alice mutters.

When they get to the door, they discover he hasn't abandoned the shop. Sendhil is perched on a high stool behind the till, hunched over a paperback. He's wearing a black wool cardigan that's far too big for him, the sleeves covering his hands so only his fingers are sticking out, curled around the book. The cats are there, sitting at either side of him on the counter, like a couple of cute gargoyles.

'Can you tell the cats apart yet?' Alice asks.

Nora shakes her head and Alice points to the one on the left. 'It's easy. Your one, Oliver, is the one that looks like a haunted Victorian child.'

Nora shouldn't laugh, but with his grey fur and permanently startled expression, as if he's just witnessed something horrific, he does resemble a haunted Victorian child.

Sendhil looks up then and Nora sees that he's wearing a pair of those thick black-rimmed hipster glasses that she usually thinks are tragic, but actually suit him.

'Busy?' Alice asks.

'What do you think?'

He says *think* like Alice does. Like it doesn't have an H in it.

'Did you sell anything at all?'

'There wasn't a rush on your homemade rhubarb and apple chutney, funnily enough.'

Nora can tell they grew up together because they immediately start bickering in that easy, affectionate way Nora and her brother do. The change in him is astonishing. In a moment, he goes from her mellow, monosyllabic neighbour, to giving as good as he gets.

'I wasn't mocking your chutney,' Sendhil tells Alice. 'It's perfectly lovely chutney.'

'There it is!' She points at him, then at Nora. 'You hear the tone, right, Nora?'

She holds up her hands, refusing to get involved.

Alice turns back to him, her gaze narrowing. 'No more chutney for you!'

'I have nothing to eat it with anyway, given that you didn't bring me back any cheese.'

'There's cheese in the fridge.'

'Yeah, but Annabelle gets that good cheese from the shop in Penzance.'

'You want cheese? You have to leave your house for cheese. Earn it. Be sociable.'

'Ah! It's not worth it.'

Alice turns to her when he goes back to his book. 'Need anything before I close up?'

Nora already knew from the glimpse she saw of it this morning that the shop was nice, but it's more than that. Beetroot juice. Organic chickpeas. Gluten-free pasta. Homemade hummus. There'd be a queue out of the door if this place was in Shoreditch.

'I've been craving a KitKat, actually,' she admits sheepishly.

As soon as she says it, Sendhil lifts his head from his book and raises his eyebrows at Alice with a sharp smirk, letting Nora know that this is a discussion they've had before.

'No KitKats.' He raises his arm with a saccharine smile, like he's trying to sell her a dodgy Mini. 'But can I interest you in a four-pound bar of handmade, Fairtrade chocolate?'

'Shut it, you,' Alice tells him, striding over to the display on the shelf by the till.

Nora follows her to the narrow bars of chocolate wrapped in thick, brightly illustrated paper burnished with gold leaf that wouldn't look out of place in Liberty.

'The pretzel and caramel is lush,' Alice tells her. 'And the dark chocolate and ginger.'

Nora takes both.

'That'll be a hundred and twelve pounds, please,' Sendhil says, holding out his hand.

'No charge.' Alice slaps it away, then winks at her as she gives Nora a hot pink and turquoise box of salted caramel truffles as well. 'Call it a welcome-to-Pidwell present.'

'Thank you.' Nora smiles, careful not to drop them as she nods over her shoulder at the door to the shop. 'I'd better go. I'm done in. See you, Sendhil.'

'See ya,' he says, like it has twenty-seven As in it.

As she's passing the window on her way back to Mrs Stroud's cottage, clutching her chocolate, she glances in to see them chatting, Alice no doubt filling him on lunch. She waves as Nora passes, then says something to make Sendhil throw back his head and laugh.

Chapter 11

To Nora's absolute horror, the cats wake her at four thirty the next morning.

Both of them.

She pulls the duvet over her head, hoping they'll give up and go away, but it's futile. They're like a couple of furry car alarms that cease just long enough to make her think they've gone, only for them to resume their assault a few moments later.

By five thirty, the sun is up and Nora has had enough. So, she drags herself out of bed. As soon as she does, the cats start *shrieking* as they twist and turn around her ankles, getting under her feet as they shepherd her towards the kitchen.

Nora knows she shouldn't or it'll be like this every morning until Mrs Stroud returns, but she can't take it any more and feeds them. As soon as she does, they shut up and she contemplates getting back into bed. It's going to be a long day, so she probably should, but her brain is already whirring ahead of the arts festival meeting later. Just thinking about it makes her stomach clench but she doesn't know why until she's passing the dining table on her way back to the bedroom and sees the new notebook she'd left there, ready for the meeting. She's nervous, she realises, as she pads through the bedroom and into the bathroom. She shouldn't be, she tells herself as she tugs off her bonnet and replaces it with a shower cap, tucking each of her curls under the elastic. After all, she's done this dozens of times at Redchurch. Not a festival, but she's managed plenty of exhibitions.

And it's not the team. She's already met them and they seem lovely so there's no need to be anxious about whether or not they'll like her, or if they won't trust her because she'll ruin their little arts festival with her big ideas. Even Kate has accepted that she's in charge, or she wouldn't be trying to endear herself to Nora with such enthusiasm.

By the time Nora climbs out of the shower, she's already made a list in her head of everything that needs to be done and heads into the living room to scribble it down before she forgets. Ten minutes later, she's still there, wrapped in a towel, adding to it.

'Parking!' she remembers, as she's heading back into the bedroom, and trots back to the living room to grab her notebook from the dining table, taking it with her this time.

Parking, she jots down. *Signage. Maps. Contact list. Catering.*

I'll have to do a risk assessment, she thinks, grateful that rooting through Mrs Stroud's desk drawers last night resulted in finding the Wi-Fi code so she can google a form.

But there isn't a printer.

Maybe she can borrow one.

On it goes, the list getting longer as she dresses and puts on some makeup.

By the time she's done, Nora notices that the cats are gone. No doubt next door, pestering Sendhil for their second breakfast. According to the art-deco-style wooden clock on the mantelpiece, it's not even seven. The meeting isn't for another three hours. *I'm going to work myself into a right state by then*, she thinks, studying her list.

When her phone buzzes, it's Luce, texting to ask if Nora's up yet. It's already proving to be another glorious day. So she tells Luce that she'll ring her in ten, then makes herself a coffee and takes it – with her notebook – to Meredith and Annabelle's bench.

As soon as Nora opens the front door, the sunlight hits her. *It really is beautiful here*, she thinks, as she steps outside. The sea pinks are blushing on the cliffs, the sea obscenely blue. But, just as the valley isn't simply green, the sea isn't merely blue: rather every shade from the softest baby-blanket through Bombay Sapphire to navy and every shade in between.

She can see why Ottessa Bellow referred to her time in Pidwell as her Blue Period.

As Nora is heading towards the shop, an elderly green Land Rover chugs towards her. When it pulls up, Nora stops beside it to say good morning to Megan. She nods, her smile a little less tense this morning, as Alice tumbles out, clutching a basket of bread that, even with the Land Rover between them, Nora can smell has been freshly made.

'Morning!' Alice sings, as Megan reverses and pulls away.

'Morning,' Nora replies, surprised by how pleased she is to see her.

Alice has obviously just got out of the shower because she has that whole surfer-babe-fresh-from-the-sea thing going on again, her cheeks flushed and her green eyes bright.

'Where you off to so early?' she asks, resting the basket of bread on her hip.

'The cats woke me at four thirty,' Nora tells her, rolling her eyes. 'So, I'm going to drink this very strong coffee and have a think about what we need to do for the meeting later.'

Alice nods, then says, 'Once we get going with the festival, you're welcome to work here, you know.' She turns to look at the tables outside the café, then back at Nora. 'I know how small Mrs Stroud's cottage is. So, if you fancy some company, we have coffee and Wi-Fi.'

'Thanks. That's good to know.'

Nora means it because she doesn't really do alone. Not really. She's never been very good at it. She tries, usually the weekend before pay day, when she only has £3.37 in her account and she tells herself she should stay in and sort out her room. So, she'll get home from work on a Friday night, change into sweats and, after dinner, she'll really go for it. She'll dance to Stevie Nicks while she vacuums or listen to one of her murder podcasts while she picks her clothes off the floor and sorts through her books, deciding which ones she wants to keep and which she should drop off at the charity shop the next day.

But then she'll reach for her phone to skip a song and find a text from Luce, or one from her brother with a link to an article about racial and ethnic health disparities in healthcare and, before Nora knows it, she's pacing around her room, chatting to one of them.

So she's surprised that she hasn't freaked out about being in Mrs Stroud's cottage by herself yet. In fairness, she hasn't stopped since she got to Pidwell. Still, she hasn't felt the need to double-check the front door and windows are locked before she goes to bed or woken with a start, sure that someone is lurking outside her bedroom door, like she does at home. Which is surprising, given her brush with the Barefoot Killer the night she arrived.

She's beginning to understand why everyone feels so safe here.

When she gets to Meredith and Annabelle's bench, Nora opens her notebook and begins scribbling, then tells herself to stop. *Give yourself a minute, Nora. It might be the only one you get today.* She forces herself to take a deep breath and looks out at the sea, listening to the steady push and pull of the waves until each breath comes a little easier.

Then she closes her notebook and sips her coffee.

When she gathers herself enough to call Luce, she answers on the second ring.

'Nor!' she says, turning down the Missy Elliott song she's listening to. 'How you doing?'

Nora fills her in on everything that's happened since she got to Pidwell. Luce thinks the shower incident is hilarious, of course, but then she asks, 'Is he hot?'

'Who? Sendhil? I guess.'

Luce shrieks and Nora almost jumps clean out of her skin. 'What? What happened?'

'I googled him! Are you kidding me? Is this him, Nora?'

She has no idea what Luce is looking at so spells his name, just in case.

'Nora! This guy is *three hundred per cent* your type! Total art-school trash.'

'I don't have a type,' she says, with a huff.

Nora definitely has a type. Not necessarily in looks, rather in attitude. She tends to go for guys who don't toe the line, who don't always wear what they're supposed to or say what they're supposed to and go left when they should go right. And while that can lean towards pretention, which often means lengthy, breathless conversations that aren't actually conversations because she can't get a word in, for the most part, guys like that – guys she's been into in the past – tend to be kind. Gentle. More aware of the world around them and their place in it. They want to leave a mark. And, as Nora has come to realise, there is nothing more attractive than someone with a talent who is in absolute, complete command of it.

He certainly fits that mould, she thinks as she looks across the cove at his cottage.

~*~

Talk of Sendhil soon shifts to the podcast Nora started listening to before she went to bed last night about a woman who was murdered in West Cork, which makes Luce gasp with horror.

'How can you listen to stuff like that when you're alone in the cottage, Nor?'

She shrugs as she walks around the cove, then waves back at Alice as she passes the shop. 'I don't know. Pidwell's tiny, but I don't feel alone, you know? It's so safe here.'

But as soon as she and Luce say their goodbyes, Nora is immediately punished for her hubris when she approaches Mrs Stroud's cottage to find the front door ajar.

''S all right,' a voice says, somewhere behind her, and she jumps.

It's Sendhil. He's barefoot again, this time in a pair of black jeans and a black cotton shirt buttoned to the neck. He's heaving a cardboard box into the bed of his pickup and, when he's done, he walks the few steps towards her, then waves at the open front door. 'That lock hasn't worked since the Second World War. It does this all the time.'

'Okay,' she manages, but her heart is beating so hard she can feel it in her fingers.

'You need to use both locks or this happens.'

Thanks for warning me, Mrs Stroud. She'd left detailed instructions about how to clean Oliver's ears, but hadn't thought to mention the dodgy front door.

It's okay, Nora tells herself, forcing herself to take a step towards it. *There's no one in there. Sendhil's right. It's just the lock.* But as soon as she's brave enough to peer through the gap, she jumps back when she sees an axe murderer-shaped shadow in the living room.

He laughs, but has the grace to look contrite when she glares at him.

'Sorry.' He holds his hands up. 'But seriously. There's no one in there, I promise.'

He's probably right, but she still stays exactly where she is.

Sendhil thumbs at the open door. 'I can go in and check if you like?'

'No.' She shakes her head. 'No. No, it's fine. I'm fine. It's fine.'

When she says *fine* a few more times, he slips past her and pushes the door open. Nora doesn't stop him, but curses herself because she wishes she wasn't That Girl. The girl who needs rescuing by the Big Strong Guy. Not that Sendhil is particularly big or strong – he's so skinny that a particularly strong wind would knock him off his feet – but he's brave enough to go into Mrs Stroud's cottage right now and she's not.

To be fair, Nora is brave about a lot of things. She catches spiders in her hands, and came here by herself, even though she knew nothing about Pidwell and no one but her uncles. Plus didn't she stand up to Roland on Friday and tell him to stick his job?

But she definitely saw someone in the living room, okay?

So, if Sendhil wants to go in there and check, she's going to let him. Besides, do you know what her mother would do to her if Nora woke up in a bathtub of ice with no kidneys?

So, she waits on the doorstep and asks herself how much damage she can inflict with an empty travel cup, if she needs to. Maybe she can use the notebook as well.

Paper cuts are painful, right?

Nora can hear Sendhil moving around inside the cottage but, just as she's brave enough to take a step closer to peer through the open door again, the cats come flying out.

'You all right?' he asks, from inside, when she screams as Oliver and Dodger run past.

All Nora can manage as she tries to catch her breath is 'Cats.'

He calls them something she won't repeat, then doesn't say anything for a long time – so long that she's about to check he's okay, when a shadow passes through the living room.

'It's me,' he calls, which is good, because she almost hurls the travel cup at him.

Then Nora hears him opening and closing the cabinet doors in the kitchen. It seems to be taking an inordinate amount of time, but she's grateful that's he's being thorough.

Finally, he appears on the doormat and says, 'All clear.'

'Are you sure?'

He nods.

'Did you check the utility room?'

He nods.

'And under the bed?'

He nods again.

'And behind the shower curtain?'

He nods again.

She nods this time. 'Okay.'

'There's no one in here, I promise.'

'Thanks.' She forces herself to smile even though she's still shaking. 'Thank you.'

'No problem.' He slips past her and heads towards his cottage.

Nora still hesitates before she goes inside. He must notice because, as he's heading into his cottage, he stops and says, 'Don't worry. Whoever it was changed the sheets.'

~*~

Twenty minutes later, Nora is still trembling from the whole ordeal. Trembling so much that when she heads out for the meeting, she stops at the shop for a latte to steady her nerves.

Plus she has no idea where the town hall is.

'Hey!' Alice beams as she steams a jug of milk.

Sendhil is in front of her, on the other side of the counter, eating an apple, and as soon as she sees him, Nora's cheeks warm, suddenly ashamed for being so silly earlier.

Luce is right, she realises. Maybe she needs to lay off the murder podcasts for a bit.

Before she can thank him again, Alice holds up the stainless-steel jug and says, 'I'm doing everyone's drink order for the meeting. You want a latte, right?'

'Please,' Nora says.

Alice winks at Sendhil as though she's won a bet.

'Thank you,' Nora says, then says the same to him.

'For what?' Alice asks, over the splutter of the coffee machine.

'I just got back to Mrs Stroud's cottage to find the front door was open and Sendhil kindly went in to check that no one was in there,' Nora explains sheepishly.

'Oh, God. It's so annoying. Tommy keeps trying to fix it but I think the place is haunted.'

'Nice.' Sendhil rolls his eyes. 'That'll make her feel safe, Alice.'

'Sorry!' She winces as she puts Nora's coffee into a cardboard box with the others, then gestures at the orange Jacob's cream crackers tin next to it. 'Can you grab those?'

Sendhil perks up. 'What's in there?'

'I made Figgy 'Obbins for the meeting.'

'Yeah?' he murmurs, trying to open the tin, but Alice slaps his hand away.

'If you want one, you have to come to the meeting.'

He huffs and goes back to eating his apple. 'No, thanks.'

'Thought so,' she says, then holds out her hand to him. 'I need to borrow the truck.'

He looks appalled. 'You're not *driving* to the town hall?'

'I'll never gonna get this coffee up there without giving myself third-degree burns.'

He mutters something about her carbon footprint, then reaches into the pocket of his jeans and pulls out his keys. Before he hands them to her, he says, 'I need it back.'

'I'll come straight here after the meeting,' she promises, as she grabs the box and walks around the counter to join Nora. 'Sell lots of rhubarb and apple chutney while I'm gone.'

'Save me a Figgy 'Obbi-whatever.'

'Bye, Sendhil,' Nora says, as she follows with the tin.

But he just tips his chin up at her and goes back to the apple.

~★~

Nora could have driven, she realises, as they're heading back to the cottages, but it all happens so quickly. The next thing she knows, she's getting into Sendhil's pickup truck with the tin of Figgy 'Obbins and Alice is handing her the box of hot drinks, telling her to be careful.

They hit a pothole as they're heading up to the valley, so Nora holds the box as though it's a newborn baby. Luckily, they aren't going far, which explains Sendhil's reaction to them driving. The town hall is on the way to Meredith and Annabelle's house, but because she and her uncles went through the valley yesterday she didn't see it.

Referring to it as a hall is rather grand, Nora discovers, when they pull up outside. It isn't a hall, rather a house that looks remarkably like Meredith and Annabelle's. Alice runs around to grab the box from Nora so she can clamber out. The front door is open so Alice heads in and Nora follows to find it bare inside. It seems to be the same layout as Meredith and Annabelle's, a large room to her left, another to her right, with the hall and staircase in the middle. It's hardly a wreck but, with the grubby windows and the floorboards that belch dust as she walks across them, it could do with a good scrub and a lick of paint. But, then, there's little point, she supposes. It doesn't look as if the 'town hall' gets used very much.

If Pidwell ever held a village meeting, about six people would show up.

Everyone is already waiting in the room to the right. There's a fireplace that clearly hasn't been used for years and someone has set up a circle of five orange plastic chairs in the middle. Kate is holding court, standing over Tommy and Megan, who are sitting with their arms crossed. Again, she's immaculate, in a pink-and-white houndstooth skirt and jacket that looks like vintage Chanel, a string of pearls and pair of pink heels too high to walk far in.

Nora has no idea what Kate was saying before she and Alice walked in, but Tommy and Megan look so relieved to see them that they almost smile.

'You're here!' Kate claps. 'How exciting!'

'How you doing, guys?' Nora asks, as Kate strides over to kiss her on each cheek, complimenting Nora's pink-and-red heart-print shirt dress and white Converse.

Nora knows full well that Kate is buttering her up, but smiles sweetly anyway.

Tommy and Megan aren't as enthusiastic. They merely nod at her as Kate finally sits – in the middle, of course – and Nora heads for one of the two empty chairs. Alice hands out the drinks and Figgy 'Obbins on brown paper napkins, saying they're vegan. Kate refuses one, saying she's meeting friends for lunch in Penzance after the meeting, but smiles and thanks Alice for what looks like a tea, judging by the string hanging from the paper cup.

Alice sits in the empty chair opposite Nora, and when they all turn to her, Nora remembers she's the one leading the meeting.

'Okay,' she says, putting her coffee on the floor and resting the napkin with the Figgy 'Obbin on her knee as she reaches into her tote for her notebook. 'Thanks for coming.'

'Of course!' Kate holds out her hand across the circle. She's not close enough to touch her, although Nora's sure she would if she could. 'We're all so excited about the festival!'

She wiggles in her chair while Tommy and Megan shift in theirs.

'Sorry,' Alice says. 'Before we begin, I meant to say that I've started a group chat. We're all on it. I just need your number, Nora, so I can add you.'

Kate winks at her. 'Our fearless, curly-haired leader.'

Nora nods. 'I was about to suggest we do a contact list, so thanks for sorting that.'

A group chat sounds like a nightmare, actually, Nora thinks. *But let's see how it goes.*

Kate points a glossy pink fingernail at Nora. 'Speaking of your list, I was just saying ...'

That's it. Nora barely has time to open her notebook before Kate is firing ideas at her. Then Alice joins in. A launch party! A parade! A children's art tent! Painting lessons! Walking tours of the village and valley! Themed cocktails! Merchandise! Kate even has a friend at Farrow & Ball whom she wants to ask if they can mix a shade of paint called Pidwell Green.

When they finally run out of steam, Nora's hand hurts from writing everything down. She looks at Tommy and Megan, holding her breath as she waits to discover if they have anything to contribute. Mercifully, they don't and just gaze at her, looking equally startled.

Actually, Tommy does say something. He leans forward and points at the Figgy 'Obbin still sitting on Nora's knee and asks, 'You gonna eat that?'

She hands him the napkin, then looks up at Kate and Alice. They seem so happy that Nora is going to have to choose her next words carefully so she doesn't dampen their enthusiasm. The truth is, though, even if they had the budget – which Kate keeps telling her not to worry about – there's five of them and they have only three months until the festival.

There's no way they'll be able to do all of these things.

'I'm loving your enthusiasm.' She beams at Kate and Alice. 'We're gonna need this energy over the next few months. I can't wait to implement some of these ideas.'

Kate and Alice beam back at her, settling in their chairs with their paper cups.

That was easy. The next bit won't be, she knows, as she tries not to say 'but'.

'*However,*' Nora says instead. 'As this is our first meeting, let's start at the beginning.'

Kate and Alice look baffled.

'What have you guys done so far?'

Now they all look baffled, muttering and glancing around the circle at one another.

So, nothing then? Nora realises, her smile a little tighter.

'The date.' Alice points out. 'We picked a date. August bank-holiday weekend.'

That's the one thing they didn't have to do, actually – the festival was always on the August bank-holiday weekend since Meredith started it in 1967 – but Nora lets them have it.

'Yes!' She makes a show of writing it down. 'Good. Excellent.'

Kate smiles proudly and raises her cup to Alice, as though their work is done. So, Nora knows she needs to handle this part with the sort of care usually reserved for persuading a cranky toddler to go to bed. Luckily she's had four years' experience of dealing with Roland.

'Excellent. So, the festival will be on the bank-holiday weekend. The *whole* weekend?'

Kate shrugs gracefully. 'Of course. Friday. Saturday. Sunday. Monday.'

'Okay. Four days is a lot of time to fill, don't you think?'

Kate shrugs again, as if to say, *Well, that's your problem, surely.*

'And having the festival across four days will double the budget—'

'Don't worry about the budget,' Kate interrupts, waving a hand at Nora.

She smiles. 'Thank you, Kate. That's very generous. Having the festival across four days means we'll have to hire more staff, though, who'll need to be managed. I'm happy—'

'Staff?' Alice interrupts this time, gesturing around the circle. 'But you have us.'

'Of course.' Nora really tries not say *but*. 'There's only five of us, though.'

No one seems concerned at that.

'And I assume the festival is going to be across several sites, right?'

They all nod.

'So who's going to escort people between them so they don't get lost?'

They obviously haven't thought about that.

'And who's going to show them where to park?'

They obviously haven't thought about that, either.

'Or help someone if they have difficulty walking? Or administer first aid if someone hurts themselves? And who's going to manage the children's art tent all day,' she adds, letting them know that she listened to their ideas. 'And teach the painting lessons?'

They all turn to one another and start muttering, even Tommy and Megan.

'If we're interacting with children, everyone will need to be DBS checked.'

Alice looks at Megan, then at Nora. 'What's a DBS check?'

'A Disclosure and Barring Service check to make sure that none of us are . . . you know.'

Nora pulls a face. It takes Alice a second, but she looks horrified. 'Ah. Okay.'

'Then there's the set-up,' Nora says, when an uneasy silence settles. 'Getting the event spaces ready. Cleaning. Painting. Repairs. Risk assessments. And even if we rent them, like the children's art tent, we still have to order them, organise delivery and make sure they're up and ready to go for the festival. Then we'll need tables, chairs, art supplies.'

They all stare at her.

'And we have to take everything down after the festival. Having visitors means there will probably be rubbish all over the valley and village that we'll have to clear up.'

Kate is clearly appalled, letting Nora know that she will not be involved with any of that. But, then, Nora wasn't expecting her to. Her contribution, Nora suspects, will be *this*. An initial flurry of impossible-to-implement ideas and she won't see her again until the festival.

Alice seems slightly nauseous. 'That's a lot of stuff, Nora.'

'It is,' she agrees. 'So I suggest that as it's the first festival we keep it simple.'

Everyone is visibly relieved.

Everyone except Kate, who is obviously waiting to see where Nora is going with this.

'Why don't we do the Saturday and Sunday?' Kate's face tightens, her right eyebrow twitching up and hovering there before it lowers when Nora adds, 'We can see what we learn this time, with a view to expanding the festival and making it longer next year.'

Kate brightens and joins in with the nodding.

'And it will give people a day either side for travel. Like your London friends, Kate.'

'Oh, yes,' she says, lips pursed. 'Of course. It is rather a long drive, isn't it?'

'So, it's agreed?' Nora checks, looking around the circle. 'The festival is going to be on Saturday the twenty-eighth and Sunday the twenty-ninth of August?'

They all nod.

'Excellent!'

That's one thing decided, at least. Only another 512 to go.

'So, now we have a date, guys, we can tell people about it, can't we?'

There's a small cheer at that, but Nora is dreading her next question.

'Has anyone started mocking up a poster?'

Evidently they haven't, because they just look at her.

'That's okay. We've only just decided on the date. Is there a website?'

Everyone shrugs.

'How about social media? Facebook? Twitter? Instagram? TikTok?'

There's another beat of silence. Then Alice holds up her hand. 'I can do the poster.'

Megan adds, 'And I can do the website.'

It's the first time Nora has heard her speak, and she's so shocked she drops her pen.

'I did one for the shop,' Megan goes on. 'So I can do something similar for the festival.'

'Thank you, Megan.' Nora smiles, writing it down. 'We just need a holding page with some basic info about what we'll be doing, the date and a map. Maybe some contact info.'

'I can create a bucketmail address, or something.' She lifts her right shoulder, then lets it drop. 'And I can do the Facebook page. I did one for the shop as well.'

Before Nora can thank her, Tommy says, 'And my daughter, Lottie, can help with the other stuff, I'm sure. She's always on Instagram. I'll ask her about it when I get home.'

'Thank you!' Nora is stunned by the sudden burst of enthusiasm. 'We can pay her.'

'Paid to be on her phone!' Tommy crosses his arms. 'She'll love that.'

Okay, Nora thinks. *Maybe we're getting somewhere.* 'Excellent!' When she looks up, her smile feels less tight. 'Is a week long enough to sort all of that out?'

Alice, Megan and Tommy look at one another and nod.

'So, if all goes to plan, we can go live next Monday?'

Kate leans forward. 'Shall we have the launch party then?'

'A party would be great!' Nora pauses as she tries to think of a way to steer Kate away from that. 'Why don't we have one *after* the festival to thank everyone for their hard work?'

'We could do both!'

'Okay.' Nora really doesn't want to be the one who keeps saying no, but she has to be honest with them. 'Here's my concern. Annabelle said that Sendhil came here because he was looking for her, because he needed sanctuary.'

Alice's cheeks flush.

'Well, if word gets out that he's here, what's going to happen?'

They all go quiet. Even Kate.

'He's here to avoid the art world. How's he going to feel when it descends on Pidwell?'

'He'll freak out,' Alice says, her cheeks even redder.

'Then, and this is honestly no disrespect to Sendhil,' she extends her hand to Alice, 'the festival will cease to be a celebration of Meredith, her life and what she did here. It'll be about Sendhil's first showing in three years, which, I'm pretty sure, he doesn't want.'

'No.' Alice looks at her wife. 'He'd hate that.'

'So,' Nora says carefully, 'I suggest we keep it as low-key as possible. Keep it local. Let's not say who's exhibiting and make it more of a celebration of Meredith Murphy.'

Nora isn't convinced Kate agrees with that.

'I'm sure people will find out eventually we're showing Sendhil's stuff – that will be unavoidable once the festival begins – but we can't advertise it or have a launch party because Pidwell is tiny. We can't cope with hundreds of people turning up. Think about parking.' Nora counts off each thing on her fingers. 'Toilets. And, like I said, with people traipsing through the valley, having picnics and doing who knows what else, there will be rubbish *everywhere*.'

Kate recoils. She doesn't quite clutch her pearls, but it's close enough.

There's a murmur of agreement and, hopefully, it's enough to convince Kate that throwing the big, busy festival she was hoping for isn't such a good idea, after all.

'We already need security, but if that happens, we'll need even more.'

Alice nudges Tommy with her elbow. 'We don't need security.'

'Tommy is clearly a very capable man,' Nora says, and he salutes her with two fingers, 'but he can't possibly keep an eye on *all* of the art work at once. What if someone tries to nick something? Or a kid with jammy hands climbs on one of Annabelle's horses?'

Again, Alice looks like she's going to throw up. 'Oh, Christ.'

Nora's losing them, she knows, the energy in the room duller now.

Even Kate looks concerned.

She decides to ramp it up again. 'Speaking of which,' she says brightly, 'we haven't discussed the art yet, have we?'

She thought that might perk them up – especially Kate – but they still look forlorn.

'Annabelle's handling that,' Alice says, sounding exhausted.

'Where is Annabelle, by the way?' Nora had thought she'd be there.

'London. She's giving a talk at the Whitechapel Gallery,' Alice tells her.

'Okay. Do any of you know what Annabelle has for us?'

That gets Kate's attention, her eyebrows shooting up. 'Quite a lot, actually.'

Alice squints as she thinks about it. 'Her stuff, Meredith's and Sendhil's. Plus, she has a Malcolm Pidwell that's currently on loan to the Newlyn Gallery, which they're returning for the weekend. And Ottessa Bellow is lending us a piece she did here.'

Wow. She had no idea there would be so many. It makes her stomach tense again as she scribbles it all down. They're going to be showing stuff by some of the best artists in the country, so keeping it low-key is looking increasingly unlikely.

'And your stuff as well, of course,' Nora says, without looking up from her notebook.

That makes Alice falter. 'Wait. What? My stuff? No.' She shakes her head, but Megan sits up straight and beams at Nora, clearly thrilled that she's thought to include her wife.

Kate glares at Alice, but laughs lightly when Nora adds, 'And yours, Kate.'

She's also beaming while Alice looks stunned, her lips parted.

Before she can object, Nora says, 'We have the art covered. What about the venue?'

'We thought the gardens at the Trefelyn,' Kate says. 'Tie in with the reopening.'

'That's perfect!' Nora agrees. 'For the sculptures. But what about the paintings?'

Kate frowns. 'What do you mean?'

'I know it's August, but it's still England. What if it rains? Everything will be ruined.'

There's a nervous titter around the circle.

'Or it's windy? And the Ottessa Bellow flies off into the sea?'

Nora's losing them again as they look around at each other, whispering fiercely, so she tries a different tack. 'How about this place? We can dedicate that room to Meredith and this one to the Pidwell Arts Club. We could play on the abandoned-house thing. Make it more Pidwell than a stark white art gallery. Think plants and ivy and cobwebs, so it looks like the valley is taking the house back. It'll be like people have stumbled across a secret place.'

Alice obviously loves that, because she points at her. 'And candles!'

Electric candles, Nora is careful to write down in her notebook.

Kate raises her arm. 'And the newer work can be upstairs.'

'We can't use upstairs, sadly,' Nora tells them and instantly feels awful.

All she's done since the meeting started is tell them no.

'Don't worry,' Tommy tells her. 'The stairs are in pretty good nick.'

'I was thinking more if someone has access needs?'

Kate looks at Tommy, then at her. 'Access needs?'

'Like if they can't get up the stairs.'

It takes them all a minute, but they turn to one another and say, *Oh*.

'The festival has to be accessible to everyone,' Nora says, as the penny drops.

'Yes, of course.' Kate nods furiously. 'Of course it does.'

'There's the silver bus,' Tommy pipes up then.

Nora frowns at him. 'The silver bus?'

'Meredith used to have this double-decker bus for the festival. Apparently, she used it to drive people from and to the station. Maybe we could use that for something.'

'Yes!' Nora points her pen at him. 'Where is it?'

'My barn. It's not roadworthy, but my mate Terry has a trailer.' He scratches his neck. 'I'm sure we can get it down here. We can park it there.' He gestures out of the window. 'I can take the seats out downstairs and build a ramp up to it. If I give it a clean and another lick of silver paint, we can put Alice and Kate's stuff there. Like an old and new school thing.'

'Yes!' Kate is so excited, she rises out of her seat, her hands clasped, then sits down again. 'What a wonderful idea, Thomas! Wonderful!'

'Perfect!' Nora tells him, so relieved she has to fight the urge to kiss him.

Tommy is obviously going to be a Godsend.

And she hasn't even had to give him a bottle of Jack Daniels yet.

'We have a camper,' Megan says then. 'We used to take it to festivals, selling tea and cake. We could park it next to the bus and do the same. Take some pressure off the shop.'

Nora makes a note. 'Alice can run it. Then she'll be on hand to talk about her art.'

Megan beams with pride again as Alice splutters next to her, her whole face scarlet.

Nora points at Kate. 'You can be the bus conductor, ushering everyone on and off.'

She's beside herself at the idea. 'I have the perfect hat!'

Alice puts her head into her hands and groans. When she lifts her chin again she looks distraught. 'Jesus wept, Nora!'

'What's wrong?'

'This is *so much stuff*. You thought you were coming here to help us with our little arts festival and look at *all this stuff*. Who's going to do it? I mean, I can help when I'm not at the shop, but Megan has the orchard. Your uncles are renovating the Trefelyn. Kate has the farm.'

Given that Kate's currently wearing a Chanel suit and five-and-a-half-inch heels, Nora doubts she's doing much around the farm but, still, Kate nods sombrely.

'So, that just leaves you and Tommy doing *everything*,' Alice adds despondently.

Nora nudges him with her elbow. 'We'll be okay, won't we Tommy?'

'Course we will.'

'Actually, are you around tomorrow morning?'

'Tomorrow? Yeah. Should be.'

'Shall we meet back here at nine and have a look at this place?' Nora holds her pen up, circling it around the room. 'See what state it's in. I'll need to do a risk assessment—'

'Nora!' Alice interrupts, clearly panicking. 'You don't understand. We need help.'

'It's okay,' she says gently, closing her notebook. 'It'll be fine, I promise.'

Alice pulls a face as if to say, *Really?*

'My boss once gave me a day,' she holds up a finger, '*one day* to organise an exhibition for an artist who was going to Tibet to become a monk, vowing never to return. I mean, he came back six months later, and is married with a couple of kids and works for the Hayward now, but that's not the point. The point is, I got it done. *And* we'll get this done as well.'

Alice still doesn't look convinced.

Chapter 12

'I was thinking,' Nora says, as she and Alice are heading back, the valley a blur of green Alice is driving so fast. 'You know that canvas over Meredith and Annabelle's front door?'

'The *COME AS YOU ARE* one?'

'Yeah. I think that would be perfect for the poster.'

'I can definitely do something with it.'

'Excellent,' Nora says, as she opens the car window to let in the smell of the valley.

'And *I* was thinking you need to make a list of everything that has to be done and divvy it up. I know Lady Kate won't get her hands dirty, but she can make some phone calls.'

'Don't worry,' she promises, as the trees give way and there's the sea again. 'I will.' She'll have to. There's no way Nora can do it all by herself.

'Tommy's great, isn't he?' Alice says, as they drive around the cove towards the shop and pull up outside. 'He's quiet, like Sendhil, but he hears everything.'

'I love his idea for using Meredith's silver bus.'

'It'll be our mini Silver Factory.' Alice grins as they head into the shop.

Sendhil doesn't look up from his book, just says, 'Hey.'

'Busy?' Alice asks, looking around at the empty shop.

'It was *roaring*. The builders from the Trefelyn came in and I sold, like, four coffees.'

'Megan and I can retire soon, then,' she tells him, handing him the Jacob's tin.

'Did you save me a Figgy 'Obbi-whatsit?' He grins, shaking it.

'Tommy ate them all,' Alice says, and passes him the keys to the pickup.

'Ah, what's the point of you?'

'Love you too,' she tells him, then blows him a kiss as she disappears through the door behind the counter, leaving it open so Nora sees that it leads to a small white kitchen.

'Oh, hey,' Sendhil says, almost falling off his stool when he spots her in front of him.

He hadn't even noticed her.

That's nice.

Alice returns, wearing a navy and white striped apron and punches Sendhil's shoulder.

'Ow!' he yelps, looking up at her with a frown. 'What was that for?'

Alice points at him. 'You need to help Nora with the festival.'

'It's okay.' Nora waves her hands at them as she remembers what Annabelle said about leaving Sendhil alone to finish his piece. 'Me and Tommy have got it covered.'

'You two can't do *everything* by yourselves!' She punches Sendhil again. 'Help Nora!'

He rubs his shoulder and glares at her. 'I would, but I'm too busy!'

'We're all busy.' Alice gestures at the shop. 'Megan's busy at the orchard and this place is quiet now, but the weather's turning, so people will be venturing out along the Path again soon and, by the time school finishes for the summer holidays next month, this place'll be rammed. But I'm still going to help Nora with the festival and so should you.'

She punches him again before he can object. 'I know you're showing your work for the first time in ages and that's a big deal, but Nora needs your help. She came here all the way from London to help us revive the festival and we can't just abandon her. Her uncles are flat out trying to get the Trefelyn ready, which, if it gets done in time, will be a miracle, frankly. And what's Lady Kate gonna do? Write a cheque and throw a party?'

'But I have so much—'

She doesn't let him finish. 'You will help! You will! You'll do it for Meredith!'

'Nice.' He nods. 'Play the Dead Friend card.'

Alice points at the door. 'Go outside now and listen to what Nora needs you to do.'

'I can't! I have to be in Penzance for half twelve. That's why I needed the pickup back.'

'Well, take Nora with you, then. You can talk about it on the way.'

Sendhil glares at her, and Nora is mortified.

Alice shoos him off the stool. 'Ah, get over it, Sendhil. We've no time for your brooding-artist nonsense. It's

Tommy's wife's birthday tomorrow and I need to make a cake.'

With that, she ushers them out of the shop and, before Nora knows it, she and Sendhil are standing outside, bewildered, while a gull pecks a circle around their feet.

'It's okay,' she tells him. 'Me and Tommy have got it covered.'

When he paces over to his pickup, she doesn't know what to do and stays there.

'Nora, go!' she hears Alice call from inside and she runs over to the pickup.

He's holding the door open for her and she thanks him as she gets in, watching carefully as he closes it, then stalks around the front of the truck to jump in on the driver's side. Sendhil slams the door so hard the whole pickup shakes and Nora's cheeks flush.

'You don't have to help with the festival,' she tells him, as he tugs on his seatbelt, then waits for her to do the same before he starts the engine. 'I do stuff like this all the time.'

'It's fine,' he says, even though it clearly isn't as he turns in his seat to look over his shoulder while he reverses, then pulls away and heads around the cove towards the road.

The light changes from yellow to green as his pickup is swallowed by the valley and Nora doesn't know how it happened. One minute she was talking to Alice about Meredith's silver bus and now she's in his truck going where, exactly? Penzance, did he say?

So much for leaving him alone. Nora sinks into the passenger seat.

'Listen,' he says, when they leave the safety of the valley and turn onto the road towards Penzance. 'It's not that I don't want to help with the festival. I do. I will.' He takes off his glasses, tucking them into the pocket of his shirt and replacing them with the Ray-Bans on the dashboard. 'It's just that I have a lot on my mind right now.'

I know, she nearly says, but stops, unsure how he'd feel about her talking to Annabelle.

'So, if I'm being moody, that's why. It's nothing to do with you.' He scratches his eyebrow, a pained look on his face. 'Plus I'm not like Alice. She's good at the talking thing. She's the social one. I'm usually the one at parties, sitting in the corner, talking to the dog.'

Nora chuckles. 'I understand. My brother, Ben, is the same. Last New Year's Eve, I walked into my friend Luce's kitchen to find him refilling the ice trays.'

He laughs at that, the sound filling the truck. Laughs in a way that she's only ever seen Alice provoke. It shouldn't feel like a victory, but she takes it as one anyway.

'So, don't worry,' Nora reassures him. 'If you'd rather not talk, I won't be offended, I promise. To be honest, I've had a bit of a morning. Between the cats waking me up at four thirty, getting back to the cottage to find the front door open and spending an hour and a half trapped in the town hall with Lady Kate and her *ideas*, I'm happy to sit here in silence.'

So that's what they do.

He drives while she catches herself sneaking looks at him. Each time she does and he doesn't notice, it gives her the courage to study him for a little longer. His profile.

The curl of his thick eyelashes. The tiny dot on the top of his cheekbone, like a fleck of ink. The sharp sweep of his nose and the sharper sweep of his jaw, softened by a couple of days' worth of stubble. His right arm bent, elbow resting on the open window, half in and half out, his left a straight line, fingers curled around the top of the wheel at twelve o'clock.

The cuff of his sleeve has ridden up to reveal the round bone in his wrist. It's the same size as one of the pearls in the necklace Kate was wearing earlier, Nora notes, his skin stretched tightly over it. She's never noticed someone's wrists before, but they're perfect.

'It's just a lot, you know?' he says, so suddenly that Nora sits up and tries to look awake in the way she used to when she was a teenager and her mother came into her room to see how she was getting on with her homework.

'The festival,' he clarifies, when she doesn't say anything. He exhales sharply, a deep groove appearing between his eyebrows. He doesn't look at her, though, only at the car with the GB bumper sticker in front of them, his jaw clenched.

'People are gonna know ...' He gives her a sideways look. But as soon as their eyes meet, he looks back at the road. 'Everything's going to change.'

'Maybe it needs to,' she tells him, thinking about everything that led to her sitting in his truck right now. Usually at this time on a Tuesday she'd be looking at the clock, counting down the minutes until Roland went for one of his three-hour lunches.

He just shrugs as they turn into an open-air car park. They must have arrived, she realises, with a twist of dis-appointment. That was quick. Her uncles told her Pidwell was twenty minutes from Penzance, but it feels like they've only just left the village.

He turns off the engine, but they sit there for a moment or two, watching someone trying to back an SUV into a space that clearly isn't big enough.

Finally, Sendhil asks, 'How long do you need?'

'Huh?' she mutters, still distracted by the SUV.

'Here, in Penzance. I have a thing so I need a couple of hours.'

'That's fine,' Nora says. Happy to explore. 'I need to get a printer, actually.'

'If you go down there,' he points through the wind-screen to the other side of the car park, 'you'll find a shop called Benson's Electronics. Speak to Lou. He won't do you over.'

~*~

Lou does not do Nora over. Or, at least, she doesn't think he does. She's sure she could have got the same wireless printer online for cheaper, but doubts anyone delivers to Pidwell.

There's still time to fill before she has to meet Sendhil, but Lou lets her leave the printer there so she can pick it up on her way back to the car park and she goes for a wander.

Penzance is lovely. With its quaint pubs and £5 bags of Cornish clotted-cream fudge, it's clearly geared towards tourists, but once she strays off the high street, she's rewarded with several narrow roads of independent boutiques and art galleries. As she's ambling down one of them, she sees a cheese shop and stops outside, wondering if it's the one where Annabelle gets the good cheese that Sendhil hoped Alice would bring him back last night.

As soon as she walks in, she's confronted with the heady smell of ripe cheese. Her parents would *love* this place, but Nora has always been more fond of the taste of cheese than the smell. They abide by the stinkier-the-better rule. Her mother always says that if it isn't smelly enough to clear the room, she doesn't want it, so she'd be in Heaven.

It *reeks*, so Nora decides to make her escape. But, as she's leaving, she sees they do a mini cheese plate for one and buys it for Sendhil to thank him for the door thing.

As she's leaving the shop, she hears her phone ringing in her bag.

'Nora, darling, where are you?' Mark asks, before she's even said hello.

'Penzance.'

'What on earth are you doing in Penzance?'

'I don't know,' she admits. 'It just kind of happened.'

'Alice?'

'Yeah.'

She doesn't need to elaborate on that because he says, 'So, the grand tour's off, then?'

Nora curses under her breath. She'd forgotten she was supposed to swing by the Trefelyn after the meeting. 'I'm sorry,' she says, pressing a hand to her forehead.

Mark laughs. 'It's okay. A builder's just drilled through a water pipe so it's chaos here. I actually forgot you were supposed to be coming, too, until James reminded me.'

'That's good,' Nora says, then feels bad. 'Not about the water pipe, of course.'

'I think James is going to have a stroke.' Mark groans. 'Hey. What you doing tonight?'

'I haven't even thought about it.'

'Why don't we come to yours? I'll cook. James needs a break from this place.' As if on cue, someone starts drilling and Mark has to raise his voice. 'We both do.'

'Of course! That'll be lovely.'

'Where are you now?'

She looks up at the shop she's standing outside. 'By a very fancy boutique called Salt.'

'I know it,' he says. 'Can you see an alley directly in front of you?'

'Yeah.'

'Go through there.'

She walks through the alley to find it opens into a much bigger street.

Nora smiles when she sees the green-and-white-striped stalls. 'A farmer's market!'

'That's St John's Hall,' Mark tells her. She assumes he means the old biscuit-coloured building the stalls are pitched in the carpark of. In the middle, there's a long narrow table with a pale blue and white check table cloth that people are sitting around, eating whatever they've bought, and Nora is suddenly *ravenous*.

'It's usually only there on Friday mornings,' Mark explains, shouting over the drilling, 'but they do it on Tuesdays as well in the summer. They're packing up soon, so hurry.'

He tells her what to get from where. Mackerel from a guy called Ron, who insisted that Nora tell Mark his daughter got into Manchester University. Fennel from a woman called Liz, who told Nora to remind Mark that she's not there next Friday, but Johnny will be.

Finally, she buys an obscenely expensive bottle of olive oil from a guy called Frank. When Nora reminds her uncle about the thirty-mile rule, Mark tells her that she has to inform James that she brought it with her from London, which, they both know, he won't believe.

By the time she's done, it's almost two thirty so she has to run to pick up the printer, almost dropping it, and everything else she's carrying, as she races to the car park.

'Sorry!' she says, when she finds Sendhil, leaning against the pickup in his Ray-Bans, his face tilted towards the sun. He looks like a poster for the indie album of the summer.

''S all right.' He nods at her bags. 'You should have said. I've got loads of totes.'

'I didn't know I'd be going to the farmer's market. This is for my uncle Mark.'

He takes the printer, putting the box into the bed of the pickup and covering it with a worn grey blanket. The cardboard box he was putting in there earlier is gone now and she hopes it wasn't stolen while they were gone. Sendhil doesn't seem concerned, though, as he goes to open the passenger door for her. She wasn't expecting him to, though, and was about to open it herself so their fingers graze as they reach for the handle at the same time. The shock makes her whole arm jolt and she wonders if he feels it too as he steps back.

'Sorry.' He holds up his hands. 'Go ahead.'

And, with that, Sendhil goes from chill to the point of looking like he's about to fall asleep to standing at attention, his back straight and his hands still in the air.

Nora is equally startled as she opens the passenger door, but before she climbs in, he reaches for her bags. Their hands graze this time and it's enough to make her stop, half in and half out of the pickup and look at him. He peers at her from under his eyelashes as he takes the bags from her. The tips of his fingers touch the centre of her palm as he does and hers instinctively curl up to touch them, but his hand slips away before she can.

'You in?' he asks, when she slides into the passenger seat.

'Yeah,' she murmurs, her face burning as he shuts the door.

Nora still hasn't caught her breath by the time he ambles around the front of the truck. The cab is already stifling from sitting in the sun for two hours, but feels noticeably warmer when he climbs in. He shrugs the canvas tote off his shoulder and when he turns to reach between their seats to sling it onto the back seat, his knuckles catch on her bare arm. It's only for a second, but she has to swallow a gasp at the fleeting moment of skin on skin.

Then they're back on the road to Pidwell and Nora's unspeakably grateful for the breeze passing through the open windows as she asks herself if he meant to touch her hand.

The first time – when they both reached for the car door – was definitely an accident.

But the second time, there was definite contact and …

'Nora?'

She turns to him with a frown. 'Huh?'

'Is that your phone?'

'Oh!' she gasps, bending down to retrieve it from her tote bag. By the time she finds it, it's stopped ringing and she peers at the screen. She doesn't recognise the number, but it's a mobile, so she calls whoever it is. 'This is Nora Armstrong. I just had a missed call from—'

'Thank God!' Alice screeches. 'I hope you don't mind, but Mark gave me your number.'

Sendhil must hear her because he asks, 'Is that Alice?'

When she nods, he tells her to put her on speaker and she does to hear Alice wailing.

'What?' Nora asks, her eyes wide. 'What's wrong? Who died?'

'My scanner!' she shrieks.

Sendhil curses under his breath. 'Ah, for God's sake. You scared the life out of us!'

'Sendhil?' Alice asks, with a heave and a sob.

'Yes! You're on speaker. Nora and I driving back from Penzance.'

Alice wails at him now, her accent getting thicker and thicker until Nora can only pick out certain words like *scanner* and *festival* and some others she won't repeat. Still, she manages to piece it together. Alice did the poster while she was waiting for Tommy's wife's birthday cake to bake, but as she was scanning it in, her printer died before the file made it to her laptop and now it's gone. Plus, while all of this was going on, the cake burned.

Or, at least, Nora *thinks* that's what happened.

'You scan things in by opening the top of the printer, right?' he asks, when she calms down enough to let him get a word in.

Alice sounds confused. 'Yeah? Why?'

'Open it.'

'Sendhil, I've tried everything. I've even unplugged it, but it's dead, I'm telling you!'

'Just open the top of the printer, Alice.'

'That won't work, Sendhil. The printer's dead. The file is gone. *Gone*. It took me ages and I'm going to have to start again,' she mutters sourly, but does it anyway, then gasps. 'Oh my God! I forgot! I still have the hard copy!' Nora hears the sound of paper fluttering through the phone. 'See,' she adds smugly. 'This is why I illustrate by hand! I don't trust technology.'

He turns to Nora and rolls his eyes.

'Hey!' Alice snaps. 'I can hear that face you're pulling, Achari!'

'All this crying and for what, Alice?'

'Well, *excuse me* for having an existential crisis.'

He scoffs at that. 'An existential crisis?'

'I'm stressed, Sendhil! You know I haven't drawn anything for months. And you know I'm not great at showing people my stuff. I thought *you* of all people would get that.'

He lets out a tender sigh. 'Uh-huh.'

'I don't know why I offered to do it. Now everyone on the group chat's pestering me to see it! And by *everyone* I mean Kate. You'd think the whole festival hinged on this poster! But I want to get it right because it's for Meredith, and I really like Nora,' she says, then stops when she remembers she's on speaker: 'Oh. Hey, Nora.'

She chuckles. 'Hey, Alice.'

'All right. Fine,' Sendhil says, rolling his eyes again. 'When we get home, I'll come get the poster, scan it and email it to you so you can send it to everyone. If they like it, and by *they* I mean Kate, then I'll send it to my print guy.'

'You have a print guy?' Alice asks.

'Yeah.'

'Who is he?'

'You don't know everyone I know.'

'Why are you being weird about your print guy?'

And, just like that, they're back to bickering, as Nora holds out the phone for them.

'Listen. We're home,' Sendhil says, beeping as they pass the shop. 'So go away. You're wrecking my head, and if I'm not careful, I'll run over one of the cats.'

'Tell him I hate him,' Alice says, as soon as Nora takes her off speaker.

'Between this and the builder drilling through a water pipe at the Trefelyn earlier,' Nora says, which makes Alice gasp in horror, 'it sounds like everyone has had a bit of a day.'

'You know what, Nora Armstrong? I have had a bit of a day.'

'Mark and James are coming to mine for dinner if you and Megan wanna join us?'

Alice doesn't hesitate as Sendhil pulls up outside the cottages. 'What time?'

'Seven?'

When she hangs up, Sendhil has his head in his hands.

'You know what will help with that?' she tells him.

'Tequila?' he says into his hands.

'Well, yeah. But also this?'

He looks up as she reaches between her feet and holds up the paper bag.

Sendhil peers inside and smiles. 'The good cheese.'

'To say thank you for the door thing.'

'Ah, you didn't have to,' he tells her. 'To be fair, I was pretty confident that no one was in there. I honestly don't know what I would have done if someone had been.' He raises his eyebrows over his sunglasses. 'You might have had to deploy your travel mug.'

Nora laughs, but stops when he says, 'I got you something too, actually.'

Her heart hiccups as he reaches between their seats. 'You did?'

He roots around in the canvas tote he slung into the back and produces a small box.

Nora cackles when he holds it up. 'Ear plugs.'

'Those bastard cats.'

As he's about to get out, she says, 'Hey. Did you hear what I was saying to Alice?'

'I zoned out after she demanded to meet my print guy.'

'My uncles are coming over for dinner. She and Megan are as well, if you fancy it.'

Sendhil shrugs. 'All right.'

~*~

As soon as Nora walks into the cottage and sees the sofa, she sighs and says, 'Hello, friend.'

She shouldn't, she knows. She has a dozen things to do for the festival before she meets Tommy tomorrow. Plus she should probably set up the printer so she can print out the risk assessment forms. And, she remembers, with a heavy sigh, she *still* hasn't unpacked. But it's been such a day and the sofa is right there and it looks so comfortable.

Nora finds a box of Peace Tea in the kitchen, which sounds like exactly what she needs, and makes herself a cup, taking it and the salted caramel truffles Alice gave her last night to the sofa. She puts them on the coffee-table and heads into the bedroom to retrieve her book from the bedside table, grabs her phone, and settles down. As soon as she sits down, she sees the sofa gives her a perfect view of the sea and *this* is what she daydreamed of when her uncles told her about Pidwell.

After a few minutes, she reaches for a cushion to put it on her lap. But, as soon as she does, the cat – who she hadn't even noticed was asleep on the armchair – stirs. Nora isn't sure which one it is. Dodger, she thinks, since he looks more curious than haunted.

When he jumps down and stalks towards her, she freezes, watching as he leaps into her lap, sits on the pillow then nudges her cheek with his furry grey head.

'Hello,' she says, watching as he turns in a circle in her lap – around and around and around – his little paws kneading the cushion, then stops, lies down and curls into a ball.

'Comfortable?' she asks, but he's already asleep, purring so contentedly that Nora can't help but stroke the top of his head with her finger. He responds with another purr so, she does it again, scratching him this time, which prompts more satisfied purring.

She hears her phone buzz on the coffee-table and reaches for it to find a text from Luce, asking if she's around. Before she can unlock her phone to respond, she gets another, this time from her brother, asking the same thing. After batting a few texts back and forth, she discovers that Luce is on the bus, having just finished at the salon, and Ben is about to start his shift in A and E. So, in an increasingly rare moment of synchronicity, the three of them are free for twenty minutes at the same time and decide to FaceTime.

'There's that face! I've missed that face!' Luce grins as soon as hers appears on screen.

Her brother isn't as enthusiastic. But she knows him well enough to know that despite his sniff and shrug, he's pleased to see her as well. 'All right, Nor.'

They demand to see the cottage, which she shows them from her vantage point on the sofa, but when they ask to see the rest – and the cove – she tells them she can't, lowering her phone to show them the cat fast asleep on her lap.

After that, they have only fifteen minutes, so they each get five. Luce tells them about her last client, who had nits, and Ben regales them with a story about a man who came into A and E with an electric toothbrush inserted somewhere they're not designed to be inserted.

Nora tells them about the festival and they both agree that it sounds amazing (Luce wants Kate to adopt her), but they don't know how she's going to get it all done in time. And they definitely don't know how she's going to keep the Sendhil thing a secret.

She calls her mother next and it's *so nice*. She can't remember the last time they talked for so long. Now when they talk, it's usually in passing, as one of them is heading out of the front door. *Don't forget I'm staying at Luce's tonight* or *Do you need anything from Waitrose?* Or, it's over Sunday lunch, with her father, uncles and brother there, and they're talking at once while they fight over the crispiest roast potatoes.

So Nora hasn't talked to her mother like this – just the two of them – since she was a teenager and she would lie in bed with her on a Sunday morning, telling her about whatever adolescent melodrama she was weathering that week. And much like she used to when she was thirteen, it comes out in a breathless rush. Nora tells her everything. About how beautiful Pidwell is. And the festival. And the cats waking her up that morning. And Lady Kate and how she was kidnapped in Kentucky and her husband refused to pay the ransom.

Jennifer has a four-thirty meeting, so has to go. Nora blows kisses, promising to call her again tomorrow. When she hangs up, Dodger is still fast asleep on her lap, but Oliver – definitely Oliver judging by his haunted expression – is now sitting on the footstool, staring at something over her shoulder with such focus that Nora turns to check if someone's there.

No one is, but when she turns back, Oliver lets out a single plaintive miaow.

As soon as he does, Dodger stirs, letting out a sleepier one.

'Do you even know why you're miaowing?' she asks. He stretches and yawns.

Then Oliver starts up again and Nora realises what time it is. 'No,' she tells them. 'It's only four thirty.'

Nora has already messed up by giving them their break-fast too early.

She's not doing it with dinner as well.

So, she ignores them, opening her book. That makes them worse, though, because they start yowling fiercely, Dodger is now sitting up on the cushion, staring at her, while Oliver jumps from the footstool onto the sofa beside her, doing the same.

'No,' she tells them again, refusing to look up from her book. 'Not until five o'clock.'

Dodger paws at her book and would tug it out of her hands if she didn't hold on tighter.

'No!' she says, more firmly this time, raising her voice over the miaowing.

It doesn't work. Dodger headbutts the book while Oliver jumps onto the back of the sofa, pacing back and forth along the cushions, whacking the back of her head with his tail.

'I will not be bullied like this,' she tells them, but the miaowing is frenzied now and so loud she can barely hear her own voice, let alone focus on what she's trying to read.

After another few minutes, Nora slaps her book shut. 'Okay! Fine! Enough!'

They jump down at her feet as she stomps to the kitchen to feed them. It's four forty-one, so she's not feeding them *that* early. Or, at least, that's what she tells herself as she heads back to the sofa, like it was her decision and she wasn't terrorised into it.

The next thing Nora knows, she wakes with such a jolt, she hears herself say, 'Oh!'

What's happening?

What time is it?

What's going on?

When her eyes refocus, she looks around the cottage to find that it's still daylight. The sea is still blue. The gulls are still calling to one another. And she's still on the sofa.

She hears a knock then.

'Nora? You there?' she can hear Mark asking on the other side of the door.

'Coming!'

As soon as she opens the front door, her uncles start talking. Complaining about the builders and the burst water pipe and telling her they're late because they were waiting for a delivery of timber and the driver couldn't even find Pidwell, let alone the Trefelyn.

When they barrel in, the cats barrel out, no doubt in search of some peace and quiet.

Or, more likely, another dinner from Sendhil.

Nora doesn't blame them. Given she was fast asleep three minutes ago, her uncles' arrival is *a lot.* As is the fact that they're even there. *It can't be seven,* she thinks. She can't have been asleep for *two and a half hours*. But, according to her phone, it's only six o'clock.

'Thought we'd get dinner started before Alice and Megan get here,' Mark explains, as they head for the kitchen. He grabs three glasses out of the cupboard while James opens a bottle of red wine and demands to know how the first meeting went.

When Nora fills them in, they say that the festival sounds like it's going to be amazing, but agree – along with Ben and Luce – that people are going to find out about Sendhil.

'I feel so bad,' Nora admits, as she heads into the bedroom to grab her wireless speaker, then points it at them when she returns. 'This festival is supposed to a celebration.'

'Don't feel bad,' Mark tells her, as he takes the mackerel out of the fridge. 'It's not your fault. Sendhil must have known this would happen when he agreed to it.'

'Maybe that's the point,' she wonders aloud, as she connects the wireless speaker to her phone then looks for an appropriate playlist. 'Maybe he knows he can't keep where he is a secret much longer and he wants to do it on his own terms.'

Mark nods as he inspects Mrs Stroud's spice rack. 'You could be right.'

'Maybe he's decided to move on,' James suggests.

'And go where?' Nora asks, with an uneasy shiver.

'Well.' James picks up a tub of sea salt from the counter and shakes it. 'If he's decided it's time to get back out into the art world, London would make the most sense.'

She almost laughs at the thought of Sendhil in London. He seems so rooted here that she can't picture him anywhere other than Pidwell. It would be so strange to step onto a tube carriage and see him sitting there, cradling a book, or strolling along Marylebone High Street with a coffee. Like the parakeets in Kensington Gardens.

Mark must agree, because he shakes his head. 'No way. He'll never go back to London.'

James shrugs. 'Cork, then?'

'Not now Alice is here.'

Nora traces the rim of her wine glass with a finger as she thinks about what Sendhil said earlier in the truck, about how everything was going to change. 'Maybe Pidwell will lose some of its magic when everyone finds out he's here.'

Mark tilts his head at her and smiles. 'Pidwell will never lose its magic.'

'He doesn't need to leave, though,' James says. 'So what if people find out he's here? Yeah, it might encourage some of them to visit, but he's hardly Harry Styles. People like his work, not him. It's not like anyone is going to be camping outside his cottage or anything.'

'Or breaking in and taking a shower,' Mark says, winking at Nora.

~*~

Sendhil arrives at seven with his own chair, which is good, because Mrs Stroud only has four. He also brings beer, a saucepan and a small bowl of what looks like orange couscous.

'What's that?' Nora asks, when he puts them on the kitchen counter.

'Aubergine curry.' He points at the saucepan, then at the bowl. 'And coconut sambal.'

Nora stares at them, then at him. 'You cook?'

He shrugs. 'You don't?'

Her uncles erupt into laughter.

'Yeah, right,' James tells Sendhil. 'Nora's favourite recipe is Deliveroo.'

'Remember last summer?' Mark flicks James with a tea-towel. 'When we were in Italy and Jennifer and Alex were in Beijing and Nora tried to make that stir fry?'

'It wasn't so much fried as incinerated.' James arches an eyebrow at Sendhil. 'Nora called us because she couldn't get the smoke detector to stop going off.'

Mercifully, Alice sweeps in then.

She doesn't bother knocking, just walks through the front door. She had some left-over batter and buttercream from the lemon and elderflower almond cake she made for Tommy's wife's birthday, so she's brought a mini – if much less elaborately decorated – version of it and a salad, in case Nora's uncles have forgotten that Megan is gluten-free.

Which, of course, they haven't.

The noise level increases considerably as Alice heads into the kitchen to oversee what Mark is doing. Sendhil, rather sensibly, takes a bottle of beer and retreats to the living room, while Alice tells Nora's uncles about the drama with the scanner.

When Nora next looks for Sendhil, he's sitting on the footstool in the living room with the cats. One is in his lap and the other draped around his neck like a scarf. He's talking to Megan who has appeared from nowhere and is sitting on the sofa, drinking one of his beers.

Dinner is cramped around Mrs Stroud's small table, but lovely, Nora's uncles and Alice leading the conversation while Nora tries not to be too enthusiastic over Sendhil's aubergine curry in case she offends Mark, showering his rice with compliments instead.

But the truth is, Sendhil's curry is divine. As is his coconut sambal, which is nose-running hot, so she's surprised when she has to fight Alice over it.

'Are you kidding?' she says, when Nora comments on it, pointing her spoon at Sendhil. 'My family used to live next door to his, I grew up on stuff like this. You should try his hoppers.'

After dinner, they wash up, Mark at the sink and the rest of them forming a production line to dry and put everything away, while Nora tells Ben's story about the electric toothbrush. Everyone except Megan, who drives to Penzance station to pick up Annabelle. They return as

Alice is complaining at the lack of tea that isn't herbal, and the noise level ramps up again as they greet Annabelle, rushing over to hug her and ask how London was.

They sit in the living room with Alice's cake, squeezing onto the sofa and chairs while Sendhil lies on his back on the rug in front of the woodburner, playing with the cats. One is curled up on his chest while the other is kneading Sendhil's hair with his paws. Judging by the face Sendhil is pulling, it's as uncomfortable as it looks.

Annabelle tells them about her talk at the Whitechapel, which is one of Nora's favourite galleries, and she feels her first pinch of yearning for London. She doesn't think Sendhil is paying attention, but when Annabelle stops to sip her wine, he looks up. 'How's Fran?' he asks, his hand under Dodger's stomach, pulling him out of his hair.

'Good.' Annabelle nods. 'She's busy getting the Yinka Shonibare exhibition ready.'

'Yinka's exhibiting at the Whitechapel?'

'Yes, in October. It's quite a coup. We must go.'

'No London,' he mutters, raising his arm and holding Dodger aloft. 'I'll never go back.'

'You can't ignore London for ever,' Annabelle tells him.

'Yes, I can.' Sendhil laughs, but something about the way he says it makes Nora frown.

She's about to stand up and collect the empty plates, when Annabelle turns to her. 'Fran's frantic with the exhibition,' she says, tucking one of her curls behind her ear.

'I can imagine.'

'I told her about all the wonderful work you've been doing for the festival.'

Nora's cheeks warm at that. 'You're very kind, Annabelle.'

'I also told her that you're available from early September and Fran was thrilled.'

She isn't sure what she's getting at until Annabelle adds, 'She just needs help with the Yinka Shonibare exhibition to begin with, but after that, who knows what it could lead to?' she says, with an eager smile. 'So, what do you think? Can I pass on your number to Fran?'

Nora is surprised at the tug of hesitation she feels, but shakes it off and smiles back. 'Yes! Yes, of course. Please. Thank you so much, Annabelle.'

~*~

There's another round of washing-up while Megan drives Annabelle home. Then everyone is saying they should go as well, Alice reminding them that she has to get up at four to make bread while Nora's uncles grumble about having to let the builders in at seven.

They're already saying their goodbyes by the time Megan returns, but Sendhil is still pinned to the floor by the cats and only manages to get them off him as they're leaving.

'I'll collect my chair in the morning, if that's okay,' he says, as the others are heading out, then the corners of his mouth twitch when he adds, 'And my towel.'

'Sorry!' she gasps, pressing her hands to her face. She'd totally forgotten about it.

'Don't worry about it,' he says, nudging her with his hip on his way out.

She doesn't know if it's an accident or if he meant to do it and is so startled that she almost doesn't notice that he's walking out with the printer under his arm.

'Um,' she says, pointing at it, 'if you're gonna rob me, can you not be so brazen about?'

When he realises what she's saying, he chuckles. 'It's just the box. I'll take it out to the recycling bin by the shop.'

'Just the box? Where's the rest of it?'

He points over her shoulder and she turns to see the printer sitting on the desk.

She blinks at it, then at him. 'Did you set up my printer?'

That's what he must have been doing when he was rooting through the desk drawer earlier. He was probably looking for the Wi-Fi password so he could connect it to her laptop.

'There was no dog to talk to or ice trays to fill,' he tells her with a wink.

Chapter 13

God bless Sendhil Achari because the ear plugs work. They work so well, in fact, that Nora sleeps through her alarm and wakes up twenty minutes before she has to meet Tommy.

Luckily, there's no point in having a shower because she's only going to get filthy poking around the town hall and the silver bus, which, Nora suspects, isn't much cleaner. So, she washes her face, brushes her teeth then runs back into the bedroom to tug on a pair of black leggings and her black Ivy Park hoodie, then wraps her curls in a leopard-print scarf.

Nora has no idea where the cats are and should probably be concerned that they're not pestering her for their breakfast, but she really doesn't have time.

Besides, they're hardly going to starve, are they? Sendhil will feed them.

Better get out of here before they come looking for their second breakfast, she thinks, grabbing the risk assessment forms she printed off last night, and charges out of the door.

As she's approaching the shop, she sees Alice in the doorway, gazing at the sea.

'Coffee?' she asks.

'I'd love one,' Nora tells her, with a pout. 'But I'm late to meet Tommy.'

She doesn't seem concerned. 'It's Tommy. He won't mind.' She walks into the shop, and the promise of a latte is enough to make Nora follow as she checks the time on her phone.

'I haven't got my purse,' she remembers. Maybe she can run back and get it while Alice is making the coffee.

But she waves her hand as she heads behind the counter. 'Don't worry about it.'

It occurs to Nora then that she hasn't paid for a coffee since she got here. 'You can't keep giving me free coffee,' she tells Alice. 'That's no way to run a business.'

'Business?' She turns to open the fridge beneath the coffee machine to grab a pint of milk. 'God, if I was in this for the money, Nora, I'd have given up long ago. Besides,' she says, pouring some milk into a stainless-steel jug, 'I can stretch to the odd latte.'

'I drink *a lot* of coffee, though,' Nora warns, tilting her head at Alice and raising her eyebrows. 'So you have to let me pay otherwise I'll bankrupt you.'

'Seriously. Don't worry.' She lowers her voice then, even though they're the only ones in there: 'Meredith left us some money. Not loads, mind, but enough to keep this place going.'

'That's so nice.'

'Meredith was all about going for what you want.' Alice's smile flattens when she says *was*. Then she turns to the coffee machine to steam the milk, raising her voice over the hiss. 'No excuses. She said that if all I needed was money, I can have it. *It's only money, honey.*'

When Alice's smile brightens again, it's enough to make Nora smile as well.

'From what everyone has told me, Meredith must have been a very special person.'

'She was,' Alice agrees says with a tender sigh. 'I wish you could have met her.'

Me too, Nora thinks.

~*~

Alice is right. Tommy isn't bothered that she's five minutes late. Especially when she gives him the oat milk cappuccino Alice sent her off with. And the vegan blueberry Danish.

The town hall is hardly the Louvre, but it's in surprisingly good shape, especially if they're embracing the whole enchanted fairy-tale house thing. Some of the windows are cracked and there are a few uneven floorboards, but it's solid, and when Tommy confirms there's nothing structurally wrong with it, Nora can stop worrying about the ceiling caving in.

'First things, first.' She jabs her notebook with her pen. 'Before we do anything, we need to make sure that the gas, electricity, water, all that stuff, is sound.'

He doesn't seem as worried, though. 'I can do that.'

Nora frowns at him. 'You can?'

'Yeah. I'm a qualified spark and I'm gas-safe-registered.'

'Okay,' she says, slightly stunned. Tommy is clearly a man of many talents. 'I think we should focus on these two rooms.' She points the pen at their feet, then at the room they had the meeting in yesterday. 'This one can be for Meredith and that can be for everything else.'

'When are you seeing the art?' Tommy asks.

'After this. I'm going straight from yours to Meredith and Annabelle's.'

'So we'll know then if everything's going to fit?'

'I *hope* these rooms are big enough.' She bites her bottom lip for a second, then says, 'If they are, we just need to give them a scrub and get rid of any loose nails, that sort of thing.'

When they walk into the hall, she points her pen at the staircase. 'We'll have to rope this off so no one goes upstairs. We don't want randoms wandering around.'

'True. Didn't think about that.'

'And we'll need *at least* one person in each room to keep an eye on the art. God. We'll need insurance, won't we?' She mutters to herself as she makes a note.

'Why don't we limit the number of people in each room?' Tommy suggests, scratching his neck. 'We could say that only four people are allowed in at a time.'

'Yes! Brilliant! It'll be easier to manage and make it feel more exclusive. I hate when exhibitions are so busy that you can't actually *see* any of the artwork.'

She's still scribbling in her notebook as they head to his house to check out the famous silver bus. They amble through the valley, the rush of the stream drowning her mumbling as she runs through the list of everything she needs to do before they announce the festival.

Nora checks off each thing on her fingers. Alice has done an incredible job with the poster. It's even better than Nora expected, and it's Lady Kate approved. Megan's working on the website. And Tommy's doing *everything else*. Plus, as promised, he spoke to his daughter, Lottie, about handling the social media. So, now Nora has to create a master contact list and a spreadsheet for the budget, then decipher the scribbles in her notebook and work out what needs to be added to the schedule, which, she's almost certain, they're already behind on.

She's so distracted by everything that needs to be done that she doesn't notice the massive dog coming towards them until it's almost on top of them.

'It's all right.' Tommy pats the beast on the head when Nora steps back. It's so big he doesn't even have to bend down. 'This is Archie. I know he's a lump, but he's soft as anything.'

This is Archie? she thinks, maintaining a safe distance.

Nora was expecting a chocolate Lab or a fierce chihuahua, if only to see long-haired, leather-jacket-wearing, tattooed Tommy carrying a tiny dog with a bow. Not a Rottweiler.

'Soft lad, ain't ya, Arch?' he says, patting the dog's back this time.

Archie tilts his considerable head to look at Nora, and when she sees that he's nothing but big eyes and glossy, folded-over ears, like the cats', she feels herself soften.

'Pleasure to meet you,' she says, as he plods along between them.

Tommy's house is the same as Meredith and Annabelle's but with a barn, which, Nora knows, is where he's storing the bus. Inside the layout is the same, but they couldn't be more different. It looks like any other family home. The hooks on the wall by the front door are heaving with coats, shoes and wellies piled up beneath them, none of them seeming to match. The television is on in the living room, even though no one's in there. There's a pair of muddy football boots resting on a sheet of newspaper on the table in the dining room and a pile of bills and a chewed-up tennis ball on the much smaller one in the hall.

It's like any other family home, but with shelves of vinyl, a guitar in every room and framed gold records, sitting between photos of babies and weddings and holidays.

When they head into the cluttered kitchen, the radio is on and a tiny woman with big hair is singing along to 'What's Love Got to Do With It' while she arranges pink roses in a vase.

'Nora!' she says when she follows Tommy in. She turns down the radio, puts the vase in the middle of the equally cluttered dining table and walks over to give her a huge hug.

Nora tenses, still not used to the hugging thing they do in Pidwell, but makes a point of smiling when Vanessa steps back and looks at her, her eyelashes stiff with mascara. She smells of Elnett and Estée Lauder's Beautiful and it's strangely comforting.

'This is my better half, Vanessa,' Tommy says, as Nora casts a quick glance around the kitchen to find a cluster of pink foil balloons in the corner and a crowd of cards on the island.

Nora smiles sweetly. 'Lovely to meet you, Vanessa. Happy birthday.'

'Thank you! But, please, call me Van.'

Vanessa tells her to sit at the table, by the cherry-red drum kit, and proceeds to feed her tea and Bourbon biscuits. The two of them may look alike – all in black with unruly hair and tattoos – but Nora learns, almost immediately, that Vanessa couldn't be more different from her husband. She's loud and curious with a filthy laugh that fills the whole house

As Nora is refusing a second cup of tea, Lottie wanders into the kitchen. She's a perfect balance of the two of them, as tall as her father, with her mother's dark hair and big eyes, if none of her energy. Lottie is scrolling through her phone so doesn't see Nora as she traipses past the table. Or, if she does see her, she doesn't acknowledge her as she heads to the fridge.

'Lotts, this is Nora,' Tommy tells her, when she does. 'The one I was telling you about yesterday, who needs you to do that Instagram stuff for the arts festival in August.'

'Oh. Yeah. Hi,' she mumbles, head inside the fridge.

'Don't be offended, Nora. *This* is sociable for Lottie.' Vanessa nods at her daughter. 'Most of the time, she doesn't come out of her room until I call her for dinner.'

Nora chuckles. She isn't offended at all, actually. She remembers what it was like to be sixteen and come downstairs in your pyjamas with a spot the size of a small planet on your chin, only to be confronted by one of your parents' friends and have to be nice to them. So, if Lottie wants to get out of the kitchen as quickly as possible, Nora understands.

'Lotts,' Tommy says, the already creased skin between his eyebrows creasing further.

When she doesn't acknowledge him, Vanessa says it louder, 'Lottie!'

'What?' She emerges from the fridge with a can of Red Bull. 'Why are you yelling?'

'Why aren't you at school, Lotts?' Tommy asks, now he has her attention.

'Sports Day,' she mutters, going back to whatever she was looking at on her phone.

'Why aren't you at Sports Day, then?'

But she ignores him, heading back out of the kitchen.

'And that.' He thumbs after her. 'Was our darling daughter, Lottie.'

'Don't worry,' Vanessa tells Nora. 'She's much better at talking to strangers online.'

Tommy looks slightly concerned at that. But then he slaps the table. 'Shall we go and look at this bus?'

They head out of the French windows, past Archie who is flopped on the lawn in the sunshine and doesn't flinch when they walk around him and head for the barn.

'She's a beaut, ain't she?' Tommy says, slapping the side of the bus with his hand.

Beaut might be stretching it. The tyres are flat and it's so filthy that it's not so much silver as a dull, muted grey.

The inside isn't much cleaner, the ceilings softened with cobwebs and the seats torn and taped together with duct tape, which is in keeping with the silver theme, at least. But Tommy's right: with some work, it could be perfect.

Pidwell's own Silver Factory.

Nora's list is even longer as she asks the way to Meredith and Annabelle's.

Tommy points directly ahead of him, along the stream, between a thick tangle of trees. 'Just walk that way for about five minutes and you'll see their house. You can't miss it.'

She thanks him, then thanks him again five minutes later when, sure enough, there's the house. She looks up to find Annabelle waving from an upstairs window as she approaches, her long grey curls everywhere, and waves back. Annabelle is coming down the stairs as she walks through the open front door and hugs Nora tightly, then ushers her into the garden.

They sit at the table, Annabelle showing Nora printouts of the art. It's all incredible. Pretty much what she expected. Except Alice's, which, Annabelle tells her, Megan had to surreptitiously email when Alice kept saying she would, but never did.

Nora thought Alice's paintings would be like her. Bright. Breathless. A fever dream. Like Basquiat and Pollock and Motherwell, all at once. But the printout Annabelle shows her is much more precise. Lots of sharp, straight lines and blocks of bold colour.

'She's *really* talented,' Nora says, relieved that she won't have to pretend to like it.

Nora looks up to find Annabelle holding a piece of paper.

'As for Kate.' Annabelle's eyes widen slightly as she blinks. 'There is honestly nothing I can say that will prepare you for this so I'm just going to show it to you.'

Annabelle hands her the piece of paper and Nora turns it over, bracing herself to be confronted by an insipid watercolour of a bowl of misshapen fruit that she will have to compliment constantly. But when she turns it over, it isn't that at all and Nora is so shocked that she screams and drops the piece of paper as though it's burned her.

She covers her mouth with her hand and stares at Annabelle, who looks remorseful for her part in what she just saw. Finally, she takes her hand away and asks, 'Is that Kate?'

Annabelle nods solemnly.

'Is she ...'

She nods again.

'She's ...' Nora can't even say the word and mouths instead '... *naked*.'

'That's all she paints.'

'That's it? Like, nothing else?'

'Only nude self-portraits.'

'Don't get me wrong,' Nora starts to say, then stops, concerned that Annabelle will think she's a prude. 'Figurative art, particularly nudes ...'

Annabelle holds up a hand, letting her know that she doesn't need to explain. 'Her work is harrowing, Nora. There really is no other word for it. And it's not because they're self-portraits. I honestly don't care that they're self-portraits. If she was Lucian Freud, we wouldn't be having this conversation, but they're terrible. Just *terrible*.' Annabelle presses a hand to her chest. 'It honestly pains me to say that, because I really do think that, with the right encouragement, everyone can paint *something*, but this ...'

They gaze down at the piece of paper face down on the table between them.

When they look up, Nora frowns. 'What am I going to do?'

'I don't know about you, darling,' Annabelle pushes her chair back, 'but I need a gin.'

~★~

Nora regrets passing on the gin as she walks back to the cove for her last stop of the morning.

What am I going to do? she asks herself, as she turns up the path to the Trefelyn.

Seriously. What *is* she going to do? She has to show Kate's paintings. They got Arts Council funding for the festival, but it's nowhere near enough. Alice has never organised anything like this before, so only asked for five hundred pounds in the application, figuring that would cover it when it will barely cover the cost of hanging the art.

So, the truth is, without Kate's contribution, there is no Pidwell Arts Festival.

And without Kate's paintings there's no Kate.

'Sorry, love! Didn't see you there!' a disembodied voice calls out.

Nora leaps out of the way as a piece of wood falls from somewhere above, narrowly missing her as it lands in the skip she's walking past. She's almost sorry it didn't hit her. *That would certainly solve the Kate Dilemma*, she thinks, as she heads into the Trefelyn.

Nora stops, her eyes wide as she looks around. It's a mess. There are ladders everywhere, in the middle of the room or propped against walls, the wallpaper peeling off in places to reveal more layers of it. Years – generations, probably – of different patterns, each one betraying the age of the Trefelyn, like the rings of a tree.

As she takes another step inside she has to walk around a table saw, its lead trailing across her path. She almost trips on a paint-spattered dust sheet in her effort to avoid it, kicking it away to reveal floorboards that look original, but will need more than a polish.

Nora can hear shouting coming from somewhere deep in the house. Friendly builder banter as a Coast FM jingle plays from a radio she can't see. *Hammer my arse, Mick!* someone yells, and she really shouldn't laugh, but she can't help it as she looks for her uncles.

'Nora!' Mark cheers when she peeks around a sheet of plastic to find him and James holding up a set of blueprints. 'You're here! Finally, we can give you the grand tour!'

'You okay?' James asks. 'Did you see the Trefelyn ghost?'

'Yeah,' Mark says. 'Now you come to mention it, you do look like Oliver.'

She mock-shudders. 'Annabelle just showed me one of Kate's paintings.'

'Oh, no! You poor thing! No wonder you look like Oliver!' James's eyes widen.

But her uncle Mark just throws his head back and claps his hands, cackling wildly.

'*You*'ve seen her stuff?' she realises.

James nods, knuckles white around the blueprints. 'She has one in her bedroom.'

'Her *bedroom*?'

'She gave us a tour of her house the first time we went.' Mark is quick to clarify.

'She's very proud of it, but can we ... I'd really rather not think about it.' James shakes his head at her, then at his husband. 'Please. I can't think about it ...'

Mark strokes James's back. 'It's okay, dear.'

That reaction seems pretty accurate, Nora thinks, as she nods at her poor uncle.

'You warned me her stuff was bad.' She shudders for real this time. 'But I thought it would be *boring* bad, you know? Hotel art. A nice fishing-boat or some flowers, but *my God*.'

'Please.' James is suddenly so pale, he looks like he's about to faint. 'I can't ...'

'It's okay.' Mark continues rubbing his back. 'How about we show Nora around?'

There are builders *everywhere*, so the grand tour doesn't take long, every floor and surface a minefield of tools, dust sheets and cans of paint. It's pretty much what Nora had pictured from the outside. Downstairs, there's a room to the left of the front door that will be the reception area and one to the right that will be the library, with a staircase in the middle and an extension out back with the kitchen and a dining room that overlooks the garden. Upstairs, there are eight bedrooms, four facing the sea and four the valley.

Her uncles are right, though. Despite the chaos, Nora can see that the bones are good. It's as solid as the other houses in Pidwell, just more generous. It's clear this used to be the quarry manager's house, whereas the others were for the workers. At the Trefelyn, the rooms are wider and the ceilings higher with intricate cornicing. Every room has a chandelier and a fire place and all the bedrooms are ensuite so, when it's done, it's going to be stunning.

It's going to take a lot *of work to get to that point, though,* Nora thinks, as her uncles lead her around. They need to update everything. The electrics. The plumbing. The car park needs resurfacing and, thanks to being so close to the sea, the window frames are rotting.

Alice is right, if it's done by the August bank-holiday weekend, it'll be a miracle.

'What do you need?' Nora asks, as they're showing her the herb garden.

'You've got your hands full with the festival,' Mark says.

She does, but it's them, so she'll find the time. 'What do you need?' she asks again.

They look so relieved, she's sure they're going to cry.

'We've got the structural stuff covered,' James says, 'but it's the stuff at the end, before we open. Paint and fabric and furniture, making everything look pretty.'

Mark thumbs at him, then at himself. 'I know we're gay, but we're *useless* at that.'

'Just tell me what you need, give me a budget and I'll sort it.'

They both come at her at once, hugging her so hard Nora squeals.

~★~

That's how she spends the rest of the week, trying to do everything at once. She's always in a hurry. Always measuring or talking to someone or trying not to forget something before she can write it down. Somehow, she even finds time to write the piece about the commodification of Frida Kahlo that she panic-pitched before she agreed to come to Pidwell.

Then, on Friday afternoon, while she's helping her uncles rip up the carpet in one of the bedrooms at the Trefelyn, Fran from the Whitechapel Gallery calls. It isn't so much the casual introductory call Nora was expecting. After they exchanged the initial pleasantries and Fran asked how the festival was going, she got to the point, telling Nora that she was *desperate* for her help with the Yinka Shonibare exhibition and asked when she could start.

And, just like that, Nora had a job to go home to.

Ben and her parents were thrilled. As was Luce, who confessed that she was getting concerned that Nora liked it so much in Pidwell she might never come back. Her uncles were pleased as well, of course, but they confessed they'd been hoping Luce was right.

Nora assured them she would miss them as well. After all, dinner with her uncles has become a nightly thing since they gutted the kitchen at the Trefelyn. Not that Nora's complaining. After spending her days charging around, juggling the festival and what needs doing at the Trefelyn, she couldn't imagine getting back to the cottage and having to cook.

Even when her uncles head home, yawning and already thinking about what they're going to make for dinner the following evening, Nora still spends a couple of hours on her laptop, sending emails and updating the schedule. So, by Sunday, when she's sitting in the sunshine outside the shop with them, having breakfast to celebrate her first week in Pidwell, she's so tired that if she lay down, she would probably sleep for a week.

'I think we're ready to announce tomorrow,' she tells Mark and James, between mouthfuls of scrambled egg. 'Megan's done the website and it's exactly what I asked for. Just the poster Alice illustrated, with a Bucketmail address in case anyone wants to get in touch.'

Add 'Check festival inbox' to daily schedule, she scribbles in her notebook.

'Oh, and I met Sendhil's mysterious *print guy*,' Nora emphasises the words with her fingers, 'when we went into Penzance to pick up the posters yesterday. Sadly, he was deeply ordinary. His name's Trevor. He did give us a decent discount, though. But I guess it will be down to me to put them up. Tommy has enough to do. I can't ask him to do anything else.'

Nora has a bite of toast and thinks about that. 'Actually, going to all the local churches, cafés and shops will be a nice way of getting to know the area, won't it? Oh, and I might pop into Penzance again tomorrow and hand out some posters in the art galleries.'

She stops to write that down as well, in case she forgets. 'Although, if I go on Tuesday morning, I can hit the farmer's market as well. Two birds, one stone, and all that. But,' she muses, tapping her chin with her pen, 'Kate wants to set up a mini farm shop out here, so the stallholders might get a bit annoyed that we didn't invite them to be a part of it too.'

When she finally looks up at her uncles, they're staring at her.

'What?' she asks, rubbing her chin with her fingers to check if she has ink on it.

James looks appalled. 'I'm exhausted just listening to you, Nora.'

'Nora, honey.' Mark reaches across to squeeze her arm. 'It's Sunday. The Lord's Day.'

'A day of rest, darling.' James reaches out to squeeze her other arm. 'I know this means a lot to you, but it's a local arts festival, not Glastonbury. You need to calm down or you'll be a wreck by August.'

'Besides,' Mark adds, 'we didn't invite you here to be running around so much we never see you. This was supposed to be a lovely summer sojourn, wasn't it?'

That's true, she thinks with a sigh.

James grins when she puts her pen down. 'See? Now close your notebook. Go on. That's it. Close it. There we go. Well done! See? That wasn't so bad, was it?'

'Okay.' Nora looks around. 'Now what?'

'You're taking the day off,' James tells her.

'To do what?'

'You'll see.' Mark winks at her. 'Now finish your eggs before they go cold.'

~*~

After breakfast, they pile into Nora's car.

Poor Ron. She's neglected him since she arrived in favour of Sendhil's pickup because, no offence to Ron, the truck is infinitely more reliable and has more space in the bed for all the things she constantly seems to be either collecting or dropping off somewhere.

Plus Sendhil is *militant* about not making any unnecessary trips to Penzance. He has to go a couple of times a week himself, so insists they time it so they can go together.

But here Nora is, back with Ron, bombing along in the sunshine. When Mark tells her to turn left onto the main road, she doesn't think anything of it, assuming they're going to Penzance. But then he points to the sign to Mousehole and she laughs.

'Here we are,' he says, when they park outside his old house. 'Home, sweet home.'

Mousehole has changed a lot since she was here as a kid, but Nora still recognises a lot of it. They get raspberry Slush Puppies from the corner shop that turn their tongues blue while Mark shows them around, throwing out his arm to gesture at everything, like a tour guide. The house he and Nora's mum grew up in. The bedroom window they used to sneak out of. Their school. The park bench where he had his first kiss – with a girl

– when he was twelve. The tree where he had his second kiss – with a boy – a couple of years later. The graveyard he used to skulk around, drinking cider and listening to the Cure.

Her uncles were right, Nora is loath to admit. A few hours not thinking about the festival was exactly what she needed. Her shoulders are looser and the ache in the small of her back has begun to ease by the time they wander back to Ron.

On the way to Pidwell, her uncles ask her to drop them at Kate's farm because she's invited them over for tea to discuss the catering for the festival after-party. They invite her to join them, but she politely declines, saying she needs a couple of hours to herself.

They understand, telling her they'll see her later for dinner. Then she's gone, the warm sea air kissing her cheeks as it passes through Ron's open windows.

I'm going to finish my book. She lets out a sigh at the thought. *I'm going to lie on the sofa and finish my book, and if I happen to fall asleep with Dodger again, so be it.*

As she's approaching the turn-off to Pidwell, she sees Sendhil's pickup on the side of the road. There's no lay-by, so Nora does what he's done and pulls over ahead of him, parking on the strip of grass that rolls down to the line of trees that signal the start of the valley.

Sendhil doesn't see her, though. He's hunched over the engine, fiddling furiously with something as she climbs out of Ron and walks towards him. He's so oblivious, in fact, that he doesn't see her until she's standing next to him and he jumps, banging his head on the bonnet.

'Sorry!' Nora says, covering her mouth with her hands to stop herself laughing.

''S fine.' He winces, rubbing the top of his head.

'You okay?' she asks, even though it's quite obvious he isn't.

'Sure. Hey! Do you want a truck?'

She thumbs back at her car. 'Ron might get jealous.'

'Ron?' Sendhil frowns, then rolls his eyes. 'Ah. Because it's burgundy.'

Nora gestures at the engine of the pickup. 'What happened?'

'No idea.' He wipes his hands with a cloth. 'I was driving through the valley, no problem, but as soon as I turned left, all the lights came on and it conked out.'

'Did you hit something when you turned?'

'I don't think so. I would have felt it, surely.' He shrugs. 'It better not be the carburettor,' he mutters, as he dips his head back under the bonnet and resumes fiddling with whatever he was fiddling with before she pulled over. 'I only had it serviced last month.'

'Do you need any help?'

'Actually,' he says, without looking up, 'do you mind trying the ignition?'

When she turns the key, nothing happens.

'I'd better not need a tow,' Sendhil mumbles, as he bends down to the toolbox at his feet to pull out a spanner. 'It's Sunday and Terry's probably already in the pub with Tommy.'

'Wait. There's a pub around here?'

Sendhil doesn't respond as he does something with the spanner. 'Can you try again?'

She jumps back into the cab and turns the key.

But, again, nothing happens.

As Sendhil's swearing, shaking his hands over the engine, like he's threatening to strangle it, Nora realises there's something familiar about this. It reminds her of the time she and Luce were driving back from Brighton after Pride. Ron did exactly the same thing. He was absolutely fine on the way there. Then, on the drive back, boom.

Dead.

Nothing.

'I think I know what's wrong,' she tells him, as she hops out and walks back to Ron.

She tries not to be offended by how surprised Sendhil is when she says that. 'Yeah?'

He straightens as he watches her open the boot of her car. When she takes out the emergency green plastic petrol can, he shakes his head. 'No! It's not that! It's not!'

'When was the last time you filled ... wait. What's your truck called?'

He looks at her like she's lost it. 'It's a truck, Nora.'

'What do I call it, then?'

'*Piece of crap* will suffice right now.'

'Fine.' She sighs theatrically. 'When did you last fill *the truck* up?'

He obviously doesn't remember so she arches an eyebrow at him. 'Humour me, okay?'

'Fine,' he huffs, holding up his hands as she starts to pour the contents of the can into the tank. The truck guzzles it all and she shakes it to show him it's empty.

Sendhil points at the truck. 'If this starts, I swear to God, Nora . . .'

She just smiles.

He jumps into the cab, turns the key and, sure enough, it roars to life.

Sendhil starts swearing, slamming the palms of his hands against the steering wheel and calling *the truck* every name under the sun as she comes to stand next to him.

'It's broken.' He jabs his finger at the petrol gauge. 'Look! See? It's broken.'

'Sure, sure,' she says, turning to swagger back to Ron.

'How was I supposed to know I needed petrol if it's broken?' he calls after her.

She puts the empty can back into Ron's boot and closes it. 'You going back to Pidwell?' she asks, stopping by the open door of her car.

'I'm going for a surf.' He nods at the board in the bed of the truck. 'I need one now.'

'Have fun,' she tells him, with a smug smile.

'I'll be home in a couple of hours,' he tells her, as she's getting into Ron.

Home, Nora thinks, as she heads for the turn-off to Pidwell.

Chapter 14

After that something changes. Shifts. Everything becomes easier. Nora doesn't know what she and Sendhil are. Friends, she hopes. Neighbours certainly. He swings by most evenings to check if she has anything for the compost or to return whatever she's left in his pickup.

Sometimes he stays for a glass of wine with Nora and her uncles. Most of the time, though, he ambles off, reminding her not to feed Dodger and Oliver again or they'll explode. He's always there, though. Even when he isn't. She's aware of him through the walls. She can hear him moving, his music or him yelling at one of the cats to get down, and it's nice.

Like he's only in the next room.

Then, one afternoon, she gets back to the cottage to find Tommy fixing the lock on her front door. He didn't say it was because of Sendhil, but she thanked him anyway. A couple of weeks after that, she rescues him from a spider in his bathroom (not without teasing him mercilessly first) so he drives her to Trungle to pick up a sideboard she'd found on eBay for the Trefelyn. A few weeks after that, on the last Sunday of June, he talks her into going with him to Penzance early one morning to help with the beach clean-up he volunteers for every month. In return, he has to show her how to make his coconut sambal.

But it's the same with everyone in Pidwell. Tommy needn't have bothered fixing the lock on her front door because there's always someone popping by. Her uncles, in the evening, as soon as the builders leave the Trefelyn, bustling in with bags of what they're going to cook while they complain about whatever went wrong with the renovations that day. Alice, for a glass of wine when she shuts the shop before she heads home. Annabelle, whenever she feels like it, but always with a hug and a compliment about how well Nora is doing with the festival. They all just move in and out of each other's lives with such ease that Nora doesn't know how it happened, just that she's there and no one had to make space for her.

She just fits.

Then something changes again. Not them, but Pidwell. It's July and summer is in full voice, the sun high in the sky, and the village goes from sleepy to wide awake.

It's no longer just them any more. When Nora goes in the shop now, it's full of builders from the Trefelyn in orange neon vests and hardhats waiting for their teas and the bacon sandwiches Alice has started doing because most of them aren't interested in feta and basil omelettes and sourdough toast. And the *noise*. God, the noise. Nora can no longer hear the lap of the sea against the granite and the gulls chattering. The soft, soothing soundtrack of Pidwell that she used to close her eyes and listen to every morning when she sat on Meredith and Annabelle's bench, drinking her coffee. Now all she can hear is drilling and hammering and the unescapable *screech* of a saw cutting wood or tile or pipes or whatever the hell it's cutting that she can feel the buzz in her teeth. She may as well be back in London.

They're all weary of it. Her uncles have decamped to Meredith and Annabelle's house because they can't take the chaos at the Trefelyn any more. And Alice has had enough of going home with tender feet, her hair smelling of bacon fat. After all, it was never her plan to open a greasy spoon but, as Mark and James keep reminding her, it's not for ever. And, in the meantime, at least, she's making a fortune. Even if the builders don't appreciate the bread she gets up at four every morning to make.

But if everyone else has had enough of it, Sendhil is going out of his mind, locking himself into his studio most days and refusing to come out until they've gone.

By the middle of July, something shifts again. The days are longer and it's as though Pidwell has been turned up to eleven. Not just the volume, but the colours. The sea is bluer, an unreachably deep neon blue that reminds Nora of the raspberry Slush Puppies she and her uncles had that afternoon in Mousehole when she first arrived six weeks ago. The valley is *wild* and as green as the Palm House at Kew. It's their only respite, cool and quiet except for the white noise of the stream that swallows the relentless racket rising from the cove.

Sendhil keeps threatening to go full Unabomber and move out there. She has to stop him buying a tent one afternoon in Penzance. So, when Tommy offers him his barn, which is empty now the bus has been moved for the festival, Nora knows Sendhil considers it.

If she hasn't seen him for a few hours – espccially in the evening – she'll ask herself if he's finally snapped, and is relieved when the warm smell of onions and garlic frying wafts her way from his cottage. She'll wait for a bit, then wander over to let him know not to feed the cats and listen to him ranting about the rubbish and the noise while he chops chilli and rinses coriander, humouring him when he asks her to look up camp beds on her phone because he's going to live in Tommy's barn.

Before Nora knows it, it's the end of July. School is out and here they are – the tourists – in their walking boots and backpacks, stomping back and forth along the South West Coast Path. Then it gets so busy Alice has to hire Lottie, who stands outside with her arms crossed, selling homemade ice cream and sneering at anyone who remarks on what a nice day it is.

It's a bit like living in a goldfish bowl, a steady procession of tourists peering in through her living room window as they pass. That would usually make Nora murderous, but she's never there and, by the time she is, they're gone. Back at their hotels, soaking their feet and congratulating themselves on how many miles they walked that day.

And, with that, the festival is a month away.

Her uncles were right – she should have paced herself – because Nora is already exhausted. Her whole body *aches* from cleaning and sweeping and painting and heaving boxes. Aches so much that she can barely muster the energy to eat most nights, her arms too sore to lift a spoon while Sendhil tries to bribe her, saying she can have the last roti.

It would help if she could actually get some sleep, those halcyon days of dozing on the sofa with Dodger long gone. Now she gets barely a few hours, and even they're interrupted when she wakes during the night to reach for her phone and make a note of something else.

Pace yourself, everyone keeps telling her. But if she'd paced herself, they wouldn't be on schedule now. Even so, they're only *just* on schedule, the whole thing such a precarious balance that one late – or, worse, missing – delivery and the whole festival will unravel.

But as she counts the days, Nora is becoming increasingly aware of another deadline.

Mrs Stroud's return.

Everyone is so focused on the festival – the festival, the festival, the festival – but Nora is already thinking about what happens when it's over. She was hoping to have a few days to catch her breath, but she won't be able to now. Not after speaking to Fran at the Whitechapel Gallery last week, who was so frantic getting the exhibition ready that Nora found herself agreeing to start the day after the August bank-holiday. So she'll be back in London before Mrs Stroud returns to Pidwell and won't even have a chance to meet her.

Every time she thinks about it, her heart clenches like a fist. She puts it down to nerves at starting a new job, but then she'll catch herself watching Sendhil padding barefoot around his kitchen, the cats at his feet. Or when they're driving back from Penzance, the windows of his truck open. Like her, his skin is darkening from the sun, threads of bronze appearing in his curls that make her want to sift through them and count each one.

He was the first to mention it, while they were standing by his living-room window last night, eating the Greek salad he'd made and looking out at the sunset. 'Who'm I going to cook for when you go?' he'd said, without looking at her.

Nora was so startled that she made a joke. 'Salad isn't cooking, actually.'

Because she couldn't say the other thing.

The thing about maybe not wanting to go.

~★~

'Of course you're in love with him,' Luce tells her, when Nora calls to say it to her instead.

'Don't be so dramatic, Luce. I'm not in love with him,' she's quick to say, as she sits on Meredith and Annabelle's bench, looking out at the sea. 'I just like being with him.'

And she does.

Nora doesn't know when it happened, just that it crept up on her after weeks of sitting in his truck, going back and forth to Penzance every day, or hanging out in his cottage every night, bickering over what record they should listen to while he cooked.

Sendhil, who everyone told her was so quiet, so private, so sensitive yet had turned out to be anything but. Who had turned out to be the most open, honest, gentle soul she's ever met. Who hadn't even flinched when she'd charged out of his bedroom with that can of deodorant and has been as steady ever since. He's as much a part of her life now as her first coffee of the day and Nora doesn't know when that happened. It's as though they just made space for one another and now there's no room for anything else.

'So, what are you going to do about it?' Luce asks, and Nora almost laughs.

'What can I do? I start at the Whitechapel on the first of September.'

She hears Luce start to say something, but then she goes quiet.

'What?' Nora asks, when she does.

'Well, if it was anyone else, I'd tell them to have a summer fling, but you two are way past that. I mean, he *cooks* for you, Nor.' Luce chuckles. 'Not that you've ever been the summer-fling type. God. Remember that bloke you met in Rhodes?'

'Don't remind me,' she mutters, shuddering at the memory.

Nora had thought he was the love of her life, but he was married with three kids.

'Oh, well,' she says, with a defeated sigh. 'It is what it is.' It is what it is.

~*~

206

Still, Nora can't stop thinking about it.

About him.

Them.

If there even is a *them*.

'You okay, Nora?' Sendhil asks her, one afternoon in early August.

'Yeah. Yeah. Fine.'

'You thinking about the festival?'

'Yeah,' she lies, turning back to the window, the sea a steady smear of blue beside her as they drive back from Penzance after picking up some paint for the Trefelyn.

Usually he'd be right. She would have been thinking about the festival. That's all she's thought about for weeks. Everything – every thought, every delivery, every trip back and forth to Penzance – has been meticulously timed to line up for one thing.

The August bank-holiday weekend.

So, she hasn't had a moment to consider what happens after that.

But now here it is. September 1st. Right there. On the horizon, waiting for her.

If she told him that, he'd probably ask her if she's excited about going back to London.

About her new job.

She should be, so why isn't she?

It can't be because of Sendhil. She sneaks a look at him. Yes, she likes him. Okay. She *more than* likes him, but she can't honestly be considering staying? She can't be considering turning down a job at one of her favourite galleries to stay in Pidwell?

To do *what*, exactly? She won't even have anywhere to live once Mrs Stroud comes home. And while she knows everyone in Pidwell well enough by now to be sure that she'll be neither jobless nor homeless for long, is that really what she wants? To live in Pidwell?

It's nice for the summer, but could she really *live* here?

But if she doesn't, what's the alternative? Sendhil is never going to move to London. He's talked about moving back to Cork one day, but not London. He's made it abundantly clear that he *loathes* London. Loathes how the bars are too busy to sit down in, let alone hear what anyone is saying, and how people (i.e. Nora) take spin classes, but would never get on an actual bike and ride somewhere. And he especially loathes the 'art scene'.

He loathes everything about her life, basically.

Besides, why should I be the one to compromise if he won't?

It's great that he's found his place in the world, but what about Nora?

Doesn't she deserve to find that as well?

They could do the long-distance thing, she supposes, but Nora knows what she's like. As soon as she gets back to London, to that loud, busy life he hates so much, she'll start working at the Whitechapel Gallery and that'll be it. Then it'll just be work. Spin on Saturday mornings. Lunch with her parents on Sundays. Dumplings with Luce and Ben during the week. She won't have time to drive back and forth to Cornwall.

'No-*ra*!' Sendhil says, so loudly she rises out of her seat, her head almost hitting the roof of the pickup as she reaches for the dashboard. 'What's got into you?'

'Nothing,' she tells him, aware that she's still gripping the dashboard, which isn't very convincing. So, she lets go. 'I've just got a lot on my mind, that's all.'

'Right,' he mutters, pulling over so suddenly, she thinks he's about to drive off the cliff.

But he doesn't. He pulls into a car park. Actually, it's too small to be considered a car park. It's more of a lay-by with just enough room for three cars to park, side by side.

When Sendhil turns off the engine and reaches between them to grab the beach towel on the back seat, Nora shakes her head. 'Thanks, but I'm not dressed for a swim.'

'We're not going for a swim.'

'Where are we going, then?'

He doesn't tell her, just jumps out of the pickup, saying, 'You'll see.'

Curiosity gets the better of her and she walks over to stand next to him on the edge of the cliff as he looks out at the wall of blue. Then he peers down, and when she does the same, she sees a small beach about the size of the one in Pidwell, but there are no pebbles.

You could just step into the sea.

'This is my favourite cove,' he says, throwing the towel over his shoulder and lifting his chin to gaze out at the horizon.

It's beautiful, she thinks.

'Come on,' he says, leading her along the edge of the cliff.

When he stops, she thinks he's suggesting they climb down to the cove.

I'm wearing flip-flops, she almost says, but is relieved when he stops at some steps.

'I have no idea who built these,' he tells her, as they begin walking down them. 'But whoever it was, I'm very grateful. Especially when I've got my board.'

'Is this where you come to surf?'

'Yeah. But it's too calm this time of year. So, I just paddle out and sit on my board.'

As soon as they get down to the beach, she kicks off her flip-flops, letting them hang from her fingers as they walk side by side, the sand getting damper beneath her feet.

'I've never seen anyone down here,' he tells her, turning his head to look out at the still, blue line of the horizon. 'Not once in three years.'

'Thanks for showing me it.'

'I think you need it right now.' She can't see his eyes because he has sunglasses on, but she wishes she could as he smiles and says, 'Now come. Stand.'

Nora does as he says, standing next to him on the sand, facing the sea.

'Don't,' he tells her, when she jumps back as the tide reaches out to touch her toes.

This is the point, she realises, as the water bubbles over her toes. Her feet sink deeper into the sand, which should make her feel less steady, but it grounds her, somehow.

'This is nice.' She sighs, closing her eyes and taking a deep breath.

It is nice, the water cooling her feet. She hadn't realised how hot she was from charging around every paint shop in Penzance, trying to get the right one for her uncles.

'This place saved me when I got here,' he admits.

When she opens her eyes, all she can think is *Please, take off your sunglasses*. She wants to see his eyes. Wants to see the sunlight catching on his eyelashes. To touch his hair. Separate each curl and search for the threads of bronze the summer sun has teased out.

But he doesn't take off his sunglasses.

He merely says, 'It's okay, you know?'

'What is?'

'To not have it all figured out yet.'

Nora nods, letting out a tender sigh.

'When I showed up here, three years ago, I was your age,' he tells her, sliding his hands into the pockets of his black jeans. 'There's something about being twenty-seven. Twenty-seven is a weird age. It feels like you've only just graduated from uni and you're still cool and restless and constantly on the verge of something. But then, one day, you look around, and all your mates have got their shit together without telling you. They have jobs and flats and are getting married and having babies, and there you are, staring down the barrel of thirty, and you don't even know how it happened, because you still feel twenty-two.'

'You're really good at this motivational-speaking thing, you know? Truly inspiring,' she tells him. 'Have you considered doing a TED Talk?'

He laughs, then nudges her with his hip. 'What I'm trying to say, not articulately, apparently, is that it's okay to need time. Three years ago, I was exactly where you are now.'

'Where am I?'

'Out there.' He tips his chin up at the sea. 'I was as well. The being twenty-seven thing is weird enough, but try winning the Turner Prize and the Hepworth *in the same month*.'

Nora stays very, very still because they talk about everything. The festival. The cats. The correct way to peel garlic. (He prefers to smash the cloves with the side of the knife while she prefers the jam-jar method, which, he refuses to concede, is much easier.)

But they've never talked about this.

'Imagine,' he says, with a slow nod, 'getting everything most artists spend their whole careers dreaming about in a month. I got it, Nora. Everything I wanted. So, what happens after that? When your career peaks at twenty-seven, there's only one way for it go.'

He laughs.

Nora doesn't.

'Then, all of a sudden, my parents are telling everyone that their son is an artist after begging me to get a proper job for years. And the galleries that wouldn't email me back are inviting me to exhibit. Then no one could understand why I wouldn't move to London or let *Vanity Fair* photograph my studio or go on Radio 4 to discuss how my work reflects my *pain*.' He chuckles sourly. 'My pain. Come on. My dad's a mechanic in Clonakilty, not a Tamil Tiger.'

He mutters something under his breath. 'Then I wasn't an Irish sculptor any more, I was a Sri Lankan one, and when I wouldn't talk about how hard my life was, which it isn't, by the way, they turned on me. They started talking about tokenism and how the art world shouldn't bow to pressure to be more diverse. That good art is good art, whoever does it.'

Nora's jaw clenches.

'Then it felt like I was out there.' He tips his chin up at the sea again. 'Kind of like when you were kid and you swam out too far and didn't know how you were gonna get back.'

She looks out at the sea, then back at him.

'I did that once,' he admits. 'In Sri Lanka, the beaches are *wild*. It's not like the Caribbean. The Indian Ocean is *rough*. One day, when I was twelve, I got cocky and swam out too far. I nearly drowned. Thank God my dad saw and swam out to get me.'

'That must have been terrifying,' Nora tells him.

'It was. But that's how I felt before I came here. Like I was out there, in the middle of the ocean, waving madly, but my dad wasn't there to see me this time. So I came looking for Annabelle. As soon as I found her, I could see the shore again, and started swimming towards it. Swimming and swimming and I'm almost there. I can almost feel the sand under my feet.'

Nora thinks about everything she was considering in his pickup before he pulled over and made her come down to the cove and stand still. Staying in Pidwell. Going back to London. This life. That life. Something in between with her driving back and forth. It's ludicrous to be considering it when she doesn't even know if he wants that too. If he even wants *her*. But as ludicrous as it is, right now – in this moment – there's nowhere else she wants to be.

'I can't feel the sand at all.'

She doesn't realise she's said it out loud until he says, 'You will. Just give yourself a minute to figure it out. In the meantime, trust me, this is as good a place as any to do it.'

She nudges him with her hip. 'Thank you.'

He nudges her back. 'You'll be okay, Nora Armstrong.'

And she believes him.

Nora still doesn't have a clue what she's going to do, but she needs to get out of this holding pattern she's found herself in with Sendhil. The pair of them orbiting one another – around and around – before finally colliding in a few bright, brilliant moments, like this one.

God. It's worth it, though.

Those moments.

Those collisions.

Seeing the things no one else sees. When his eyes are wild and he's shrieking at her not to harm the spider she has cupped between her hands, but to get it out of his house.

When he's just woken up from one of his stress naps and clearly isn't listening to a word she's saying. When he's talking to Dodger and Oliver and thinks she isn't listening.

She sees all of it.

Every single thing.

~*~

After that, going to the cove becomes their thing. Every time the festival gets too much, they get in his pickup and head there. He paddles out on his surf board. She reads. There's just one rule. She's not allowed to bring her phone. She has to leave it in his pickup.

There's a storm rolling in tonight from France and the wind is already picking up, so it's perfect weather for surfing. Nora watches him from the beach, cutting through the waves on his board. A thin black line against the blue sky. He looks so free, and she wonders what that feels like as she lies back and watches the clouds thicken.

An elephant, she thinks, looking at the shape of the one directly above her.

India.

A mountain.

A sheep.

A sheep.

A sheep.

The next thing Nora knows, Sendhil is standing over her with his surf board.

'Get up!' he tells her, grabbing her by the wrist and pulling her to her feet.

She barely has time to grab the towel she was lying on and her sandals as he starts running. It's dark, she realises. So dark that she asks herself how long she's been asleep as he pulls her towards a crack in the cliffs. When they get closer, she sees that there's an opening. But before she can ask him what he's doing, he tugs her in.

Inside, it's dark and damp and there's only just enough room for the two of them, the granite so low he can't stand up straight. Why on earth has he dragged her in there?

'What?' she asks, turning to look out at the beach. 'What's going on?'

Then there it is.

Lightning.

But Nora doesn't get a chance to be scared before there's a rumble of thunder so near it feels like it's about to roll in and knock her and Sendhil down like bowling pins.

No, Nora thinks. You're supposed to count the number of seconds between seeing the lightning and hearing the thunder, then divide by five. That tells you how near the storm is.

That's what Ben says.

But there was no space between the two.

'I thought the storm wasn't coming until tonight,' she says, panic licking at her palms.

'This isn't the storm. This is just a warning shot.'

'A warning shot?' Nora jumps when another crack of lightning illuminates the crevice they're huddled in.

There's a hammer of thunder and it sounds like the sky is splitting in two. With that, the heavens literally *open*, rain, loud and fast, hitting the sand like bullets.

'It's okay.' Sendhil cups her elbow with his hand when she tries to step back, but can't because there's no room. 'It won't last long. The rain here is sharp, but short.'

'Are you sure? It sounds like the world is ending.'

He squeezes her elbow, which makes her feel steadier.

'Are you cold?' he asks, reaching for her other elbow as well. 'You're shaking.'

Another spike of lightning flashes between them and she doesn't get a chance to jump this time before it's followed by a growl of thunder she feels in her teeth.

'You okay?' he asks, when it passes.

Nora laughs uneasily. 'Is this a good time to mention that I'm terrified of storms?'

'Okay.' He nods, hands still cupping her elbows. 'This must be fun for you, then.'

When she doesn't respond, just peers out at the rain hammering the sand, Sendhil lets go of her elbows to tug the towel from her clenched fist.

'Here,' he says, wrapping it around her shoulders.

He fists his hands in the front of it, holding it tight.

'What was that?' she yelps, when something drips onto her scalp in the dark.

'It's just water from the rocks. You're fine.'

'Am I? Am I, though?' she asks, fully aware that she's bordering on hysterical, but unable to pull herself back from it. 'I don't want to die in a cave, Sendhil!'

'It's the safest place. These cliffs have been here for thousands of years.'

'Yeah. Until they're struck by lightning. What then?'

'Well, *then*, I hope Moira Rose sings "Danny Boy" at my funeral.'

That almost makes her laugh.

Almost.

'What about Dodger and Oliver?' she gasps. 'Who's going to feed them if we die?'

'Ah, don't worry about those two. They'll be fine.' Sendhil adjusts the towel around her shoulders. 'Did you know that they go on a grand tour of Pidwell every morning?'

Nora did not.

'They start with you, then come to me, then the shop, then the Trefelyn. Then they go through the valley to Meredith and Annabelle's and finally to Tommy's before coming home to sleep it off until it's time for their supper. Trust me. Those bastard cats will be fine.'

That elicits a snigger.

Just a small one.

'They'd go to Kate's for smoked salmon as well, if they weren't scared of the road.'

'Stop it,' she tells him, trying not to smile.

'Why do you think Mrs Stroud and I called them Dodger and Oliver?'

Nora's never thought about it before, but of course: Oliver Twist and the Artful Dodger. 'That's perfect, actually,' she says, managing a chuckle this time.

'An actual laugh,' he says, tugging on the towel. 'See? I'm helping.'

He waits for her to look up at him, then nods through the opening. 'What did I say?'

It takes Nora a second, then she gasps, with delight this time. 'It's stopped!'

It isn't even raining, blue seeping back into the corners of the sky.

'Told you,' Sendhil reminds her. 'I'd never lie to you, Nora Armstrong.'

The sun pushes through the clouds, sending a thread of light between them. It strikes his cheek and, for the first time since he pulled her into the dark, she can see his face.

It's only then that she realises how close they are, their bare toes almost touching, his hands holding onto the towel around her shoulders the only thing separating their chests. Then Nora can't catch her breath for an entirely different reason as their eyes meet and she sees the glassy pearls of seawater falling from his hair, chasing one another down his cheeks. Each one catches on the V of his Cupid's bow then drops onto his bottom lip before skidding off. She's transfixed, glad that her arms are trapped under the towel because she's sure that she'd reach up to catch them with her fingers.

But then the towel is gone, fluttering to their feet, and Sendhil's hands are on her face. When she doesn't stop him, his eyelashes flutter shut and what little space there was between them closes, their mouths meeting in a kiss that surprises her as much as the storm.

Nora forgot that her flip-flops were still in her hand until she lets go of them as she reaches for him. His solid shoulders, then the back of his neck, the zip of his wetsuit cold against her fingers. Then finally – finally – up, up to his hair.

He tilts his head as she tilts hers and they just fit, his tongue slow in her mouth. He's so close that she can feel the heat of him, the front of her T-shirt damp from his wetsuit.

But, much like the storm, it passes almost as suddenly as it begins, his mouth sliding away from hers as he breathes something against her lips. He tries to step back, but there's nowhere to go because there's no room and her hands are still in his hair, still holding on until her mouth finds his again. The sound he makes then is a little like defeat as he wraps his arms around her back, the soles of her feet leaving the sand as he pulls her to him and they kiss again, deeper than before, Sendhil's back against the granite.

Then they're stepping on each other's toes, his hands in her hair, cupping her head and sighing into her mouth. Or maybe that's her. Nora doesn't even know.

All she knows is that he tastes like the sea.

But he pulls away and, before her mouth can find his again, his hands reach for her face, fingers pressing into her cheeks to stop her as he looks at her from under his eyelashes.

'I'm sorry,' he says, his voice rough with something she's never heard before.

'It's okay,' she breathes, nudging him with her nose to let him know that it is.

But he doesn't kiss her, just curses under his breath.

'It's okay,' she tells him again, trying to lean in, but he won't let her, hands still on her face.

'I can't believe I did that. I've been trying not to do that for two and a half months.'

'Sendhil, it's okay.' She smiles, hands falling from his hair, reaching for his face.

But before she can, he shakes his head. So hard that it sends another shiver of sea water down his cheeks that she wants to reach up and catch with the tips of his fingers.

'I'm sorry, Nora,' he says again, his forehead creased. 'I shouldn't have done that.'

But before she can tell him she's glad he did, he's gone.

Chapter 15

They drive back to Pidwell in silence.

Sendhil hasn't said a word since he muttered another breathless apology, then stumbled back into the light of the beach, grabbed his board and walked away.

Nora wanted to call after him, ask him what was wrong – what she did wrong – but she was too stunned to speak, the corners of her mouth stinging from his stubble and the taste of him lingering on her tongue. The sea and summer and melted strawberry ice cream.

She didn't know what to do. Should she follow him? Did he even want her to follow him? She had no idea, unsure if he'd still be there when she'd gathered herself enough to bend down and snatch her towel and sandals before stumbling out into the light.

Nora followed his footprints in the sand and was relieved to find him waiting at the foot of the steps back up to the road. But as soon as he saw her, he started walking up them. She had to take them two at a time to keep up, and when she walked into the stark sunshine of the road, he was slinging his surf board into the bed of his pickup.

He opened the door and jumped in without changing out of his wetsuit or at least peeling it down to his waist and throwing a T-shirt on, like he usually did. He slammed his door so hard the truck shook and Nora half expected him to roar off without her.

He didn't, and when she realised he was waiting for her to get in, she did. She hasn't dared look at him since. Even when he muttered another apology before he pulled away.

She doesn't know why he keeps apologising, but she feels the shift immediately, Sendhil tight as a guitar string, his eyes fixed on the road as they drive back to Pidwell.

It's more than a shift, actually. It's a crack. She felt it open when he pulled away from her at the cove and put his hand on her face to stop her kissing him again. Her cheeks scorch with shame at the memory, her fingers curling around the handle of the door.

Nora doesn't know what happened, just that he's driving too fast. So fast that the leaves on the trees at either side of them whip past so quickly, it's like they're waving at them as his truck tears through the valley. Then they're passing the shop, but Sendhil doesn't beep. He pulls up outside the cottages and jumps out before he's taken the keys out of the ignition.

With that, he's gone, all but falling out of the truck in his haste to get out. He doesn't look back. Doesn't apologise. Just leaves Nora sitting there, her fingers still on the handle.

She watches as he strides over to his cottage, sweeping in without so much as a glance over his shoulder. Then he slams the front door behind him so hard it makes her jump, and one of the cardboard boxes he's left outside to take to the recycling topples onto its side.

Nora can't move, because if she moves, she's going to cry and she absolutely will not cry because she hasn't done anything wrong. She hasn't. Sendhil kissed her. Sendhil kissed her, then ran away, and she doesn't know why he did either of those things.

But she will not cry.

So, she snatches her stuff and climbs out of the pickup. She slams the passenger door so loudly that she hopes he hears it as she paces over to Mrs Stroud's cottage.

She can't find her keys in her ridiculous TARDIS of a bag. *Here they come*, she thinks, as she roots through it, the corners of her eyes stinging as the tears gather. She manages to get the door open just as they rush down her cheek. Big, hot tears that skid off her jaw and land on her T-shirt, which is still damp from Sendhil's wetsuit. She lets them fall as everything else falls from her hands as she closes the door and presses her back to it.

Nora can hear her phone ringing in her bag and ignores it, letting it go to voicemail. She can't talk right now. It's all she can do to focus on each shallow, shuddering breath as she waits for it to pass. But as soon as it stops ringing, it starts again, and she wonders if it's him.

Calling to explain.

Apologise.

Anything.

She reaches down for the handle of her bag, lifting it off the floor to look for her phone.

It's her uncle Mark.

She can't. Not right now. He'll know that she's upset and she can't.

Nora lets it go to voicemail again, but he calls straight back.

Something's wrong.

'Uncle Mark?' she says, hoping he puts the weirdness in her voice down to panic.

Actually, she is panicking now.

He just called three times in a row, which he never does.

'What's wrong?' she asks him, before he can ask her. 'Are you okay?'

'Nora, thank God!'

'What's wrong? What happened?'

He doesn't tell her, just barks, 'Come here now.'

'Come where?'

'To Meredith and Annabelle's.'

'Why?'

She hears Annabelle in the background. 'Is that Nora?'

'Yes,' he says, his voice quieter, obviously moving the phone away from his mouth.

Then Nora hears Annabelle ask, 'Is she coming?'

'I'm telling her to now.'

'Tell her she must come.'

'I'm telling her now.'

'Nora!' Annabelle calls to her. 'You must come quickly, darling.'

Her fingers curl around her phone. 'What is it? What's going on? What's happening?'

'What do you mean what's going on?' Mark says. The storm, Nora!'

She curses under her breath, pressing her hand to her chest. 'I thought someone died!'

'This storm isn't a joke, Nora! Didn't you see the preview?'

She'd almost forgotten about it, thanks to Sendhil. As distraction techniques go, that was certainly more effective than most.

'I called to check you were okay while it was happening, but you didn't answer.'

'Sorry,' Nora says, with a sullen sigh. 'I was in a cave.'

'A what?'

'It's a long story.'

'Listen,' Mark says, when Annabelle asks him again if Nora is coming. He tells her that Nora is, then says, 'We were panicking because we didn't hear from you and we know how scared of storms you are. We thought you might be cowering in the bathtub, like Archie.'

'Archie? Tommy's dog?'

'Yes.'

'That dog is scared of everything,' Annabelle says. 'A Chihuahua in a Rottweiler suit.'

When Nora hears James cackling, she wonders if they've already started on the gin.

'Listen,' Mark says again, as though she's the one not focusing, 'James just checked that radar app he's so obsessed with and the storm is hitting us earlier than we thought.'

'When?'

'In about an hour, so you can't wait until seven.'

'Seven?'

'You're coming over for Games Night, remember?'

Oh, God.

Games Night.

Between all the kissing and running away, she'd totally forgotten.

'It's a shame.' Mark tuts. 'Alice just shut the shop or she could have dropped you off on her way. I don't like you driving around in that clapped-out old heap.'

Nora gasps. 'Ron has never let me down and he never will because he loves me.'

'Sure. Sure. Just grab your stuff and come.'

'How long have I got?'

'James says an hour.'

'Okay. Let me just jump in the shower and I'll come straight there.'

'Shower? Nora, there's no time!'

There has to be. She needs a minute to wash away what just happened and gather herself so she can spend the evening pretending to be okay while James and Mark get increasingly competitive over Articulate! Usually, she loves that, but Games Night is the last thing she needs. Although she'll take it over being in the cottage by herself during a storm.

'But you said I had an hour!'

'Fine,' Mark says through his teeth. 'But no exfoliating or deep conditioning.'

'I'll be in and out and at Meredith and Annabelle's in half an hour, tops.'

'Promise?'

'Promise.'

'And bring some stuff in case you need to sleep over.'

Nora blows him a couple of kisses then hangs up, leaving her phone on the kitchen counter. She stops to look out of the living-room window at the horizon on her way to the bedroom. It looks pretty normal. There's a ceiling of cloud forming, the blue beginning to drain from the sky again. And she can see from the trees that the wind is slowly picking up, but it hardly looks as if Pidwell is on the verge of the apocalypse.

The instant the hot water of the shower hits her, she feels better. She wishes she could stay in there longer, but she has to be quick, she knows, giving her face a good scrub to make sure that whatever trace of mascara she just cried down it is gone.

When she climbs out of the shower, she brushes her teeth, gets dressed, then starts grabbing whatever she'll need for the night and stuffing it into the gym bag she rather optimistically packed before she left London and hasn't even unzipped. But when she heads into the living room to look for her charger, she looks up at the window.

No.

I had an hour, she thinks, pacing over to it. The sky is grey now, great black clouds galloping towards her like a string of horses. She's never seen clouds move so fast. Never seen the sky get so dark, so quickly. Then, there it is, an electric white crack of lightning that lights up the living room as Nora turns, chased out by a rumble of thunder.

She grabs her gym bag from the bed, furious with herself for not leaving as soon as her uncle Mark told her to. She curses herself again when she hears another vicious crack of lightning, the long grumble of thunder that follows so close she doesn't get a chance to count the seconds between the two as she asks herself if she still has time to get out of there.

Another snap of lightning answers that question, the thunder that follows so loud it seems to make the whole cottage shake. Then she can hear them – the waves – this rush, then crash. Rush. Crash. Rush. Crash. Rush. Crash. The wind whipping back and forth around the back of the cottage with such force Nora can hear the shed creaking outside.

Then here it is.

The rain. Throwing itself against the bedroom window like handfuls of gravel. The sound makes the hair on her arms bristle as the white sheets ripple on the bed.

'What the–' Nora steps back, then screams as the bathroom and bedroom doors slam shut at the same time. Suddenly, a picture frame falls, hitting the floor, the glass shattering.

Nora has barely caught her breath before there's another loud bang, from the living room this time. Then another. Then she feels it. A breeze. She opens the bedroom door to see that the front door is wide open, the rain so loud now it sounds like white noise.

She runs over to close it, but the wind is so strong, she has to use her hip. Eventually, she succeeds, but as she asks herself where her keys are so she can double lock it, she hears her phone. She runs over to the kitchen counter to grab it, thinking it's her uncle Mark.

But it's Alice.

'You okay?' she asks, before Nora has even said hello. 'Do you have power?'

'I don't know.' Nora has to shout over of a *roar* of thunder.

After that, she can't hear a thing as it all – the lightning, the thunder, the wind, the waves, the rain – combines into a rolling sonic stew so loud, she wonders if the storm will swallow the cottage whole and spit it out into the sea.

The front door blows open again and Nora screams.

'What? What?' Alice asks.

'Door,' she manages, as she runs over to shut it, using her hip again.

She stands with her back against it, trying to catch her breath.

'Have you got power?' Alice asks again.

'I don't know,' she whimpers, looking around the cottage.

How would she know?

'Check, Nora.'

She runs into the kitchen and when she opens the fridge, the light doesn't come on.

Then she tries to turn on the kettle.

Nothing.

'The power's out,' she tells Alice, with another whimper.

How did the power go out already?

Alice doesn't hesitate. 'Go to Sendhil's. He has solar panels. He'll have power.'

Nora laughs at that, but it's drowned by another rumble of thunder.

'I'll be okay,' she tells Alice, reasoning that she'd rather risk whatever's going on outside than ask for Sendhil's help. 'It's only, like, five minutes to Meredith and Annabelle's.'

'You will not drive to Meredith and Annabelle's now, Nora Armstrong! Are you mad?' Alice screeches, and she's louder than the storm, somehow. 'Even if that heap of a car makes it there, what if you're hit by a falling tree, or something?'

'It's fine. I'll be fine.'

'Go to Sendhil's right now!'

'Alice, it's fine. Seriously. It's not that bad.'

As if on cue, the front door blows open again.

'Was that the door?' Alice yells.

Nora ignores her as she's pelted with rain trying to get it shut.

Where are her bloody keys?

If she double locks it, this will stop happening.

'Nora, get to Sendhil's right now!'

'I'm fine.'

She was aiming for casual, but lands on too loud as she finally gets the door shut.

'Nora, what are you doing? Will you just go!'

'Alice,' she says, trying not to cry again. 'It's a long story, but I can't go to Sendhil's.'

'I know,' she says, her voice so low, Nora can barely hear her. 'He told me.'

'He did?'

But before she can ask *what* he told her, Alice snaps, 'I'm not getting involved! All I'm saying is that you cannot stay there by yourself with no electricity and the door blowing open.'

Nora is about to protest, but Alice tells her to go and hangs up.

She's not going anywhere, though.

If she's missed her chance to get to Meredith and Annabelle's, she'll have to retreat to the bathtub, like Archie. *It won't be so bad*, she thinks, as she looks for her keys. She can take the duvet and some pillows in there. Shut the shower curtain and listen to Yo-Yo Ma.

It'll be fine.

She just needs to find her keys so she can double lock the front door before it blows open again. They're not on the kitchen counter, where her phone was when Alice called, so she runs to the front door, realising she must have dropped them on the floor with everything else when she got in. She lifts up her towel and shakes it, then bends down to grab her tote bag. She's in such a panic, that she grabs it at a weird angle and everything falls out.

It's good, though, because she hears her keys hit the floor, but when she bends down to look for them, the front door swings open again, sending her flying.

The force of it knocks her into the living room. She falls sideways so, before she can put out her arms to break her fall, Nora catches the side of her head on the corner of the coffee-table. She goes down so hard, she's sure cartoon bluebirds are circling her head as she lies on the floor, the wind rushing through the open door, ruffling her curls.

Oh, God. She slammed into the floor with such force that everything hurts. Everything. Her hip. Her shoulder. Her elbow. Her whole right side, actually. And her head.

Oh, God.

Her head.

Nora can feel her hair is damp and hopes it's rain. But when she presses her fingers to her temple, she pulls them away to find they're wet with blood.

When she looks at them, there's Sendhil, standing over her, looking distraught.

'Jesus, Nora! Are you okay?' he gasps, pulling her to her feet.

Chapter 16

It's just a cut. Still, Nora won't let Sendhil touch her, insisting that she's fine. So, he leaves her in his bathroom with the first-aid kit he finds in the cupboard under the kitchen sink.

Nora's glad he's gone because, between the cut and the storm, she's miserable.

Absolutely, utterly miserable.

It doesn't help that she jumps every time the bathroom window rattles, the rain hitting the glass with such urgency, it sounds like someone is banging on it to come in.

Please stop so I can go, she thinks, because she doesn't want to be here. She doesn't want to be here, in his cottage, with him being nice to her and asking her if she's okay.

Granted, she had a lucky escape. She could have knocked herself out when she hit her head on the coffee-table. Or, worse, split her head open. So, yes. She's very grateful that Alice sent Sendhil to check on her. As did her uncles when Nora didn't answer the phone.

'You all right?' Sendhil asks, leaning against the doorframe, his arms crossed.

'It's just a cut,' she tells him again, dabbing it with a piece of folded-up kitchen towel.

'So, Alice doesn't need to send the air ambulance out? Because I'm pretty sure she's about to. Otherwise, your uncles will. Or Annabelle. Or Tommy.'

'Tommy?' She frowns, finally looking away from the mirror.

But as soon as their gaze meets across the tiny bathroom, she looks away again.

'Yeah,' Sendhil says. 'He called me when you didn't answer your phone.'

'He did?'

'He was worried about you.'

'He's such sweet man,' she says, then winces when she dabs at the cut again.

She hopes she's cleaning it, not making it worse. She can't call Ben over a cut, can she?

'None of those people called to check on me, by the way,' Sendhil points out.

'Well, it's very sweet of all *those people* to call and make sure I'm okay.'

When she sneaks a glance at him, he's smiling, his arms still crossed.

'I would have checked on you, you know. I didn't need to be told.'

'Mm-hmm.'

'Do you think I would have left you alone in a storm after I saw the state of you earlier?'

'Mm-hmm.'

'I was asleep.'

Nora gestures at the storm howling outside. 'You slept through *this*?'

'I was having a stress nap, okay? It's been a stressful day, Nora.'

'And whose fault is that?' she reminds him, as she curses at the rattling window.

'Can I see?' he asks, when she peers into the mirror again to inspect the cut.

'No,' she snaps, then gasps and turns to him. 'Where are the cats?'

'Ah, don't worry about them. They're currently under the desk in my studio.'

Nora lets go of a breath and resumes fussing over the cut in the mirror.

'Can I see?' he asks, but walks over anyway.

She scowls at him in the mirror when he stands behind her. 'I told you, *I'm fine.*'

'Can I just check to see if it's still bleeding?'

'It isn't.' She turns the folded kitchen towel over to the clean side, presses it to the cut and holds it up to show him there's nothing there. 'See? I'm fine. So, I can go now.'

'You're not going anywhere.'

Their gaze meets in the mirror – for a beat longer this time – then immediately parts again as Nora turns to toss the piece of kitchen towel into the bin by the washbasin.

She hopes he takes the hint, but he continues standing between her and the bath.

'Can I see?' he asks again.

'No,' she tells him again.

'Humour me?' He arches an eyebrow at her in the mirror. 'Like I did with the petrol?'

'Well, I was right about that,' she reminds him. 'And I'm right about this as well. I don't need you to check.' She flashes him a sour smile in the mirror. 'My brother Ben's training to be a doctor in A and E at the Royal London. So, if I need any medical advice, I'll ask him, okay?'

Sendhil nods. 'Fair enough.'

'So, can you …' She gestures at him to move.

He does, but there's only enough room for him to take a step back. She had hoped he'd get out of the bathroom altogether, but when he doesn't, she turns around with a huff. As she does so, her hip grazes his. The shock makes her look up as he looks down, his eyelids so heavy, all she can see is the fan of his lashes. It's as though they've crossed a line into the same forcefield, because suddenly, everything is blurry and out of reach and before Nora's brain even registers what she's doing, she's leaning in.

He is as well, so they meet halfway in a kiss so sudden, she gasps against his mouth and has to reach for the collar of his red and black plaid shirt and hold on. Then they're kissing again. And it's just like it was at the cove earlier. Breathless and dizzy and bewildering. A collision that has them stepping on each other's toes as they fall against the washbasin.

Sendhil wraps his arms around her back, holding her still so everything slots perfectly into place. Their faces. Noses. Mouths. His hair is dry this time, she learns when she lets go of his collar to fist her hands it. And he smells different. Tastes different. Not of the sea, but something fresher. Toothpaste. He showered when he got home as well, she realises. Showered and brushed his teeth, like she did, in an attempt to wash it away.

Wash her away.

But here they are again, crashing into each other once more.

Then her toes can't find the floor and she has to reach for the collar of his shirt again, holding on as he lifts her onto the washbasin. Her thighs hook over his hips as he moves between her legs, knocking the open first-aid kit off the edge of the basin with his hand as his right arm slips around her waist, pulling her closer as plasters tumble to the floor like confetti.

Nora's hands slip under the collar of his shirt then, seeking out the heat of his skin. Her fingers curl around his throat, pressing into it until she finds the frantic stutter of his heartbeat and tells herself that's because of her. As soon as she feels it, her hands move back to the collar of his shirt, pushing it over his shoulders to expose the black T-shirt he's wearing underneath. He's holding onto her waist so tightly that she only manages to get it down as far as his elbows. So, she leaves it hanging there, her hands moving up to the hem this time. He groans into her mouth when she slips them beneath the black cotton, his skin already warm, then getting warmer as she presses her palms to his chest, her hand seeking out the bird tattooed over his heart and waiting to feel it flutter against her skin.

That makes him groan again, but he rolls his hips against her this time, so suddenly that her whole body jerks up and their mouths miss. When their lips part and the light of the bathroom gets between them again, it's like a thread has been cut and they separate.

'Nora,' he pants against her lips, trying to untangle himself from her legs. But he still has his arm around her waist and she still has her hands under his T-shirt, so when he steps back, he takes her with him. Nora slips off the edge of the basin and into him, back into their forcefield. That invisible space that's just theirs as their mouths blindly meet in another kiss.

She hears something topple as they fall against the basin again, whatever it is joining the plasters on the floor, his hands in her hair, holding her head still as he kisses her deeply.

Nora can feel the hammer of his heart against the palm of her hand as she kisses him back. Then she can't hear the storm any more – can't hear the window rattling or the wind whipping around the back of the cottage or the rain trying to get in – only him moaning into her mouth as his hands fist in her hair until she feels the sweet sting on her scalp.

Then everything is even more blurry and out of reach as her fingers drag down his chest to find the top button of his jeans. When she undoes it, he whimpers into her open mouth and lifts her off the edge of the basin. She tries to hold on, her thighs hooked on his hips, ankles crossed, hands moving up to his hair and pulling until he whimpers again, panting against her mouth as he carries her into the bedroom without breaking their kiss.

~*~

Nora wakes up to find the sheets are warm, but Sendhil is gone.

It's still dark, so she can't have been asleep long, she realises, as she sits up and looks around the bedroom. It's funny, because she's been in his cottage so many times – almost every day – yet she hasn't been in here since the evening she arrived in Pidwell.

It looks exactly as she remembers. Still cluttered with stuff, except now she recognises it all. The framed photo of him, Meredith and Annabelle on top of the chest of drawers. The copy of *Cat's Eye* he's been nursing for the last week on the bedside table. The white T-shirt he was wearing yesterday, half in, half out of the wicker hamper in the corner.

Not stuff.

Him.

Everywhere.

Everywhere but next to her.

Nora glances at the open bathroom door. The light's on, so she can see the plasters littering the floor, the dark green first-aid box they fell out of now open on its side, spewing rolls of bandages. She holds her breath and waits to hear the shower, but all she can hear is the stuttered shudder of the bathroom window in its frame as the storm rages on outside.

The worst of it has passed – there hasn't been any lightning or thunder since Sendhil came to rescue her – but she can hear that it's still raining heavily. Even so, she suddenly becomes aware of how still the cottage is. She can't hear the kettle boiling. Or Bob Dylan calling from the living room. Or one of the cats outside on the doorstep, yowling to be let in.

Nora covers herself with the sheet, wondering if he really has gone.

If he's run away like he did earlier at the cove.

But then she hears the fridge door open and is immediately weak with relief.

Nora untangles herself from the sheet, separates her clothes from his out of the trail from the bathroom to the end of the bed and pulls them on. She gingerly opens the door to find him slumped in the brown leather chair in the living room, looking up at the ceiling.

She stands in the doorway, waiting for him to notice her. When he doesn't, she says, 'Hey.'

Sendhil's chin drops and he looks at her in a way he never has before. As though he's seeing her for the first time. He kind of is, she supposes. In another way, at least.

After all, they've never done *that*, have they?

'Hey,' she says again, managing a smile this time.

When he licks his lips and looks at her from under his eyelashes, her stomach tightens at the thought of him saying, 'Come here,' then crawling into his lap.

But he doesn't say that. He just holds up the bottle in his hand and says, 'Beer?'

He doesn't wait for her to answer, as he hauls himself out of the chair and pads over to the kitchen. He grabs a bottle from the fridge, stopping to open it, then pads back to where she's standing and hands it to her, before sitting in the armchair again.

Nora doesn't want a beer, but accepts it anyway as she moves the yellow blanket out of the way and sits on the sofa. She's grateful that she had the foresight to get dressed before she came out of the bedroom. Something tells her that she should be dressed for this.

Then it's so quiet she can hear the rush of the rain outside, the sound making her want to reach for the blanket and wrap it around herself. But she's terrified to move and stares ahead at the woodburner, suddenly fixed to the spot as she waits for him to say something.

Anything.

But he just sits there, his head tipped back against the chair, staring up at the ceiling.

So, is this him? Nora thinks.

The Sendhil everyone warned her about.

Nora hadn't believed them because he was never like that with her, but here he is.

What was the word her uncles used to described him? Reticent. Reticent Sendhil who, the first time they were alone, that first time they drove to Penzance, told her he was scared that everything was going to change after the festival. Who'd sat next to her on this sofa until four a.m. last month, with a shoebox in his lap, showing her photos of everyone. His mother. His father. His sisters. His niece, who was born last year. Reticent Sendhil, who had just breathed her name against her skin and held her like he'd never let go.

Nora knows that Sendhil.

Not this one who won't look at her.

When she's brave enough to look at him, he's doing exactly what she was just doing. Sitting there, picking at the label on the beer bottle, his jaw clenched.

Nora realises then that she's going to have to be the first to say something. 'Do you want me to go?' she asks, putting the bottle down on the coffee-table.

'Do you want to go?' he asks, still picking at the label.

'I want to know what you're thinking,' she says, before she can stop herself.

And she does.

She really does.

'What *I'm* thinking?' The corners of his mouth pull down as he nods to himself.

He finally succeeds in peeling the label off the bottle, rolls it into a ball between his fingers and throws it onto the coffee-table in front of her. Then he says, 'I'm just thinking that I can't have this conversation again.'

Nora stiffens at that. 'What conversation?'

'Oh, you know the one. "This was great, Sendhil."' He raises his eyebrows and tilts his head from side to side. '"Best summer ever. Let me know when you're next in London."'

When she'd opened the bedroom door a few minutes ago to find him sitting there, she hadn't even thought about what she'd say to him, but it certainly wasn't that.

Nora chuckles sourly. 'Had that conversation before, huh?'

'A few times.'

She presses her fingers to her lips before she can ask how many *a few* is.

He takes a sip of beer, then says, 'For a while, it felt like every few months a different lost girl showed up here, trying to find herself. And I swore,' he shakes his head so hard one of his curls falls over his right eyebrow, 'I would never do that again and here we are.'

Wow.

That hurts more than smacking her head against the coffee-table.

'Is that all I am, then?' she asks. 'Just another lost girl?'

Nora waits for him to look at her, but he won't, only at the bottle of beer in his hands. 'For the record,' she says sharply, 'I am not lost. I didn't come to Pidwell to *find myself* because I know exactly who I am, thank you. And I thought you, of all people, knew that.'

That's what hurts, she realises. What really hurts. More than the fact that he quite clearly regrets what just happened and he's doing this – whatever *this* is – to get her to leave.

So, fine.

She'll go.

But before she does, she raises a finger and tells him again, 'I am not one of your lost girls, Sendhil. I know *exactly* who I am, and if anyone has caused me to question that, it's you.'

When she stands up, he does as well.

'Don't go.' He holds out his arm, then presses his hand to his chest. 'Please. I'm sorry.'

Nora wipes away a tear from the corner of her eye with her knuckle before he sees. 'What is this, Sendhil? Who are you? Where's the guy who took me to the cove earlier and told me it was okay not to have everything figured out? And now, what? You're mad because you think I don't have everything figured out?'

'I meant everything I said earlier. Every word.' He slaps his chest. 'I could see how confused you were. How confused you've been since I said that stupid thing.'

'What stupid thing?'

'About not having anyone to cook for when you leave. The second I said it I saw it.'

'Saw what, Sendhil?'

'The doubt. I saw it in your eyes and you haven't been the same since.'

She crosses her arms and looks at the floor, scared of what else he'll see.

'I don't want that, Nora. I don't want to throw you off course. What I said then,' he turns to point the bottle at the empty armchair, 'was bang out of order because you're not lost, Nora. You're not lost at all. That's the point. You have this amazing life and now you're going to work at one of your favourite galleries and I've messed everything up.'

He puts his hand into his hair. 'This is why I don't like talking! I always say the wrong thing and make everything worse.' He tugs at his hair. 'All I'm trying to say is that this was supposed to be so simple, Nora. You were supposed to come here, help with the festival, then go home and I made you all confused. *That*'s why I took you to the cove earlier. Because I wanted you to know that you'll find your way back to what you wanted before you met me. But then I kissed you and ruined everything. And that's on me.

That's my fault. And I am *so mad* at myself for giving in to it and confusing you even more, and now …'

He takes his hand out of his hair and turns to look at the bedroom, then back at her.

'*That,*' he says, gesturing at the bedroom door, 'is my fault as well, for having no self-control, and now I've made everything ten times worse and it's gonna be even harder when you leave because, contrary to my recent behaviour, I'm not trying to get my leg over, here.'

He stops to take a swig of beer, then wipes his mouth with the back of his hand and says, 'I don't want *that,* Nora.' He tilts his head at the bedroom door again. 'I don't.'

'What do you want, then, Sendhil?' she asks, when he stops to finish the beer.

He laughs bitterly. 'What do *I* want?'

'Yes,' she pushes, when he paces to the kitchen. 'What do you want?'

'Who cares what I want if you don't know what you want, Nora?'

That almost knocks her clean off her feet.

'I can tell you what I don't want, though,' he says, opening the fridge and grabbing another beer. 'I don't want to spend the next sixteen days doing *that* until you go home.' He points the bottle at the bedroom, then snatches the opener from the kitchen counter. He flips off the cap with a sharp hiss. 'Because it's gonna be hard enough as it is when you go.'

She crosses her arms because that's fair. This was never supposed to be a summer fling. Nora has no idea *what* it is, just that she can't stand the way he's looking at her.

She watches his Adam's apple rise and fall as he says, 'And, *again*, that's my fault. I kissed you. I confused you. I made this *way* more complicated than it needs to be. And I'm so sorry.' He shrugs. 'But you have to understand, in case it isn't obvious from the absolute *show* I'm making of myself right now, I like you, Nora. I really like you.'

The rush of relief at hearing him say it out loud makes her feel lightheaded.

Nora's cheeks flush as she smiles at him. He smiles back, but then he catches himself and looks away with a sigh. 'I've made space for you, Nora, and I've only ever made space for two people outside my family. Alice, mainly because I had to. I've known her since I was five and I can't seem to get rid of her. And Annabelle, because I came here thinking she was going to save me and she says she didn't but she did. Then there's you.'

He points the beer bottle at her. 'I don't miss people, Nora. I haven't seen my parents for four months, but if I don't see you for four hours, I miss you.' He looks appalled with himself. 'I actually *miss* you. I find some lame excuse about compost or feeding the cats just so I can come over. I don't even know who I am any more. You left your hoodie in the truck the other day and I actually sniffed it. I *sniffed* it, Nora, like some sort of psycho.'

She can't help but snigger at that.

Sendhil does as well, then looks her in the eye for the first time since she walked out of the bedroom. 'You want to know what I want? I want it all. I want *you*. I want *this*. I want *us*, fighting over what to listen to when I'm cook-ing and whose turn it is to feed the cats. I want to fall asleep with our heads on the same pillow and wake up to find they're still on the same pillow. I want our kids to be friends with Alice and Megan's kids and to sit on Meredith and Annabelle's bench when we're ninety and look at each other and say, *We made it.*

'Which,' he stops to blink a few times, 'is a ridiculous thing to say given that I've known you for ten minutes, but that's the point.' He shrugs. 'I know. I knew when you ran out of the bedroom with that can of deodorant and you make me more sure every time I'm with you.'

Nora's heart shivers at that. But she doesn't have a moment to recover as he says, 'But if you don't know that I promise you I understand. I do. Like I said, we've known each other for, like, ten minutes and I'm talking about kids and sitting on benches when we're ninety. Which is a lot, I know. I'm honestly not saying this is to put any pressure on you.'

He presses his hand to his chest again. 'I'm saying it so you know what I want. And I know how lucky I am to know what I want and where I want to be. And you deserve to decide that for yourself without having it decided for you because you're with me.'

'So, there.' Sendhil holds up his hand. 'Now you know. And once you've decided, if what you want and what I want are the same thing, grand. But there's no in between for me. So, until you know, we have to stop doing this because it's not fair on either of us.'

And, with that, her options divide neatly in two.

Stay here with him.

Or go back to London without him.

Because Sendhil's right: there really is no in between.

Chapter 17

When Nora calls Luce the next morning to tell her what happened, she's appalled.

In inimitable Luce Nicolaou style, she sums the whole thing up as: 'So, you shagged once and he wants you to give up your whole life and move to Pidwell?'

When Luce puts it like that, Nora concedes, it does sound like that's what he's asking her to do. But, really, it's not about giving up her life, it's about starting a new one with him.

Besides, it's not Sendhil's fault. Nora asked him what he wanted and he told her. He was completely honest with her and now it's up to her. And while, yes, it is ridiculous – and unreasonable and maybe even a little melodramatic – to be considering it, given she's only known him a couple of months, the truth is, the thing she never said to Luce or even to him, she's never felt this much so quickly for someone. It's been six hours since she last saw him and she already misses him with a depth she hadn't thought herself capable of.

Luce doesn't even ask if she's considering it, though, just concludes that it's merely a case of the right guy at the wrong time. Perhaps it is, but isn't that what all of us want?

To turn to someone when we're ninety after a long, loud life and say, *We made it.*

Sendhil is the first person Nora has ever thought about doing that with. So, despite how ridiculous – and unreasonable and maybe even a little melodramatic – that is after only a couple of months, it's becoming increasingly impossible to ignore.

Time.

That was what they concluded Nora needed when she left his cottage last night. He told her to take all the time she needs. How much time, she has no idea. All she knows is that, this morning, the storm has passed, but the threat remains. Like everything around her is still in constant motion.

Go.

Stay.

Pidwell.

London.

This life.

That life.

When she gets off the phone from Luce, she sits on Meredith and Annabelle's bench and waits for it to pass, but it doesn't. Everything churning around and around as though the windows are still rattling and the front door is about to blow open at any moment.

So, she throws herself into the festival.

After seeing Sendhil every day, Nora doesn't see him at all. They seem to have developed an unspoken routine. In the mornings, she pokes her head out of the front door to check he isn't around, then scuttles off. A few minutes later, when she's in the shop, chatting to Alice, she'll hear him beep as his pickup passes. Then, in the evenings, when Nora is too tired to contemplate anything other than a bowl of cereal for dinner, she'll close the kitchen window when the warm smell of onions and garlic wafts in.

And while Nora is grateful for the distraction of getting the festival – and the Trefelyn – ready for the August bank-holiday weekend, she's back to being exhausted. Except this time, it's a different kind of ache. Not just a physical one, her back sore from cleaning and sweeping and heaving boxes, but something else, somewhere else. Somewhere deep in her bones.

The unreachable ache that she feels every time she gets back to Mrs Stroud's cottage and it's just her and there's nothing to clean or sweep or heave until the next day. When it's dark and quiet enough to hear Sendhil moving around, like he's only in the next room.

He's been listening to the same album for days. Each night, at about eleven o'clock, she can't hear him moving around any more, and as soon as she asks herself if he's gone to sleep, she hears it. Then, that's it, he plays it over and over. So many times that, eventually, it becomes a lullaby. The last thing Nora hears before she falls asleep.

She has no idea what it is. So, after the third night in a row, curiosity gets the better of her and she downloads an app to find out. As she holds up her phone to the song playing through the walls, the app tells her it's 'You're A Big Girl Now' by Bob Dylan.

Nora downloads the album the next morning and listens to it all day, seeking out the secret messages in each song, hoping to decipher what Sendhil is thinking. Then, that night, when everything is quiet on the other side of the wall, she cues it up, and as soon as Sendhil starts playing the album, she does the same, so they're listening to it at the same time.

Nora shouldn't intrude on him like that. He deserves to be left alone to stew or mourn or whatever it is he's doing. After all, it's four a.m., when the night is at its most tender, and it feels like they're the only ones in Pidwell still awake. Them and the moon while they wait for the sun to come up so they can tell themselves they've survived another night. Even if it means they have to spend the rest of the day pretending everything is okay.

But it's the first thing they've done together for two weeks.

So, she lies there, on the sofa, listening to the album and looking up at the ceiling, while she pictures him on his sofa in his cottage doing exactly the same thing.

It's moments like this when Nora thinks she can do it. She can stay. She can work at the Trefelyn. Strut around in colourful Diane von Fürstenberg dresses, like Lorelai Gilmore. Have lunch every Sunday with Annabelle and her uncles and organise the festival every year.

That's enough.

That sounds like a lovely life, doesn't it?

What more does she need?

But then she thinks about Sendhil, locked into his studio, working on whatever he's working on, and she doesn't feel an ache, she feels an itch. An itch to check if the tickets to the Yinka Shonibare exhibition are still sold out. Or an itch to check the Royal Academy of Arts website to find out if they've put up any more videos from their Summer Exhibition.

It's the first Summer Exhibition she's missed since she was fourteen and it doesn't even matter, but, with that, the uneasiness is back. Go. Stay. Pidwell. London. This life. That life. Back and forth. Back and forth. Around and around. Like the storm is in her chest now, everything moving at once. Her bones rattling. The door in her heart about to blow open.

Something's off, Nora realises, as she lies on the sofa, mouthing the words to 'If You See Her, Say Hello'. Her shared moment with Sendhil through the walls has passed.

It's the song.

They're no longer listening to the same one.

When she lowers the volume, she hears that he's not listening to 'If You See Her, Say Hello', like she is. He's listening to the next one, 'Shelter from the Storm'. He skipped it, Nora realises, as she listens to Bob Dylan lament a girl he lost, but won't stand in her way.

As soon as the song ends, she listens to it again, closing her eyes and hanging on to each lyric as she asks herself if he skipped it because it makes him think of her, her hands trembling at the thought. But as it concludes with Dylan telling the girl he's not that hard to find if she's ever heading back this way, Nora knows why Sendhil can't listen to it.

Because he knows, doesn't he?

He knows what Nora has been ignoring for the last two weeks.

He knows she can't stay.

~*~

Then it's the day before the festival and she and Ron are bombing through the valley, late to pick up Luce. She booked the weekend off from the salon to come early and 'help'. Help with the Sendhil Situation, that is, rather than the festival because, Lord knows, Nora needs it.

After two weeks of almost acrobatic avoidance – Nora all but threw herself into a bush the other day when she saw him ambling through the valley, talking earnestly to Annabelle – she hasn't seen Sendhil at all. So, when Luce swaggers out of Penzance railway station, her holdall banging against her hip, Nora is barely able to get out of the car before she's crying.

Luce.

She's here.

Luce is here and she looks the same. Her curls are green now but, other than that, she looks exactly as Nora remembers. As though she could be strolling across Hoxton Square, in a pair of black denim dungarees, rolled up at the ankles, and a black crop top underneath.

'Luce!' Nora says, with a heave and a sob, as they fly at each other, falling against Ron as they hug with such enthusiasm, the strap of Luce's holdall slips off her shoulder.

Everything is going to be okay.

~*~

They don't stop talking as Nora drives back to Pidwell. To her amazement, the Trefelyn has come together in time so Luce is staying there. Along with Ben, Nora's parents and the other friends and family her uncles have invited for the soft launch in the hope they'll go easy and not complain about the smell of paint and that the coffee machine hasn't arrived yet.

Nora parks at the inn and, once they've said hello to her uncles, she and Luce head to the shop, promising to see them for dinner. Alice and Luce are so similar that this could go either way. Plus it doesn't help that Alice has been noticeably cooler with her since the night of the storm. Mercifully, she is sweetness and light. To Luce, at least, Alice complimenting her hair while Luce flicks it and tells her that she mixed the colour especially for the weekend. She's calling it Pidwell Green. It isn't quite the Farrow & Ball shade Lady Kate was hoping for, Alice notes, but it seems perfectly appropriate for the festival.

'You hungry?' Alice asks, heading behind the counter. She doesn't wait for them to answer, and immediately stuffs a paper bag with fairings and asks what they want to drink.

When she's made their coffees, she sticks her hand out across the counter.

'Hand over the bag, Armstrong.'

'But I need it. It's got all my stuff in it. My phone. My notebook.'

'I know. That's the point.'

Nora is horrified. 'But it's the day before the festival, Alice!'

'*Exactly*. You need an hour with your friend before it all kicks off tomorrow.'

'But what if there's an emergency?'

She gestures at her for Nora to hand the bag over. 'I'll deal with it.'

Nora hands it over with a petulant huff.

But before she does, she tells her, 'The T-shirts are arriving at six.'

'Go, will you?' Alice hisses. 'Your coffee's getting cold.'

~★~

It's almost five thirty so, while it's still warm, the sun has lost its urgency as afternoon melts into evening, the light going from an intense yellow to a warm gold. It's enough to make the muscles in her shoulders unclench, but as soon as they do, Nora stops as they tighten again.

There he is.

Sendhil.

Or his pickup, at least, backing down the slip, one of Annabelle's driftwood horses strapped to the bed. Or Meredith's horses, as they're all referring to them now, which, Nora supposes, they are. She sees then that one is already on the beach, exactly where Annabelle wanted it, half in, half out of the water, so it looks like it's running into the sea.

Nora knew from the schedule that they were being installed today, figuring she'd miss it because she was with Luce, but she's glad she didn't.

Tommy and Terry jump out of the passenger door. Then the driver's side opens.

'That him?' Luce asks, but Nora can't catch her breath as her heart answers the question for her, immediately leaping up in her chest at the sight of him, like *It's him!* She can hear the paper bag rustling in her hand as they walk over to join the crowd that's gathered.

'Okay,' Luce says, as they watch him walk to the back of his pickup. 'I get it.'

If Nora could still breathe, she'd laugh.

He does look good, actually. He looks like *him*. In his Ray-Bans, black jeans and a white T-shirt that is so bright in the sunshine, she almost looks away.

But she can't of, course, because it's him.

She hasn't laid eyes on him since she almost jumped in that bush in the valley. Even then, she didn't see him, just enough of him through the trees to know it was him. The slow swing of his hips and the determined turn of his hands as he spoke to Annabelle. And his voice, that syrupy, sing songy lilt, each word seeming to call out to the birds in the trees.

But now, here he is.

All of him.

In a few days, his stubble will be a full on beard and he hasn't had a haircut for so long that the weight of his curls are pulling them down into his eyes, but other than that, he looks the same. Nora catches herself smiling as she watches him, aware that the crowd is getting thicker. Some have their phones out, filming them trying to navigate the driftwood horse off the bed of the pickup. It must weigh a *tonne*, but Sendhil doesn't seem to be struggling.

'Let's go,' Nora tells Luce, when a man with white hair and a navy jumper draped over his shoulders turns to the woman at his side and asks, *Is that Sendhil Achari?*

He'd hate this. Everyone watching. Not that he seems bothered, too focused to notice as they finally get the horse down from the pickup to an exuberant round of applause.

By the time she and Luce reach Meredith and Annabelle's bench, the high of seeing him has dipped to the pitiful low of not knowing what she's going to do.

Luce nudges her when Nora's shoulders sink. 'You know what you need, don't you?'

'Don't say it,' she warns, as she reaches into the paper bag for a biscuit.

'Come on.' Luce grins at her. 'What do we always ask ourselves in these situations?'

Nora refuses to give her the satisfaction.

'Come on.' Luce elbows her again. 'What would Ben do?'

No. She's not doing it.

'Sing it with me, Nor.'

'No,' she says, with a surly sigh, as she bites into the fairing.

'Come on.'

When Nora ignores her, Luce does it anyway, cupping her hand to her mouth and tipping her head back to sing, 'A Ben Armstrong Pros and Cons List of Indecision!'

'Absolutely not,' she tells her, feigning disgust.

But the truth is, Nora's already done one and it didn't help in the slightest.

'It'll help,' Luce promises, with a hopeful smile.

It won't, but who knows? Perhaps Luce will magically find a solution to all of this.

She's determined like that.

'As you know,' she holds up a finger, 'you must abide by the ruling of the Ben Armstrong Pros and Cons List of Indecision. *Unless . . .*' she raises her finger higher when Nora starts to object '. . . you disagree with the outcome, in which case, that's your answer.'

That actually makes sense, Nora thinks.

'So.' Luce turns her knees towards Nora and puts her coffee down on the bench between them. 'Come on, then. What are your options?'

Nora really only has two. 'Stay or go.'

'What about in between?'

'What's in between?'

'The long-distance thing.'

'I guess,' Nora says, around a mouthful of biscuit. 'But it's a five-and-a-half-hour drive with no traffic or over-turned lorries. It took me *nine hours* to get here the day I arrived.'

'That sounds exhausting,' Luce says. 'Even if you took it in turns every weekend.'

It does sound exhausting, Nora thinks, with a heavy sigh, as she finishes the biscuit.

'What's the halfway point between here and London?'

Nora's already looked it up. 'Yeovil. It's two hours and fifty seven minutes.'

'So you could move to Yeovil.'

Nora blinks at her. 'Why in God's name would I move to Yeovil? Aside from it being *Yeovil*, I'd be constantly driving between here or London. How is that any less miserable?'

'True,' Luce says, as Nora roots around for another fairing. 'Stay or go it is, then.'

Nora pulls a face at her as if to say, *See?*

'Right.' Luce claps her hands together. 'Let's start with the Pros. Pidwell. Go.'

Nora panics, stuffing the whole fairing in her mouth so that she doesn't have to say it.

'Babe, it's me,' Luce reminds her. 'I'm not going to judge you for saying Sendhil first. Besides, who the hell am I to judge? Mo has a face tattoo and a boyfriend.'

'Who's Mo?' Nora frowns.

'That guy I met at Dalston Superstore last month.'

'So are you guys, like, a throuple or something?'

'No!' Luce shakes her head. 'I don't know.' She suddenly looks concerned. 'Maybe. Anyway, Sendhil's the root of all of this indecision, so he should be the top of the Pro list.'

'Fine,' Nora mutters, biting into another biscuit.

Luce holds up her thumb. 'So, Sendhil.'

'My uncles,' Nora adds, then points at her. 'Don't tell them they weren't first.'

Luce crosses her chest with her index finger.

'Annabelle.' Nora looks up at the sky stretching over them as she thinks about it. 'Alice. Everyone here, really. They're all lovely. And you know . . .' She looks down, gesturing at the sea. It's postcard-perfect. The bluest Nora has ever seen it. So blue it almost doesn't look real, like it's been Photoshopped. The whole of Pidwell does, actually, as though someone's applied an

Instagram filter, and it's making her question how she can consider leaving.

'Excuse you.' Luce reaches for her coffee. 'This place is pretty, I suppose, but they just put one of those planter things with marigolds outside Tooting tube. Take that, Pidwell!'

'Let's save that one for London's Pros List.'

Luce throws her head back and laughs, then points the coffee cup at her as she thinks of something else. 'Oh, and the art scene in Cornwall is kind of not terrible, right?'

'True.' Nora hadn't considered that. 'There's a Tate in St Ives now, and there are loads of galleries in Penzance. I mean, it's not London but it's pretty cool.'

'There you go.'

'Plus, Pidwell's chill, you know? No traffic or running for the last train.'

'And it must be cheap-as round here. You could probably afford a house.'

That's true, Nora thinks. 'But I'd earn a lot less in Cornwall, compared to London.'

'Yeah, but you wouldn't be spending it all on rent and commuting, so it evens out.'

Also true, Nora notes.

'Is that it for Pidwell's Pros?' Luce checks, when Nora resumes gazing out at the sea.

'I guess,' she says, somewhat surprised at how long the list is. Perhaps it's Luce's uncontainable enthusiasm for *everything*, but Pidwell might actually be a contender now.

'Right. Okay. Pidwell Pros. Done.' Luce claps. 'Now. London. Go.'

'The marigolds outside Tooting tube, of course.'

'Obviously!'

'You.'

Luce grins so hard her eyes disappear. 'Of course!'

'My parents. Ben.'

Luce rolls her eyes and sticks out her tongue. 'Them too, I suppose.'

'Everyone I know, basically.'

'What else?'

Nora tries to find a way of saying it that doesn't sound like she's being a snob, but she can't. '*Life*, I suppose,' she says sheepishly. 'Culture. I just missed the Summer Exhibition at the Royal Academy for, like, the first time *ever* this year. And I miss trying not to lose you at gigs. And the smell of art shops. And sitting in the pub with you and Ben, eating crisps. And wandering around Borough Market, trying all the cheese knowing full well I can't afford it.

'And I miss people,' Nora realises. 'Pretending not to listen to couples arguing on the tube, and giving advice to crying girls in pub toilets who keep saying, *You're so pretty, babe.*' She chuckles as she watches a seagull bobbing merrily. 'Annoying as it is, sometimes, I like the chaos of London. How unpredictable it is. The promise of it. How no two days are the same. How every day could be *the one*, you know? Your day. Your day to get the job you always wanted or meet the perfect guy or just have the perfect negroni, you know?'

'And London's stressful,' Nora admits. 'It's loud and dirty and expensive and I hate how I'm always late for something or queuing for something, but ...' She wrinkles her nose '. . . if we hadn't been waiting outside Chick 'n' Sours that night, we might never have met.'

Luce nudges her with her knee. 'In fairness to Pidwell, though, London is undefeated when it comes to that sort of thing.'

It really is, Nora thinks.

'Pidwell can't compete. But, then, *nowhere* can. Unless you move to Manchester, or something.' Luce points her coffee cup at her. 'You could move to Manchester.'

'Sure. Why not? Let's throw *another* city into the mix.'

'Okay. We've got London's Pros covered. Let's move onto the Cons. Pidwell. Go!'

There are no fairings left or Nora would stuff another into her mouth.

'Sendhil,' Nora says, with a tender sigh.

'Oooh.' Luce sits up a little, her eyes wide. 'A Pro *and* a Con? Interesting.'

Nora clears her throat as it tightens, because here it is.

The thing she can't keep avoiding.

'All those Pros about Pidwell,' she says, with a sombre smile, 'lovely as they are ...' She closes her eyes and exhales because she can't say it.

So Luce says it for her: 'You wouldn't even consider moving here if it wasn't for him.'

And there it is.

~★~

Luce slings her arm around Nora's shoulders, kissing her temple and telling her it will be okay as they head back around the cove towards the shop. Luckily Sendhil's gone, the driftwood horses alone on the beach now, and Nora suddenly feels very sad as she looks at them.

Still, when she gets her bag from Alice, she's relieved to discover there haven't been any disasters and the T-shirts arrived. Sendhil dropped the box at the town hall on his way to Penzance, so she and Luce wander through the valley to check they don't have a typo like the last ones did. Otherwise they're just going to have to call it the Pidwell Arts Festivale.

'Nor?' Luce says, as Nora's looking up at the leaves, grateful for the second of quiet.

She never realises just how much noise there is in her head until she comes here.

'Nora,' Luce says again, tugging her back.

She's about to walk into the stream and corrects herself, assuming that's what Luce was warning her about. But when she turns to thank her, Luce has stopped walking.

Nora stops as well. 'What?'

'You okay? You're being weird.'

Nora frowns. 'Weird?'

'Yeah. I thought you'd be relieved.'

'About the T-shirts?'

'No. About the decision.'

It takes Nora a moment, then she nods. 'Oh. The Pros and Cons List.'

'You should be relieved. The Pros and Cons List rules.' Luce claps. 'London.'

Nora carries on walking along the edge of the stream, listening to the rush of it.

But Luce doesn't follow this time. 'Nora?'

She stops and turns to face her again, her lips parted. 'Huh?'

'You know the rules. They were decided during the Great Coachella Debate of 2018, the Pros and Cons List for which ruled!' Luce raises her finger when Nora tries to defend herself. 'We were going. Then *you*,' she jabs a finger in Nora's direction, 'left it until the last minute to tell Roland, and he wouldn't let you have the time off so *I* missed Beychella.'

Nora crosses her arms with a huff. 'Glad you're over it, though.'

'I will *never* forgive you,' she says, only half joking. 'It's Beyoncé! You should have quit!'

She's absolutely right, of course.

But Nora still pulls a face at her.

'So, you know the rules,' Luce reminds her. 'The decision is final.' When Nora turns her face away, she adds, 'Unless you disagree with the outcome.'

Nora can't look at her, gazing across the stream instead at the cluster of purple flowers spiking through the thick grass. Purple betony, Annabelle said, when Nora pointed them out last week. Someone planted them in Pidwell in the seventeenth century because a herbalist called Nicholas Culpeper believed that they protected you from witchcraft.

It obviously hasn't worked, Annabelle told her, with a wild cackle.

'So you disagree with the decision?' Luce presses, when she doesn't say anything.

Nora still can't look at her. 'I'm not saying I disagree. I'm just not ruling it out.'

Luce barks out a laugh. 'Come on! You aren't serious?'

'About what?'

'You can't seriously be considering moving here?'

'Why?'

Luce looks at her like she's lost it. 'You've known this dude for *three months*, Nora.'

When Luce says it like that, it does sound like she's lost it.

'Don't get me wrong,' Luce goes on. She sounds out of breath and Nora wonders how long she's been holding this in. 'Pidwell's lovely in the summer. But what's it like in the winter when everyone's gone home and it's cold and dark and miserable? Remember that storm?'

How could Nora possibly forget?

'People don't *live* in places like Pidwell,' Luce tells her. 'They come on holiday to places like Pidwell or they retire here. Nora, you're twenty-seven, not eighty-seven.'

'Plenty of people live here,' Nora says, her arms still crossed tightly.

'People who *had* lives and jobs and relationships somewhere else, but weren't happy. So they came looking for something different. You haven't even *started* living your life yet.'

Nora takes a step back and Luce winces.

'Okay. That was a bit harsh.'

Nora scoffs and pulls a face as if to say, *You think?*

'Listen.' Luce takes her by the shoulders and waits for her to look at her again. 'If you want my advice and why would you? The guy I'm dating has a face tattoo and a boyfriend.'

Nora snorts at that.

'But I'm going to give it you anyway, then I'll leave it, I swear.'

Nora holds her breath as she forces herself to look Luce in the eye.

'Sendhil told you how he felt, Nor, and dropped the mic. Meanwhile, here you are making Pros and Cons Lists and it shouldn't be this hard. It shouldn't be about you giving up everything. He *has* to meet you halfway. And I don't mean Yeovil.'

Nora manages a smile, but it passes as quickly as it appears as she asks Luce the one question she's been too afraid to ask herself since the night of the storm.

'And if he won't?'

'As my nan always says,' Luce says, squeezing her shoulders with a small sigh. '"Never cross an ocean for someone who wouldn't walk through a puddle for you."'

~*~

Luce heads back to the cove saying that Nora needs a moment to think about it.

She's right. Ben and her parents are arriving soon, if they haven't already. Then they're having dinner at the Trefelyn, and tomorrow the festival kicks off so she won't get a minute to herself. She wanders through the valley, listening to the birds in the trees over her head jump from branch to branch while the stream rushes alongside her, as though it's showing her the way to go. She isn't sure where until the trees part and there's Annabelle.

She seems to appear from nowhere, like her house did on Nora's first day in Pidwell. And, like her house, Annabelle looks like she could be in a fairy-tale, in a long, loose white dress, her grey curls wild and her feet bare as she looks up at the canopy of leaves.

Nora stands there for a moment, watching her dress ripple in the breeze, and smiles, thinking of that afternoon in August, when Mark was fifteen, and he saw Meredith on the edge of the cliff and thought she was Kate Bush. Brave, beautiful Annabelle, who can name every flower in the valley and conjures horses from driftwood.

Annabelle doesn't see her, though, just keeps looking up.

So, Nora does the same and gasps.

Birds.

Hundreds of brown birds hanging on wires from the branches. Birds of every shape and size. From tiny ones, no bigger than the grey and white speckled bird that startled Nora on her first morning in Pidwell, which was how she found the path up to Meredith and Annabelle's bench, to some the size of gulls, which appear to be swooping down.

'Did you do this?' Nora asks, turning in a circle as she looks up.

If Annabelle is surprised, she doesn't show it. She merely says, 'Sendhil.'

Of course.

After Annabelle had told her to leave him be, she was so reluctant to talk about what he was doing for the festival that Nora hadn't dared push it – especially after what happened the night of the storm – knowing his sculpture would just appear one day.

And here it is.

She wasn't expecting this, though. His work is usually so rigid. Solid. Slabs of cracked stone or moulded chicken wire with light piercing out of it. But this is so delicate. So fragile.

'When did he do this?' Nora asks, squinting into the sun.

'He's been hanging them for days. He's been sleeping in Tommy's barn.'

'So *that*'s where he's been the last three nights.'

'He didn't have to, of course, but I think he was worried the foxes would get them.'

'The foxes?'

'They're made of seeds.' Annabelle points up to the one nearest her. 'He's spent months making them. The idea is that the ones the birds and squirrels don't get will eventually fall on the ground for the other wildlife to have. So, one day, like with Meredith's horses, we'll come here and they'll all be gone.'

Nora feels the nudge of something.

The nudge you feel when you've forgotten something, but can't think what.

'I'll never forget the day he first wandered into our house,' Annabelle says, as Nora asks herself if she'll ever refer to Meredith in the past tense. If it will always be *our house*. But they all do it, don't they? Even she refers to it as Meredith and Annabelle's house.

'It was almost three years ago,' Annabelle says, smiling up at the birds. 'And he was even skinnier than he is now with twice as much hair. Meredith said he looked like a bird.'

That's it, Nora realises. The thing she couldn't remember. Sendhil's tattoo. The bird over his heart that had fluttered against her palm that night in his bathroom.

'She said he was like a sparrow that had flown in through a bathroom window and couldn't find his way out. Little Sparrow. That's what she used to call him.' Annabelle looks at Nora with a smile. 'I wonder if this is his way of letting her know that he's found a way out.'

~*~

Nora doesn't see Sendhil for the whole of the festival.

She can hear him, though. His name a whisper that seems to follow her everywhere she goes. The couple behind her in the shop, while Nora waits for another latte, the pair of them talking over one another, they're so excited. Outside the town hall, everyone in the queue eagerly turning to ask each other, *Have you seen the Achari?* As she's walking around the cove and has to step out of the way so another car can park, the friends saying that it'll be dark soon as they pile out, so they should go straight to the valley.

The birds. That's all anyone talks about. Meredith's horses are enough to stop people in their tracks on the South West Coast Path, of course, and, every time Nora checks in at the town hall, people are pointing at the paintings and whispering furiously, even if those stepping off the silver bus are ashen and speechless having been confronted by Kate's art.

But the birds.

Each time Nora passes through the valley there's a crowd beneath them, lips parted. Or there's a kid, on a parent's shoulders, reaching up to touch one.

It's exactly the reaction she – and, no doubt, Sendhil – had hoped for. But it doesn't make it any less painful to think of him stooped in his studio, fingers fussing over each one. He did that every day for *months*, then headed back to his cottage in the evening to make Greek salad and tease Nora for not having sliced a red onion before, like it was nothing. Like it was just another day at the office. Like he hadn't been creating something so heartstoppingly beautiful that Nora can feel the earth turning every time she looks up at it.

She wants to tell him that. She wants him to know it. She hopes he knows it.

But Nora doesn't know where he is and she feels the loss more keenly than ever.

It doesn't help that even her parents are besotted with them. The first time she takes them – and Ben – into the valley, they stand there, looking up in awe, gushing about how beautiful it is. Telling Nora they didn't know sculpture could be like that. That they thought it was just statues that stood in the same spot for ever. And thanking her – actually *thanking* her – because they're so lucky to have seen it before it disappears. And they have no idea that she's trying not to cry because her chest hurts so much that it's unbearable. The low, steady ache that gets louder and louder every time they say his name.

And later, after the festival, when everyone's gathered at Kate's house, her parents have no idea why Nora glances back each time the door opens, fingers tightening around her champagne glass. And they certainly don't know how her heart sinks each time it isn't him.

Sendhil isn't coming, she realises, by the time Kate appears at the top of the staircase in a floor-length peacock-green silk gown that makes Nora grateful she had the foresight to pack at least one nice dress. They're gathered in the hall of the house. Unlike at the town hall, describing it as a *hall* is actually modest. It's the biggest hallway Nora has ever seen.

You could fit the whole of Pidwell in here.

Kate has certainly gone to town for what she described as a *simple dinner to say thank you.* There are candles every-where, thick church ones, tiny tealights and fine tapers in silver candelabras. And flowers. Everywhere Nora looks there are white flowers. Huge arrangements of roses and big, blowsy peonies, like the ones her uncles put in Mrs Stroud's cottage to welcome Nora the evening she arrived.

He's not coming, is he? Nora knows, as Kate waits at the top of the stairs. For what, it isn't clear, until the man in the black suit and white gloves who was opening the door to greet everyone, claps and looks around the hall. It takes a moment, but they all do the same.

The applause is tepid, to put it politely, especially given they're all holding champagne glasses, but Kate throws back her head and laughs all the same, telling them to stop as she descends the staircase. She stands a few steps from the bottom and, as soon as she does, the man in the white gloves scurries up with a glass of champagne, dipping his head as he hands it to her. She takes it, thanking him with an easy smile, then looks out at everyone assembled.

'Thank you, everyone, for coming this evening,' Kate finally says.

When she pauses, the man in the white gloves claps again and the rest of them join in, even less enthusiastically than before. Still, Kate holds her hand up to stop them. 'Please,' she says. 'There's no need to thank me. This is my way of thanking *you* for all of your hard work this weekend and making the Pidwell Arts Festival a roaring success!'

The applause is more genuine this time, everyone turning to smile and blow kisses at Nora.

'Shouldn't *you* be making this speech?' her mother notes.

'Well, *she* paid for everything,' Nora manages to say, without her smile slipping.

'And we have one person to thank for that,' Kate says.

Kate's arm swings out over the banister in her direction. 'Nora!'

The applause is positively raucous now. So ardent that her cheeks burn as her gaze dips to the glossy floorboards beneath her feet.

When she looks up again, Kate's hand is pressed to her chest.

'Nora,' she says, smiling with such genuine affection, it makes Nora's cheeks even hotter. 'Thank you for everything you've done to make the festival such a success.

273

For corralling us and encouraging us and showing everyone who came to Pidwell this weekend why we think it's so special. We are for ever grateful.'

There's another round of applause that's punctuated by her parents kissing her, and when Nora looks between them, she doesn't think she's ever seen them so proud.

When the clapping fades, Nora clears her throat and raises her champagne glass. 'And to Meredith,' she says, 'without whom none of us would be here now.'

There's an echo of *To Meredith* as everyone holds up their glasses. Annabelle turns to face her then, tears in her eyes as she takes Nora's hand and presses a kiss to it.

'And to everyone else who contributed to this weekend.' Kate continues, gesturing around the hall with a grand wave of her arm. 'From the artists, to Tommy, who got the silver bus to the town hall somehow.'

There's another round of applause as he waves while Lottie looks mortified.

'To the volunteers, who have worked so hard to make sure that no one got lost in the valley ...'

'Have we checked?' James heckles and Mark elbows him.

Kate doesn't falter, though. '... and tended wounds and reunited lost children with their parents and stopped the little darlings from climbing on Meredith's horses or trying to pull down Sendhil's birds.'

There's a titter of laughter at that.

But Nora can't join in, her heart stuttering at the mere mention of his name.

'Speaking of Mr Achari,' Kate says, her sigh more wistful, 'it's a shame he didn't get to see the reaction to his piece. But, given how reclusive he is at the best of the times, I don't blame him for running off to Cork!'

Nora almost drops her glass as Luce turns to her, eyes wide.

That's why she hasn't seen him all weekend.

'But we're here!' Kate says, with a warm smile. 'So let's celebrate! We've earned it!'

Nora raises her glass with everyone else, her heart throbbing so quickly in her throat that she can't catch her breath. Each beat is painful now. So painful it's making her dizzy.

When Kate leads everyone towards the dining room, she and Luce hang back.

'Did you know he was going back to Cork?' Luce whispers, as soon as they're alone.

'Of course not,' Nora tells her, putting her glass on a table she probably shouldn't be putting it on, but she has to. Otherwise she'll drop it.

'Do you think he left because of you?' Luce asks, with a frown.

God. That hadn't even occurred to Nora. But now it has, she puts her hands on her hips and lifts her chin to stare at Luce. 'I don't know! I hope not!'

'What you gonna do if he doesn't come back before you go?' Luce asks.

'I don't know.'

And she doesn't.

Nora hadn't even considered that.

Sendhil is always *there*. Always on the other side of the wall. From the moment she arrived in Pidwell. He was the first person she saw and the last person she thought she'd see before she left. She was going to speak to him before she leaves tomorrow. At least say something. And if she still didn't know what by then, ask for more time.

But now he's gone and she can't and what's she going to do?

'Did I take too long?' Nora asks, pressing her hands to her cheeks. 'Is that it?'

'It's only been, what? Two weeks?'

Nora nods.

'It's not like you've left him hanging for months.'

'I haven't left him hanging!'

She hasn't.

Has she?

'He … *we* said I needed time. I didn't realise there was a two-week expiry date.'

'What are you going to do?'

'I don't know,' she admits, reaching for her clutch and opening it.

When she pulls out her phone, Luce gasps. 'Are you gonna call him?'

'I can't leave it like this. I can't just let him leave.'

She was the one who was supposed to leave because *he* didn't want to.

But when she looks up from her phone, she sees Alice, and freezes.

'Luce, can Nora and I have a moment?' she says tightly, without taking her eyes off Nora. It's clear from her tone that it's not a question.

Every muscle in Nora's body tightens, all at once.

When Luce turns to check that it's okay to leave, Nora doesn't want her to go but nods anyway. Luce struts down the hall towards the dining room in a blur of pale pink tulle. When the snap of her heels fades, Alice looks down at Nora's phone, then up at her.

'Don't.'

Nora does the same, looking down at her phone, then up at her. 'Don't what?'

'Call him.'

'I—'

'You *what*, Nora? What are you going to say to him?'

'I don't know.'

And she doesn't.

She just wants to … She doesn't know what she wants, does she?

That's the point.

Actually, Nora does know what she wants. She wants to go back. Back to before the storm, when it was just her and him, in his kitchen, laughing and flicking tea-towels at each other. Back when they weren't thinking about September. When they could just be.

'Well, you can't call him,' Alice tells her, 'not until you know what you're going to say.'

She's right, but it still hurts so much that she crosses her arms, as though it will ease the ache in her chest. 'When's he coming back?'

'When you've gone.'

She's never seen Alice like this. So distant. So careful. She doesn't laugh and tell Nora not to worry about it, like she did over lunch at Annabelle's when she assured her that Sendhil thought Nora threatening him with a can of deodorant was hilarious.

It's like a door slamming shut between them.

Still, Nora has to know. 'Why did he go home?'

Then Alice is the one avoiding eye contact as she says, '*I* told him to go.'

Nora blinks. 'Why?'

'Because, Nora.'

When Alice stops to glare at her, Nora realises that she says her name like he does.

It feels like she's been punched in the heart.

'Sendhil is *really* trying not to put any pressure on you, Nora.'

'Okay,' she says carefully, aware that Alice is furious. She doesn't want to provoke her.

But that doesn't explain why he had to leave.

It must be obvious that she doesn't understand, because Alice rolls her eyes and huffs. 'He isn't like that, you know. Sendhil isn't emotionally slutty, like you and me.'

Nora shouldn't, but she can't help but smile. 'You, me and Carrie Bradshaw.'

Alice starts to smile, but stops herself. 'This isn't funny,' she snaps. 'He doesn't do that. He doesn't tell people how he feels. He's only told me that he loves me once, on New Year's Eve, when we were fourteen and drunk on a bottle of Jameson we stole from my dad.'

Alice curses under her breath. 'Soon as I saw you, I knew you were trouble, Nora.'

She blinks at her again. 'Me?'

'Yeah. *You.*' Alice looks away, obviously trying to stop herself saying any more. Nora's hands shake as she asks herself which is worse: Alice holding back or Alice letting rip.

So, Nora waits because there's obviously something Alice needs to say.

'I don't know why I'm having a go at you,' she admits. 'You've done nothing wrong.'

Nora doesn't relax because there's more, she knows.

'It's not your fault, Nora. It was bound to happen. You're *so* his type.'

She shouldn't, but she can't stop herself asking, 'His type?'

'Yeah.' Alice is still looking everywhere but at her. 'Bright. Funny. Fierce. Fierce enough not to put up with his brooding-artist nonsense, but wise enough never to ask him about his art or disturb him when he's in his studio. And the first time you drove to Penzance, when he told you he didn't want to talk, and you actually didn't, I knew it.'

Alice rolls her eyes. 'That's the thing with Sendhil. As soon as he asks a girl to leave him alone and she does, he lets his guard down because he thinks he's safe. So, I knew it was coming. That first night. After my meltdown about the printer and you asked me and Megan over for dinner. When I walked into your cottage and he was there, I knew. Two years I've lived here. *Two.* And he's never been to my place for dinner. He always makes me go to his.'

Alice's gaze slides in her direction, then away again. 'A couple of hours in Penzance with you and there he is, the gobshite. Showing off with his coconut sambal. I just didn't think it would happen *this quickly*. I mean, *my God*. It's been three months. It usually takes him three months to warm up to more than a grunt. He's lived here for three *years* and he still wouldn't be able to pick Tommy's wife out of a line-up.'

Nora tries not to laugh, pressing her lips together to stop herself.

'I kept telling him, *She's only here for the summer. She's only here for the summer*. But did he listen, the idiot? I have never seen him fall this hard, this fast, for *anyone*.'

Nora's heart starts galloping. It's so loud, Alice must be able hear it.

'That's why I told him to go home.' Alice meets Nora's gaze and holds it. 'Because what should have happened after he said what he said, is that you should have fallen into his arms and told him you loved him, too, and the pair of you should be living happily ever after by now. Because that's how it goes, right? We spend our whole lives being told by every film, every song, every book that when you meet *the one* that's it, you know? The happy ending is guaranteed. But it's not, is it?'

Nora doesn't know what to say to that.

'So, I'm not mad at you. I would be if I thought you'd led him on, but you didn't. I've seen the way you look at him. So, as difficult as this is for Sendhil, I respect you for not charging into this only to find, when the summer's over and he won't turn the heating on because he's trying to save the planet and you're arguing about whose turn it is to get up and feed the cats, that it isn't the life you thought it was going to be. Because that's the thing.'

Alice uncrosses her arms to point at her. 'Before you meet someone, you have a life and they have a life. I mean, you came here for the summer and met a guy. This mean, moody, monosyllabic guy who isn't mean or moody or monosyllabic at all, once he gives you a chance to get to know him. And he did. So now what? In an ideal world, your lives would blend together seamlessly, but when does that ever happen? You had dreams before you met Sendhil. Things you wanted to do. Places you wanted to go. Things you wanted to see. What happens to those things if he doesn't want them as well?

'The same thing happened to me, Nora. I came here for a week, two summers ago, to see Sendhil, met Megan and I never left. Luckily, she didn't know what she was doing with her life and I didn't know what I was doing with mine, so we decided to figure it out together,' she confesses. 'But this is way more complicated than that and I get that. I do.

'So, take your time,' Alice says, then points at Nora's phone in her hand. 'But, *please*, until you know what you're going to say to him, you have to leave him alone.'

Chapter 18

Of all the things to undo Nora, it's a bulb of garlic. She was doing so well. It's been a month since she came home and she's been so busy trying to keep up with the treadmill of London. Always running. Always late. Always saying *Sorry!* or *Excuse me!* That Nora hasn't even thought about how seamlessly she slipped back into her old life. As soon as Ron rolled past Richmond Green that was it. The peace of Pidwell was forgotten in favour of her old routine. Work. Spin on Saturday mornings. Lunch with her parents on Sundays. Dumplings with Luce and Ben during the week.

Her old routine, except now she doesn't have to make the sign of the cross before she walks into the Whitechapel Gallery because Fran is a *dream* compared to Roland. Nora has learned more in the last month than she did in four years at Redchurch. Watching Fran put the Yinka Shonibare exhibition together, confirming that this is what she wants to do.

That Fran is who she wants to be.

She's *brilliant*. Patient enough to explain when she asks Nora to do something she hasn't done before, but intuitive enough to take a step back when she has. She's generous with her time and praise, and she actually says thank you. Roland didn't say thank you once in the four years Nora was at Redchurch, let alone bring her a latte every morning and send her a text every evening to thank her for the work she'd done that day.

Nora was doing *so* well. But here she is, standing outside a shop on Kingsland Road on a Saturday afternoon, trying not to cry at a bulb of garlic. She doesn't know why Proust gets a madeleine and she gets garlic, but it is what it is: looking at it sends her back to Pidwell. Back to standing next to Sendhil in his kitchen as he holds up a bulb to her and insists that putting the cloves in a jam jar and shaking it isn't the fastest way to peel them. Back to flicking him with a tea-towel and ignoring the shiver she feels at the nearness of him.

Nora tries to swallow the pearl of pain that's suddenly lodged in her throat as she reaches for a bulb, but as soon as she does, she hears someone say her name and drops it.

She looks up, expecting to find Luce with whatever she'd just left in the salon.

But it's Charlie from Redchurch and she can't believe how pleased she is to see him.

'Nora! It is you!'

He seems just as pleased to see her and pulls her into a hug, even though they never hugged once in the eight months he worked at Redchurch before she quit. But here they are, clinging to one another like it's the end of the film and they survived the serial killer.

Not that Nora is calling Roland a serial killer, but the sentiment remains the same.

'Where you off to?' he asks when he steps back, then thumbs over his shoulder at the café he must have just left. 'You got time for a coffee?'

She's startled. She'd thought it would be one of those *It's so great to see you! Let's have coffee soon!* exchanges where they say that because that's what you say, but have no intention of seeing each other again. She's so stunned that she says yes.

As soon as they walk into the café, Charlie bellows, 'I was right! It was her!'

For one dreadful moment, she thinks it's Roland, but it's Jonathan Bodham. The guy who was buying art for his new place in Spitalfields the afternoon she quit Redchurch. He's slumped in a booth, looking impossibly cool in a black leather hoodie, his long, dark hair piled into a bun on top of his head. His face lights up when he sees her, and when he leaps out of the booth, she recoils, thinking he's going to hug her as well.

But he just says, 'Nora! We were *just* talking about you!'

'You were?' She frowns.

'Coffee?' he asks, when she slides into the booth beside Charlie.

'A latte would be lovely, actually.'

Jonathan turns to the counter. 'Can we get a latte, please, Jack?' He slides in, the table between them. 'Mate, how wild is this?'

'I know,' Charlie says. 'We were *just* talking about her.'

'Me?' Nora asks again, slightly concerned that Jonathan remembers who she is.

'This is Fate!' He slaps the table. 'This can't be a coincidence!'

'Right?' Charlie turns to Nora. 'We thought you were still in Cornwall.'

'How did you know I was in Cornwall?' she asks him, even more concerned now.

'I follow you on Instagram. Pidwell looks blissful.'

Nora ignores the twinge she feels and tries her best to smile. 'It's lovely.'

'My parents have a place in Lostwithiel so I've been to Cornwall loads of times,' Jonathan tugs the sleeves of his hoodie up to his elbows, 'but I'd never heard of Pidwell.'

'How was the festival?' Charlie asks as someone appears at the booth with her latte.

'I heard it was amazing,' Charlie says, as she reaches for a packet of sugar. 'I'm gutted we missed it, but I'm glad JoBo and I got to see the Achari before it goes.'

Nora almost spills the sugar as she tears into it. 'You saw it?'

Charlie nods. 'Yeah. We swung by a few weeks ago on our way back to London.'

'From Cornwall?'

'Yeah. A group of us went to Fistral Beach to surf now the tourists have gone.'

'It was incredible,' Jonathan says, his eyes bright. 'Achari is a genius!'

Charlie nods more enthusiastically this time. 'I'm *so jealous* you got to work with him.'

Nora sips her coffee, but doesn't say anything. Actually, she *can't* say anything. She just felt something come loose when she was standing outside the shop, trying not to cry at a bulb of garlic, so if she says his name out loud, she's terrified she'll unravel altogether.

She'd thought it would be easier in London, when she didn't have to go back to the cottage every evening to find his lights off and the cats yowling on the doorstep. But it isn't at all. There are fewer reminders, sure, but, in the end, it doesn't matter where she is because, as she learned outside the shop, even a bulb of garlic will send her back there.

Nora hasn't kept in touch with Alice, which is a shame, but unsurprising given she's staunchly Team Sendhil, and rightly so. So, Nora is at the mercy of her uncles who, blissfully unaware of the whole ordeal, tell her about everything – and *everyone* – but him. How the Trefelyn is booked until the end of the year. How Annabelle has adopted another adrift sculptor who arrived in Pidwell one day, saying she couldn't go home. They even tell her about Kate, who's just returned from a silent retreat at a monastery in the South of France, but lasted all of twenty-two hours before checking into the Hôtel du Palais in Biarritz.

Not a word about Sendhil, though.

'We haven't seen him,' they simply say, whenever she's brave enough to ask.

'So, while Charlie was stalking you on Instagram,' Jonathan says, tugging Nora back, 'he saw that you're at the Whitechapel Gallery.'

'Yeah.' Her shoulders fall now they've changed the subject and she won't have to hear – or say – his name. 'I'm working on the Yinka Shonibare exhibition.'

'No way!' Charlie says. 'I'm JoBo's plus one for the pre-view next week.'

Of course Jonathan's invited to the preview, Nora thinks, trying not to roll her eyes. She's managing the guest list, so she should have known. Not that she's had time to check each of the eight hundred odd names on it.

Jonathan curses under his breath, frowning at his phone.

'Is it half one already? I have to go soon. I've got to be at the Savoy for afternoon tea for my mother's birthday. I can't show up in this.'

'They know you,' Charlie says. 'They'll let you in.'

'Yeah, but my grandmother will be there and if I show up wearing this,' he gestures at his hoodie, 'she'll ask me if I've joined a gang. And after what happened in Mexico . . .'

Charlie actually guffaws at that and almost chokes on the green juice he's drinking.

'Speaking of Mexico, that's kind of related to what we wanted to talk to you about, babe,' Jonathan says, with a well-rehearsed smile that he no doubt thinks will make Nora immediately acquiesce to whatever he's about to ask.

'You don't know me well enough to call me "babe",' she tells him, sipping her coffee.

Jonathan's eyes brighten at the challenge. 'Sorry, *Nora*.'

Charlie holds his green juice up to him. 'Excellent start, JoBo.'

He's unfazed, though. 'So, I was on this farm in Oaxaca last month. Don't ask why.'

'I wasn't going to. What you do on farms in Mexico is entirely your business.'

Charlie laughs and holds his green juice up to Nora this time.

To his credit, Jonathan takes it on the chin and carries on: 'So, I'm on this farm in Oaxaca and I get arrested. Again, don't ask why.'

Again, she wasn't going to.

'My father almost had a stroke about having to fly out there and bail me out. And, when we got home, he threatened to revoke access to my trust fund.'

'Oh, the horror,' Nora says.

Jonathan smirks, then says, 'He gave me the speech about how I have to stop partying and do something with my life. Get a proper job. So, I've invested in an idea Charlie had.'

The idea is an app that is essentially Etsy for high-end art to bridge the gap between people who want more than a print but are put off by galleries like Redchurch. Jonathan and Charlie think – and Nora agrees – that the days of bricks-and-mortar galleries are coming to an end. They'll always be around, but people their age prefer to shop online. And while a three-thousand-pound painting is hardly an impulse buy, if someone will spend that much on a Saint Laurent coat from Net-a-Porter, why not a painting?

Charlie and Jonathan want to support it with quarterly pop-up exhibitions around the country that will not only promote the brand and local artists but will also include events and panels with industry experts and other artists offering advice about everything from networking to not undervaluing your work so people like Roland don't screw you over.

Everything you don't learn in art school, basically.

'That sounds amazing,' Nora tells them, when the pair of them stop for breath.

And, like all good ideas, she's stunned that no one's thought to do it already.

Then Jonathan flashes her that smile again. 'You wanna come onboard?'

Nora laughs. But when he doesn't join in, she stares at him. 'Me?'

'Yeah!' he says, as though it should be obvious. 'We need you, Nora. We need a …'

Need a what? she asks herself suspiciously, when he trails off.

'An adult.' Charlie shrugs helplessly. 'We don't have a clue what we're doing.'

Okay, Nora thinks, as she puts her cup down. They want her to do what she did at Redchurch. Be a glorified office manager, basically, who'll clean up after them and answer the phone and pay the bills so the lights aren't cut off.

'Thanks, but I have a job,' she reminds them, with a smug smile.

Granted, it's only until the exhibition ends, but Fran is taking her for lunch next week for a 'catch-up', so who knows?

Jonathan holds up his hands. 'Hear us out, okay?'

Charlie takes over. 'I'm going to handle the digital stuff and JoBo's gonna be in a prison in Mexico.' Jonathan grins, clearly unrepentant. 'So we need you to do what you do.'

'Which is?'

'Artist liaison and managing the pop-ups.'

Nora sits up then. 'Are you serious?'

'Yes!' Charlie nods at Jonathan, who reciprocates. 'You have impeccable taste and you're great with new artists. So, we need you to do what you did at Redchurch, but for us.'

She stares at him. 'What? Just looking for new artists and organising exhibitions?'

They nod.

'Like that's it. That's the job?'

'Actually,' Charlie says, 'the job doesn't exist so you can make it what you want.'

'The reason we need you,' Jonathan says, in a rare moment of sincerity, 'is because we're not going to have much control over the app. The whole point of it is to be the opposite of galleries like Redchurch. So, we don't want it to be exclusive or snobby, we want it to be open to everyone in the hope that the sort of artists you championed at Redchurch won't need to rely on the likes of Roland. They can sell their art themselves.'

'The trouble with that, though,' Charlie says, with a small sigh, 'is that by marketing it as open to everyone, it means that artists can add whatever they like.'

Nora winces.

'Exactly.' Jonathan points at her. 'So, we're investing most of our money on an algorithm that will identify the better stuff, but we have to be careful. I mean, we can't even filter for pornographic stuff in case we ban the next Lucian Freud, or something.'

Nora gets a flashback of Kate's painting and tries not to shudder.

'We can keep an eye out for anything illegal,' Charlie adds, 'but we can't police the quality, not when we're trying to be all,' he waves his hands, '*Art is for everyone!*'

'Hopefully the algorithm,' Jonathan tags in, 'will push the most popular, most ...' he pretends to clear his throat '... *skilled* artists to the top of the list.'

'Okay. So, you want me to find some ... ' She pretends to clear her throat as well. '...*skilled* artists. Let them know about the app and include them in the pop-up exhibitions, which will be more indicative of the brand, to attract more artists like them.'

'Yes!' Jonathan slaps the table. 'That's *exactly* what we need!'

'So what do you reckon, Nora? You in?' Charlie turns to her with an eager smile. 'We just secured Arts Council funding and we've already booked a gallery at next year's Affordable Art Fair, so we're legit, I promise. We wouldn't waste your time if we weren't.'

'This *has* to work,' Jonathan insists. 'It has to. If for no other reason than to prove to my father that this isn't another of my whims. I mean, I'm sinking everything I have into this so if it doesn't work I'll have to get an actual ...' he pretends to shudder '... job.'

Nora pretends to shudder as well. 'Perish the thought, Mr Bodham.'

'Exactly. So all of this makes us the perfect combination of loaded, desperate and clueless. Which also happens to be—'

'The title of JoBo's sex tape!' Charlie says, before he can.

Jonathan shakes his fist at him, then turns to Nora again. 'So?'

'Okay,' she says, then takes a deep breath as she tries not to get carried away by their enthusiasm. 'So, wait. How far along are you guys with this?'

'Once the algorithm is ready, we're good to go,' Jonathan says. 'We've got enough money to keep us afloat for two years while we get set up. The website's done. My friend Millie is going to be our CFO, so she's handling the financial stuff. My friend Victoria is doing the PR and marketing, and my father's lawyer is handling the legal stuff.'

Nora is surprised, but is still sceptical. 'I'll need to see a business plan.'

They nod.

'And I'll need to see how the app's going to work.'

They nod again.

'And what you promised to get the Arts Council funding.'

'Absolutely,' Jonathan promises.

'I need to know this is legit if I'm even going to consider it,' she warns them.

'Of course,' Charlie says this time. 'I can email it all to you when I get home.'

'What about offices? Do you know where you're going to be based?'

'We don't need offices,' Charlie tells her. 'This isn't like Redchurch. We're not actually exhibiting anything. Everything's virtual so we can work from home.'

To her astonishment, Jonathan adds, 'We'd rather spend the money on the algorithm.'

'Working from home, huh?' Nora says, hiding a smile behind her coffee cup. 'Well, not having to see you two every day is certainly a benefit. You should have led with that.'

Charlie chuckles. 'You'll be on the road most of the time so you can work anywhere.'

As soon as he says it, something occurs to her and it's like a door opening.

Nora can work anywhere.

Anywhere.

Is this it? she asks herself, her heart hysterical. *Is this Yeovil?*

But then Charlie and Jonathan bellow with laughter again, pulling her back.

'So, come on, Nora,' Charlie says, 'what do you reckon? You up for it?'

'Please. We're desperate. We need you.' Jonathan presses his palms together and holds them to his chest. 'Seriously. Just tell us what you want to be paid and we'll pay it.'

Charlie points at him and says, 'Which is also the title of JoBo's sex tape!'

'Okay.' She raises her voice as they hoot with laughter, then waits for them to stop. When they do, she raises her eyebrows. 'I'll think about it. In the meantime, I can tell you this now.' Nora points her coffee cup at Jonathan. 'I am not calling you "JoBo".'

He flashes her that smile again. 'You're very welcome to call me "babe", if you prefer.'

~*~

As soon as Nora leaves the café, she runs up Kingsland Road to Luce's salon. But she can see Luce is with a client, so motions at her through the window to call her. It's Saturday, though, so she doesn't have a chance to call until Nora's train is pulling into Richmond.

Luce is on a break, so they don't have much time as Luce chugs a can of Red Bull before her next client and Nora tells her about Charlie and Jonathan while she walks home.

When she's done, Luce is quiet for a moment or two. So quiet that Nora hears a bus pulling up and realises her friend must be standing on the pavement outside the salon.

Finally, Luce says, 'So, Pidwell's back in the game.'

Nora grins. 'She's scrappy.'

'The comeback kid.'

That's actually kind of perfect, given that's why they all ended up there. Trying to find their way back.

But then Nora sighs. 'Not that I even know if there's a game for Pidwell to be back in,' she realises, with a sore sigh. 'I mean, it's been a month since I got home.'

'Sendhil told you to take all the time you need,' Luce reminds her.

'I know he did, but what if I've taken *too much* time and he's given up?'

'Then he's an arsehole,' Luce says.

She's right, Nora knows, but the thought still makes each step a little heavier as she heads up the chequerboard path towards her front door. When she closes it behind her, she stands in the hall for a second and waits, grateful to find the house still. No one calls to check if it's her. She can't hear the vacuum cleaner upstairs or the radio in the kitchen or the steady snip, snip, snip of her father's secateurs in the garden.

These old, familiar sounds that became new and unexpected when she came home.

'I've got, like, three minutes until my next client,' Luce tells her as Nora toes off her trainers and heads up to her room. 'So, come on. Let's get straight to it.'

'Okay,' she says, throwing herself on her bed and looking up at the ceiling. 'Go.'

'The way I see it, you're back to square one, Nor.' That makes Nora's heart sag. 'Yeah, you've found a way that you can live in Pidwell and still keep doing what you love, but now it's no longer a case of Pidwell versus London. It's the Whitechapel Gallery versus Charlie and Jonathan, which will then decide whether you go to Pidwell or stay here.'

Nora groans, grabbing a cushion and hugging it.

'But first,' Luce says sharply, 'I'm gonna ask you one thing.'

Nora stiffens. 'Okay.'

'Would you even consider Charlie and Jonathan's offer if it didn't mean you could live in Pidwell?'

Nora doesn't hesitate. 'Yes.'

Of that much, she's sure.

Yes, Charlie and Jonathan are young and have more money than sense, as her mother would say, but it's an *inspired* idea, and it's exactly the sort of thing she loves doing.

Luce seems satisfied with that. 'Okay. So, the Whitechapel Gallery. Pros.'

'It's one of my favourite galleries in London. They always take risks and support emerging artists. I'm learning so much. Fran is incredible. I want to be her when I grow up.'

'Cons?'

'I don't know what's going to happen when the exhibition ends—'

'Aren't you going for lunch with her next week?' Luce interrupts.

'Yes. So, we may need to review this list then.'

'Okay. Any other Cons?'

'As much as I love it,' Nora confesses, 'I miss working directly with artists. I mean, I'm sure I'll get to meet Yinka, but it's nothing like calling someone to tell them they've sold their first painting. Like Kofi Campbell. I saw his degree show at Chelsea, got Roland to show him, then, last year, he was nominated for the Hepworth Prize.'

'I guess that leads us neatly on to Charlie and Jonathan's Pros,' Luce notes.

'Well, yeah. I'll be working with artists again. Plus the job doesn't exist so I can make it my own. And I'd be doing everything I love. Everything I'm good at. And I'll be travelling, not stuck behind a desk at a gallery. Plus I really believe in this idea. If we can pull it off, it could change everything. So, being there at the start, watching it grow, will be amazing.'

'That's also a Con, though,' Luce says then.

'True,' Nora concedes. 'The Whitechapel Gallery is definitely the safer option. It has a solid reputation and will no doubt lead to other things. And, despite Charlie and Jonathan's endless enthusiasm, and budget, they've never done anything like this before, so it's a risk.'

'Sorry, Nor. I've got to go, I can see my client walking towards me. We'll finish this later, okay?' She stops to say, *Hey, babes!* then lowers her voice. 'It sounds to me like we've got another even split, but write down everything you just said and really think about it.'

As though Nora will be able to think about anything else.

~★~

If Nora was hoping that her lunch with Fran the following Friday was going to help her make her decision, it doesn't. Fran merely thanks her for her work, then announces she's pregnant.

With that, the Whitechapel Gallery ceases to be the 'safe bet'. And while Fran asks Nora to stay on after the Yinka Shonibare exhibition to help with the transition when she goes on maternity leave, it's only a six-month contract. And, yes, as Luce pointed out, it would likely to lead to another, but it's still a risk, especially if Fran's replacement is another Roland.

Needless to say, Nora is still thoroughly confused.

It doesn't help that Luce and Ben are evenly split. Nor does it help that they land on the exact opposite of what she was expecting. Brave, relentlessly restless Luce, who changes jobs almost as often as her hair colour, thinks Charlie and Jonathan are, to use their own words against them, loaded, desperate and clueless. Whereas her judicious, hopelessly practical younger brother, having done a lot of research – and read all the stuff Charlie sent Nora – thinks there's a gap in the market for a platform like that and she should go for it.

They've been bickering about it all evening over dumplings. So, when Nora returns home to find her parents curled up on the sofa, drinking red wine and listening to Chopin, it's exactly what she needs. She sits with them awhile, but as she excuses herself, saying she should get to bed, her mother tells her there's some post for her on the island in the kitchen.

'One of them looks important,' she says. 'Special Delivery.'

Nora grabs the pile on her way up to her room and, sure enough, on top of the pile of bank statements, bills and a catalogue from a website she ordered from three years ago, but hasn't used since, is a heavy white envelope, her address written in elegant, sloping script.

Who's getting married? she wonders, then wonders why a wedding invitation is so urgent that someone needed to send it to her via Special Delivery.

As soon as she slides the card out of the envelope, she drops it as though it's burned her fingers, then covers her mouth with her hand, unsure if she just read what she read. So, she reads it again, then grabs her phone and texts Luce twenty red alarm emojis.

Before Nora has even sat on the edge of her bed, Luce isn't just calling.

She FaceTimes.

'What?' she asks, her eyes wide. 'What's wrong? Who died?'

Nora is still too stunned to speak, so is relieved when Luce tells her to hold on and disappears off-screen. 'I'm mid double cleanse, so let me put you on the shelf.'

As soon as Luce reappears, she asks Nora again, 'What? What's wrong? Who died?'

Nora still hasn't recovered enough to speak, so just holds up the invitation to her.

'What's that? I can't see it.'

That should be obvious to Nora, given Luce is smearing off mascara with a cotton pad.

'It looks like a wedding invitation,' Luce says, as she continues to rub her right eyelid. When Nora shakes her head, she looks confused. 'What is it? Who's it from?'

Nora has to wait until she's caught her breath, then says, 'Sendhil.'

She hears something clatter as Luce shrieks, 'Sendhil's getting married?'

'No,' Nora gasps, lightheaded at the thought. 'It's an invitation to his opening.'

'Opening of what?'

'His gallery.'

'Gallery? Did you know he was opening a gallery?'

'No.'

'Read it to me right now!'

Nora's hands are shaking so much, it takes a moment for the words to focus.

'"Nora Armstrong, you are cordially invited to the opening of the Penzance Arts Club, a gallery and events space for local artists, musicians and writers to collaborate and create."'

'Wait. I thought it was the *Pidwell* Arts Club?' Luce points out.

It was.

Meredith started the *Pidwell* Arts Club.

Nora's shoulders jump up then and she gasps as she remembers the conversation she'd had with her uncles the morning after she arrived in Pidwell: they'd told her that Sendhil was starting the New Pidwell Arts Club, not the Penzance Arts Club.

Even so, Sendhil never said a word to her and it stings more than it should.

'Maybe he couldn't call it that,' Nora wonders aloud, as she looks down at the invitation. 'The Pidwell Arts Club is *so* Meredith. Maybe it didn't feel right.'

'Why Penzance, though?'

'There are more artists there, I suppose. Pidwell's tiny. There are only a few.'

So, that was why he was going back and forth to Penzance so much.

'When's the opening?' Luce asks, raising her voice over the sound of the tap running.

Nora checks. 'Saturday, October the twelfth.'

'October the twelfth? That's *tomorrow*, Nor!'

'Tomorrow?'

'Talk about leaving it until the last minute,' Luce says, as she rubs what looks like cleansing balm over her face. 'He must have really agonised over whether or not to send it.' She buries her face in a washcloth and sighs.

Nora uses the opportunity to smile as she wonders how many stress naps he had to take before he decided to send it to her.

'What else does it say?' Luce asks, as she wipes under her eyes with the washcloth.

'"Saturday, October the twelfth,"' Nora reads aloud. '"Eight p.m. Fifty-seven Chapel Street, Penzance. Evening hosted by Sendhil Achari. Come as you are."'

'That's it? No *Hope you can come* or *Are you going to pick me or not, Nora?*'

Nora turns the invitation over and almost drops it again.

'What?' Luce gasps. 'Did he write something?'

Nora can only manage a nod as her heart throws itself at her ribs.

'What? What did he say?'

'"Please come." Signed S with two kisses.'

It's so him. Nothing – just a couple of words – but everything, all at once.

'*Two* kisses?'

Nora nods again. 'What do you think it means?'

'I think it means your time's up.'

'Oh, God.' Nora presses her hand to her forehead and squeezes her eyes shut.

'You have to go,' Luce tells her, and she's right.

Of course she's right, Nora thinks, as she opens her eyes and takes her hand from her forehead to look back at the invitation. She reads the words – *Please come* – over and over, grazing the pad of her index finger over them, gently, careful not to disturb the ink, seeking out the indentation from the pen as she tries to picture him writing them.

She has to go, doesn't she?

He's reaching out. It would be cruel to ignore him.

But then it would also be cruel to go, if she's not going to stay.

'Yeah, but what am I going to say?' Nora whimpers. 'I still don't know what to do.'

'Yes, you do,' Luce tells her, with a slow smile. 'You've always known.'

She scoffs at that. 'No, I haven't. I've been reeling since he told me.'

'That doesn't mean you didn't know.'

'Luce, what are you talking about?'

'All this indecision, Nora. Can you live in Pidwell? Can you leave London? Back and forth. Back and forth. For weeks. But what was the one thing you were sure of?'

'What?' Nora asks, because she honestly doesn't know.

'Sendhil.' Luce shrugs. 'We did lists for Pidwell and London. We even did one for your jobs, but we never did one for him. Because you didn't need to do one for him, did you?'

Because Nora already knew.

Chapter 19

In a way, Sendhil giving her twenty-four hours' notice is a good thing, because it means she has no time to overthink it. The next morning, Nora is in Ron, bombing up the A303, singing along to Tracy Chapman. She makes such good time that she asks herself if she can get to the cheese shop before it closes. She checks and it closes at five. So, if she continues at this rate, she can get there before it shuts and still make it to the Trefelyn in plenty of time to get ready.

But as soon as she thinks it, she angers the traffic gods who decide to punish her for being so cocky. 'No,' she whimpers, as the cars ahead of her on the A303 slow.

Three hours later, she's still sitting in the same spot, stuck behind, she discovers when she googles it, a pile-up on the Honiton bypass. This section of the A303 is only two lanes, with fields either side. So most people have given up and turned off their engines and some, like Nora, are leaning against their cars, hissing into their phones. There's not much Luce can do other than sympathise, but it helps. As does reminding her that *this* is why the long-distance thing was never an option. There's no way she and Sendhil could have taken it in turns to do this every weekend before one of them snapped and drove into the sea.

By the time she's moving again, it's getting dark. Even if she drove for the next two and a half hours without interruption, there's still no way Nora will make it to the party in time, let alone to Pidwell to get ready first. She's forced to change in the toilet of a supermarket about five minutes from the gallery. Which is hardly glamorous, but wholly necessary given that she hasn't seen Sendhil for six weeks and is absolutely not showing up in jeans and her dad's Oxford sweatshirt, which is older than she is.

Isn't it just like her? She had plenty of time yet here she is, whacking her elbow on the wall of a tiny toilet that smells of dirty nappies and something else that Nora really doesn't want to consider, while someone bangs on the door outside, telling her to hurry up.

It's dark by the time Nora trots across the car park. Luckily her dirty pink (that's what Luce calls this colour, but Nora prefers dusky pink) satin dress is just past her knees, with a split she hoped would flash just enough thigh, but is now proving to be quite helpful for running.

She adjusts the thin straps as soon as she jumps back into the car and glances into the rear-view mirror to find that at least her makeup has survived the nine-hour journey, which is something. So, after a quick blot and a smear of lip gloss, she's on the road again.

Four minutes later, she finally pulls into Quay Street car park. The one Sendhil parked in the first time he drove them there. She looks for his truck, but there's no sign of it and she tells herself not to panic. It's his gallery opening. Of course he'll be there.

Then she's in such a hurry to get out of the car that she almost forgets to grab her clutch and leather jacket from the passenger seat – because this is it. After weeks of reeling, she finally knows exactly what she wants and it's all she can do not to run towards it.

Nora knows Chapel Street because there's an art shop and a few other galleries, which she found when she was handing out posters for the festival. It's not even a five-minute walk, which she hopes is enough time to compose herself before she sees him again.

But when she finally approaches Chapel Street, she sees his pickup and her heart hammers, each step slightly quicker than the last as she walks towards it. She stops on the pavement, resisting the urge to press her palm to the glass as she peers inside, smiling when she sees his sunglasses on the dashboard and his beach towel slung on the back seat.

Nora looks up and there it is – the Penzance Arts Club – on the other side of the road.

For a moment, she could be back in London. There's a vibration in the air that she's never felt in Penzance as laughter rolls out of the open door and a group of people stand outside, talking and smoking, wine glasses in their hands.

'Excuse me,' she says, slipping between them.

'Love this for you,' a guy dressed from head to toe in black says, gesturing at her dress.

Before she can thank him, he returns to his conversation, so Nora trots up the steps to find it's a mess of people inside. She doesn't recognise any of them and she wonders how Sendhil is coping because he must *hate* this, the room packed, everyone gathered in tight knots, chatting furiously. Every now and then, there's a bellow of laughter and she wonders if he's retreated to a corner somewhere and Alice is reminding him that the host of a party actually has to speak to people.

Much like Redchurch, it's a very white, very square gallery, but this one has a staircase along the back wall that, Nora assumes, leads up to the collaborative spaces. Maybe that's where he's hiding, she wonders, as she looks for him, standing on tiptoe to see past the wall of people in front of her. But then she hears someone call out her name and Nora looks to her left to find a woman walking towards her, her arms open.

'Nora!' Mrs Stroud gasps, hugging her tightly. Nora lets her, surprised at how much affection she feels for her, given that they've never actually met. But after living in her house, much like Sendhil moving around next door, Mrs Stroud was always there. In every mug, every pillow, every fridge magnet. So, it's like bumping into an old roommate.

Except the best kind because Mrs Stroud never played loud music or ate her cheese.

Mrs Stroud, Nora is thrilled to learn, is exactly what she imagined. Small and soft-hipped with short curly grey hair. Except she doesn't have the slightly chaotic edge Annabelle has. Mrs Stroud has a grandmotherly energy that instantly calms Nora. The sort of woman who can be relied upon for a Murray Mint and a clean hanky, if you ever need one.

'Lovely to finally meet you, Nora,' Mrs Stroud says, when she lets go. The skin around her brown eyes crinkles as she smiles up at Nora and that calms her as well.

'You too, Mrs Stroud.' Nora wrinkles her nose at her. 'And thank you for the flowers.'

'Oh, you got them.'

'Yes! They were lovely, but you didn't have to.'

'Of course I did.' She frowns, then her face softens and her eyes crinkle as she smiles at Nora again. 'Thank you for taking such good care of Oliver while I was gone.'

'It was my pleasure. How is he? And Dodger, of course? I kind of miss them, actually.'

Mrs Stroud rolls her eyes. 'Holy terrors!'

Before Nora can ask anything else, she hears someone screech, *Nooooorrrrraaaaaa!* And looks up to see her uncle Mark, turning this way and that, trying not to spill the glass of red wine he's holding in the air as he slides through the crowd towards her.

'Told you it was Nora!' he calls, over his shoulder, when he gets to her.

Then there's her uncle James, doing the same thing, yelling, *Nooooorrrrraaaaaa!*

Well, she thinks, with a chuckle, *if Sendhil didn't know I'm here, he does now.*

Most of Penzance does.

They jump on her, telling her how much they miss her, even though she saw them two weeks ago when she helped them pack up their house in Richmond. And it isn't until that moment that she realises how much she's missed them as well. She's been so caught up with Sendhil that she forgot they're the reason she ended up in Pidwell in the first place.

'Hello?' James mock-gasps, a hand to his chest. 'Who is this goddess?'

He's tipsy, she realises. They both are, actually. But nice tipsy. Happy tipsy. Silly tipsy.

'Um, excuse me, Miss Armstrong!' Mark feigns shock, taking Nora's hand and forcing her to give him a twirl so he can see her dress. 'I'd forgotten you had legs!'

'And shoulders!' James mock-gasps again, before gulping down some wine.

'Too much skin?' Nora leans in, lowering her voice as she fusses over the straps.

'Not at all! You look divine,' James tells her. 'Show it off, queen!'

Mark looks appalled. 'What is it about free wine that makes you amp up the camp?'

'I don't know,' he says, with a theatrical sigh. 'All I know is that we haven't been out since we celebrated selling our house in Richmond so please let me enjoy my free wine.'

They resume telling her how lovely she looks, which is exactly the boost she needs. And perfectly timed, because Nora looks up as the crowd parts, like the Red Sea, and there he is. Striding their way, looking *devastating* in a black suit and white shirt, open at the neck.

Nora has to reach for Mark's arm to steady herself. Not that he notices: he and James are standing with their backs to him, chatting away, blissfully unaware that he's approaching.

She is, though. Very aware. Her heart, her hands, her legs trembling, all at once, as he finds her gaze from across the room and holds it as he closes the space between them.

In a few more steps, he'll be there and it's not enough time to take him all in. Only enough to note that he's cut his hair. Just an inch. Maybe two. Not enough that anyone other than her is likely to notice, but enough that the weight of his curls is no longer pulling them down into his eyes. But everything else about him is exactly as she remembers. The ink dot on his cheekbone. The shadow of stubble along his jaw. The soft sweep of his bottom lip.

Then that's it. He's there. Right in front of her. Her heart leaping up, like, *It's him!*

He's carrying a chair, she notices as he puts it down.

'Here you go, Mrs Stroud,' he says gently. 'You sit here by the door where it's cooler.'

He reaches for Mrs Stroud's elbow, waiting for her to sit, with a relieved *oof*, before he lets go again, and Nora feels a punch of pride so dizzying that it brings tears to her eyes because look at him, his hand on Mrs Stroud's shoulder, asking if she needs anything.

Then his arm is around her waist and it happens so quickly that Nora can only gasp as the space between them closes and, in one smooth motion, he pulls her to him, his mouth to the shell of her ear. 'Thank you for coming,' he breathes, and she shivers against him, the heat of him – the heat, the smell, the nearness – making her reach for his lapel and hold on.

'Of course,' she manages, finally able to lift her chin to look up at him.

As soon as she does, their eyes meet and she sees his jaw clench as she feels his arm tighten around her waist. She lets out another little gasp when it does, so close to him now that he must be able to feel her heart beating because she can certainly feel his.

'Not now,' he says into her ear, his breath making her shiver again.

Nora has to force herself to nod because after waiting for six weeks – and 279 miles, not that she looked it up or anything – she suddenly can't wait another second.

'See you later at the Trefelyn?' he says.

She nods again.

Then he's gone.

~*~

They spend the rest of the evening orbiting one another, their gaze catching every now and then across the room as Nora floats from one conversation to the next.

Everyone's there, each of them hugging her and asking question after question about London and the exhibition and telling her how pleased they are that she's visiting for the weekend. Even Kate's there, in a floor-length white silk gown that Nora is terrified to stand too close to in case she steps on it as Kate tells her about her silent retreat.

For a silent retreat, she has rather a lot to say about it, especially given she didn't even last a day.

Everyone talks to her but Alice, who sidesteps Nora every time she gets near and disappears into the crowd. Eventually, Nora takes the hint and stops trying, spending the rest of the evening chatting to everyone but him about how great the gallery is.

When Nora's uncles tell her they have to leave to set up for what they're referring to as the Afterparty, she won't let them call a cab and offers to give them a lift back to the Trefelyn. Mark asks if they'll need to lean forward up the hills with three of them in Ron.

Ordinarily, for that, she'd leave him to get a cab, but she needs to get out of there: every time Sendhil looks at her across the gallery, it's as though he's lit a match and flicked it in her direction. And if he looks at her like that one more time, she's going to charge over there and do something she really shouldn't in front of all these people.

As soon as they get back to the Trefelyn, Nora retreats to her room to freshen up. But what she actually does is pace back and forth for twenty minutes, stress-eating a KitKat.

When she's brave enough to come downstairs, the library is full and 'I Want You Back' by the Jackson 5 is blaring. Nora didn't know what to expect from the After-party (after all, she's never been to a gallery opening with an afterparty), but it's her uncles, so Mark has obviously been cooking all day and everyone's already dancing.

But there's no sign of Sendhil.

'Glass of champs, courtesy of Lady Kate?' James says, appearing at her side.

'Please,' Nora says, trying not to snatch the champagne saucer from him.

Then she tries not to drink it too quickly, but she's so nervous, she fails horribly.

'That's it. Get it down you, girl,' he tells her, refilling her glass as soon as she drains it. 'Lady Kate had a whole case delivered earlier. It'd be a shame to waste it.'

He saunters off with the bottle as Nora does what she did at the gallery, floating from one person to the next, following the flow of conversation, but not listening to a word.

An hour later, Sendhil still isn't there and Nora doesn't know if it's the four glasses of champagne she's had on an empty stomach or if she's sick with worry that he's not going to show up, but the library is spinning in a way that makes her feel less steady on her heels.

So, she decides to go outside for some air.

Or she tries to, but someone steps into her path.

'Why are you here?' Alice asks, standing between Nora and the door.

She takes a step back.

'I know he invited you,' Alice says, her jaw clenching. 'But you'd better be damn sure.'

'I'm sure.' She looks Alice in the eye, meeting her gaze and holding it.

They stare at each other for a moment longer than is comfortable, until Alice finally steps aside to let her pass and Nora realises why she was trying to stop her going outside.

There he is.

He has his back to her, the moon hanging over him, as he looks out at the sea. Nora realises then that even with his back to her she knows him. Knows the way his thick black curls start from his crown then flow up and out like waves. Knows his steady, sure shoulders. Knows his back, which she held onto the night of the storm, hands cupping his sharp shoulder-blades as he breathed her name into her ear like no one ever has before.

He turns to her, and when he looks at her, Nora wonders what he knows about her.

What he sees.

They stand there for a minute or two, looking at one another. Everything behind the door – the champagne and Tommy and Van dancing to 'Bad Romance' and the look on Alice's face when she asked Nora if she was sure – gone and it's just them, at last.

Luce is right. All those weeks of indecision and lists – Pidwell, London, this life, that life – was just noise. Now, here in the dark, the moon watching, Nora can hear what she wants.

And all she can hear is *him*.

'You came,' he says.

'I came.'

She smiles, but he doesn't. She keeps smiling because he's going to. He's going to walk over to her, kiss her under the moon until her feet leave the ground because he asked her to come and she came and why isn't he smiling?

The corners of her mouth fall. 'I thought you wanted me to, Sendhil.'

'I did,' he says, with a shrug. 'But now you're here, I'm not so sure.'

Nora has no idea how she remains upright because that almost knocks her off her feet.

When he shakes his head and turns away, something shifts. But it's not a crack, like the one that appeared after they kissed at the cove. It's a whisper. A rush of air passing between them. Like, for the first time since they began orbiting one another, they don't collide.

They miss.

Nora waits for him to turn back to her, but when he does, he looks at her in the way Alice just looked at her and Nora has to take a step back, as though trying to avoid a punch.

She takes another step back and another until she turns and walks back into the light, through the library and up the stairs and, again, it's all gone. The music. Tommy and Van dancing to whatever it is they're dancing to now. All of it replaced by an aching stretch of white noise as Nora asks herself how this happened. What changed between him sending that invitation and her standing in front of him, waiting for him to smile back at her.

Nora sweeps into her room, but when she tries to shut the door behind her, she can't. It's him, his palm against the door, following her in.

'What are you doing?' he asks, as she walks over to the chair and grabs her holdall.

She hasn't even been here long enough to unpack it, she realises, snatching her leather jacket and clutch off the bed and turning to face him.

'I'm going home,' she tells him, trying to walk around him.

But he gets in her way. 'Nora, don't go.'

'Oh, so *now* you want me to stay?' she says, trying to walk around him again.

Again, he doesn't let her. 'Of course I want you to stay!'

Sendhil reaches for her arm and misses as she finally manages to slip around him and they both charge to the door, then stop when they see Lottie passing in the hall. She stops as well, and it's the first time Nora has seen her looking anything other than completely sullen, her lips pursing into a mischievous smirk and her eyebrows rising when she sees them.

'What's going on here, then?' she asks, peering into the room.

'Night, Lottie,' Sendhil mutters, slamming the door.

Then he turns to Nora and takes a step to the side to stop her leaving again. 'Of course I want you to stay,' he tells her.

That makes her pause. 'So, what was all of that about outside?'

'I'm sorry, Nora. I shouldn't have sent you that invitation.'

Now she's confused again. 'Wait. What? So, you *didn't* want me to come?'

'I wanted you to come because *you* wanted to come, not because *I* invited you.'

'What difference does it make? Surely all that matters is that I'm here, Sendhil.'

'But would you be here tonight if I hadn't sent you that invitation?'

'Not tonight—' she starts, but he throws up his hands as if to say, *See?*

'Exactly!'

'Not *exactly*,' she says, parroting his accent, then throwing her stuff on the bed before she throws it at him. 'I might not have come *tonight*, but I would have come eventually.'

He seems startled by that and takes a step back, his lips parted.

Then he shakes his head and takes one towards her again.

'How was I supposed to know? I put myself out there when you know . . .' he points at her '. . . you *know* I don't do that with anyone, then I don't hear from you for *six weeks*.'

'That is not fair, Sendhil!' She points back. 'You told me I needed time! Before I left your cottage the night of the storm, you told me to take as much time as I needed!'

'I didn't think you'd need this long, though. I mean, *six weeks*, Nora. Come on.'

'That is not fair!' she tells him again, her hands balling into fists at her sides.

'*See*?' He points at her fists. 'This is why I don't like talking. Now *you*'re mad at *me*.'

'This isn't talking, Sendhil, this is yelling!' she clarifies. 'Also, I'm sorry it took me longer than *six weeks* to decide whether or not to give up my *whole life* and move to Pidwell!'

His whole face tightens as he blinks at her. 'What?'

'It's a big decision, Sendhil! It's okay for you. You know where you want to be. I thought I did too and it was London until I met you. My family is there. My friends. My career. I'm sorry it took me longer than *six weeks* before I was ready to give all of that up!'

'What are you talking about, Nora?'

Judging by the way he's looking at her, he really has no idea, and Nora wants to scream because she doesn't know how else to say it.

But then he takes a step back. 'No. What? *No.* Is *that* why I haven't heard from you, Nora? Did you think I was telling you that to be with me you had to move to Pidwell?'

'Yes!'

'Why in God's name would you think that?'

'Why wouldn't I, Sendhil? I mean, you're never going to move to London, are you?'

'Why wouldn't I move to London?'

'Because every time anyone mentions London, you say you hate it.'

'Oh, that's true. I do do that,' he agrees, his hands on his hips.

'And remember, that afternoon you took me to cove for the first time, when you said that no one understood why you wouldn't move to London after you won the Turner Prize?'

'Yeah, I wouldn't move to London *for my career.* That's different.'

'How is that different?'

'Because I hate that everyone thinks you'll never make it if you don't move to London.'

'Wait.' Nora is thoroughly confused now. 'So, you do like London?'

'God, no. I hate it and everyone in it.' He looks appalled, but then shrugs. 'But I love you, so of course I'd have moved there if you'd asked me to.'

317

She's so stunned by that – *love* – that she can't speak.

Then he makes it worse by adding, 'I'd move to the moon to be with you, Nora.'

Before she can recover from that, he's in front of her.

'Hey. Hey. Hey,' he says softly, hand under her chin, tilting her head up. 'Look at me.'

When she does, he cups her face, sweeping away a tear with his thumb. 'I'm sorry I made you feel like I was giving you some sort of ultimatum. I would never do that, Nora.'

'Yeah, but you love Pidwell. I'd never make you leave the place you feel safe in.'

'And *that's* exactly why I adore you, Nora.' He stops to wipe away another tear and holds her face a little tighter. 'Because you'd *never* do that, would you? Because you know. You know I love it here. And I do. The light is like nowhere else in the world. And it has this energy. It's the place I'll always go back to work. To recharge. Realign.'

He waits for her to meet his gaze then says, 'Pidwell was a port in a storm. But you need light *and* shade for art. So, as much as I love how peaceful it is, I'm starting to realise I need some noise as well. Sometimes, I just want to sit in the back of a cab and listen to the driver complain about the roadworks. Or stand on a bridge, watching the trains come and go.'

'And sometimes,' he says, with a slow smile, 'I just wanna sit outside a pub with the perfect negroni on the first perfect day of the year with the perfect girl.'

Nora reaches for his wrists then, curling her fingers around them.

His pulse is wild, as if a tiny bird is trapped beneath his skin.

'So, I'd still like to live in Pidwell some of the time,' he says, 'because I love working here. But I don't need to be here *all* the time. Why'd you think I got involved in the festival? And opened the arts club? Because I'm ready to start, I don't know . . . living again, I guess. Hey.' He chuckles softly. 'Did I ever tell you what Meredith used to call me?'

Nora knows, but she wants to hear him tell the story.

'Little Sparrow,' he says, his dark eyes suddenly wet. 'Meredith said that when I arrived in Pidwell, I was like a bird that had flown into a bathroom and couldn't find my way out. But the truth is, I was quite happy flying around the bathroom. It was safe in the bathroom.'

Nora gets that. Maybe that's why she's still living at home. Not just because it's comfortable and there's hot water and nice cheese in the fridge, but because her parents will always forgive her – *always* – however awful the misdemeanour. Nora doesn't want to fall out with Luce over whose turn it is to take the bins out. Or end up stuck living with a terrible boyfriend because they have eight months left on their lease.

'Then you showed up,' he says, arching an eyebrow, 'and threatened me with that can of deodorant. And thank God you did. Otherwise I'd still be flying around that bathroom.'

He presses his forehead to hers and they stay like that for a few moments, Sendhil holding her face while she clasps his wrists. Then he kisses her forehead and looks at her.

'Okay, Nora. Just so we're clear. *You*'ve just spent the last six weeks going out of your mind thinking I was asking you to give up your whole life to be with me. And *I*'ve just spent the last six weeks going out of my mind thinking you couldn't decide if you liked me or not.'

She gasps, squeezing his wrists. 'Is that what you thought?'

'I thought I freaked you out with the whole kids-and-bench thing. I mean I *hoped* you liked me, but I thought you didn't know if you wanted it to be more than a summer thing.'

'Oh no,' Nora realises, her eyes wide. '*That*'s why Alice hates me.'

'She doesn't hate you.'

Nora tilts her head at him.

'Okay. Yeah. She totally hates you.'

When he laughs, Nora would smack him, but she doesn't want to let go of his wrists. 'Sendhil! It's not funny. I thought she was going to murder me a minute ago. If Archie is a Chihuahua in a Rottweiler suit, then Alice is a Rottweiler in a Chihuahua suit.'

'In fairness,' he winces, 'she doesn't know about the kids-and-bench thing.'

'What did you tell her happened, then?'

'That I told you I liked you and you needed to think about it.'

'Sendhil!'

'I'll fix it. I'll fix it.' He kisses her forehead again. 'I promise.'

'I'm so mad at you!'

'She'll forgive you, I promise.'

'Actually, I'm mad at both of us,' Nora confesses with a deep sigh.

Sendhil frowns. 'For what?'

'For not talking about this. For talking to everyone else but each other.'

He feigns shock. 'So, you mean blurting out all that stuff about kids and benches then avoiding you and running away to Cork until you left wasn't the mature way to deal with it?'

Nora really shouldn't laugh but she can't help it. 'I'm mad,' she tugs on his wrists, 'because if we'd talked, none of this would have happened. Knowing that I wanted to be with you was the easy bit. I knew I loved you the moment I saw your birds in the valley. Actually,' she admits, tilting her head from side to side, 'I knew when I tasted your coconut sambal.'

She laughs again, but he wrinkles his nose and smiles.

'What?' she asks when he does.

'Did you just say that you loved me, Nora Armstrong?'

Did she?

She didn't?

Did she?

She remembers saying something about coconut sambal.

'Well,' Nora panics and bats it back at him, 'you said it first.'

'When did I say I love you?'

'Just now. You said you hate London, but you love me.'

'See? This is why I don't like talking. You've got me saying all sorts.'

Nora sneaks a look at him from under her eyelashes. 'So, you don't love me, then?'

'Oh, no. I'm out of my mind in love with you in case that isn't obvious.'

It is now, she thinks, squeezing his wrists again as his pulse slows under her fingers. 'So,' she says, with a small shrug, 'you love me and I love you. What now?'

'I think we should go home, Nora Armstrong.'

'Where's home, then?'

They still haven't worked that one out yet, have they?

Although she suddenly isn't in as much of a hurry to decide.

'Wherever you want it to be, Nora,' Sendhil says.

But she doesn't believe him. 'Sure.'

'Really.'

'So, if I told you I wanted to live in London, you wouldn't complain?'

'Oh, no. I'd absolutely complain. But I'd still go.'

'How about if I told you I wanted to live in Yeovil?'

'No one *wants* to live in Yeovil, Nora. But it's the mid-point between London and here.'

'So, you looked it up as well?'

'Of course. I considered every option.'

'So, you'd live in Yeovil?'

'Yep.'

'No, you wouldn't!' Nora rolls her eyes because he's lying. There's *no way* he'd live in Yeovil. She might tell him she wants to live there out of spite just to see if he'll do it.

'I would,' Sendhil insists. 'Do you wanna know why?'

'Why?'

'You know when you jumped into that bush in the valley to avoid me?'

Nora gulps, mortified. 'You saw that?'

'Forget it. I ran away to Cork. We're even. Anyway, while you were diving into a bush, I was talking to Annabelle about Meredith. Actually, we were talking about you, which led to talking about Meredith and how Annabelle still doesn't feel like she's gone. She says it feels like she's just gone into the next room to get something and she'll be back.'

Nora's chin trembles and he pinches it between his forefinger and thumb.

'I've never lost anyone like that,' he says, 'so I had no idea what she meant until I got back from Cork and you'd gone. I'd hear Mrs Stroud moving around and think, *It's okay. Nora's only next door.* But every time I saw Mrs Stroud, I'd feel it all over again. The loss.'

He pinches her chin once more to stop it trembling. 'The first night I got back from Cork and you were gone, I realised I didn't have anyone to cook dinner for, so I had toast. And it was weird, because I'd gone from Cork, which used to be my home and didn't feel like it any more, back to Pidwell, which was the home I'd left Cork for, which didn't feel like home any more, either, now you weren't there. And do you know what I realised, Nora?'

When she shakes her head he says, 'I realised that maybe home isn't a place, you know? Like a physical place. Maybe it's just someone you wanna cook dinner for every night. So, I don't care where we live, as long as I cook dinner for you every night, Nora Armstrong.'

It's a moment before she can speak. 'You're getting much better at this talking thing.'

'Well, now I've proved that, can we go home, please?'

'In a second. I just want to do one thing first.'

'What now? Can't it wait? Jesus, Nora, it's been six weeks and I—'

She lets go of his wrist to press her finger to his lips.

'As happy as I am that you're talking now, can you please be quiet?' Nora tells him.

Then she kisses him.

Acknowledgements

Writing often feels like a solitary pursuit. Particularly at five in the morning, when I'm tapping away at my laptop, while my dog snores steadily beside me. But then the book is done and I'm called upon to think about who I'd like to thank and I realise that I was surrounded by people all along.

My friends Suzi, Hannah, Holly, Sara, Angela, Maya and Tracy, who made sure I ate and generally kept me sane while I was Googling the mid-point between Penzance and Richmond. Hannah, I fear, bore the brunt of it during our evening dog walks, but she was still kind enough to get me laptop tray so I could continue working from bed while I was recovering from surgery and told me that if I wasn't going to reply to her texts while I was on deadline, I had to at least open WhatsApp once a day so she knew I was still alive.

The children I'm lucky enough to have in my life who don't care that I'm on deadline. Indie, who makes me play Sharky after being at my desk for thirteen hours. Eve, who wants to show me all the dresses that she got since I last saw her. My darling nephews, Jacob and Nathan, who want nothing more from me than to cheer them on while

Acknowledgements

they climb trees and watch *Baking Impossible* with them. And my brother, Martin, of course, who is the reason I see my darling nephews, even if they get their darlingness from me not him.

Everyone at Hodder & Stoughton, particularly Erika Koljonen and Steven Cooper who endure my aversion to replying to emails and the incoherent ALL CAPS responses when I finally do. Jo Myler for this beautiful cover, which made me full on swoon the first time I saw it. And, of course, my editor, Melissa Cox, for letting me tell this story and making it *so much* better than I could have if left to my own devices.

Then there's my agent, Claire Wilson, who has had to put up with me for ten years now, yet reads everything I write with the same wonder and enthusiasm as she did my first manuscript. Not a day passes that I am not grateful that she read that manuscript and decided to take a chance on me. All of this is because of her.

Finally, Jean Louise Bourne who is a constant and enduring source of inspiration. I should say, however, that while Dodger and Oliver were created in her image, there is only one Jean Louise.